East Side

D. D. Riessen

East Side - Fiction

This book is a work of fiction. Names, characters, places and incidents are either products of the author's imagination or are used fictitiously. Any resemblance to actual events, locales or persons is entirely coincidental.

Library of Congress Control Number: 2018900978
ISBN 10 - 0991663088
ISBN:13- 978-0-9916630-8-8

ddr
books

San Diego, CA 92119

We had no idea where we were heading.
It was all about cars and drugs,
rock and roll and women.
Pick any three.
And then came the war.

*W*e crossed Texas in January, driving faster than was safe through the swirling snow as the drifts snaked across the two-lane road. Sometimes we were in one lane, sometimes the other, depending on which side of the car the wind hit us and how much ice was on that section of the road. When we couldn't see anything, we just slowed down and steered straight, hoping we didn't veer off of the road. It had been straight for the last fifty miles so we figured that our chances of staying on the road were pretty good.

There was some discussion about turning around, but no one wanted to do that anymore than stopping and waiting it out. Our plan was to go as fast as we could through the blizzard, but not so fast that anyone got killed. That didn't sound like much of a plan to me, but I couldn't think of anything better.

Inside the car, nobody was talking, all of us hypnotized by the white, unfolding storm on the other side of the windshield, wipers working full speed, afraid that if we broke the silence the car might break, or something like that.

I slept all the way across New Mexico. Waking up and staring out the windows, I learned that we were in Arizona. All I could see was cactus, sagebrush, plants from a world I'd only read about. The sky was a dark blustery gray, spitting rain here and there as we sped along. The rising sun, directly behind us, cast its light beneath the clouds and brought a bright sheen to one side of the plants and long dark, extended shadows on the other across a barren unpopulated land that seemed to go on forever.

We came across a section of desert, miles of sand and not much of anything else. Everyone wanted to stop. Getting out of the car, I felt warm rain hitting my skin, more like a heavy drizzle. We'd just come from two feet of snow in Chicago. This felt like summer.

I raced up the first dune as fast as I could, tripping and

i

sliding along the way, filling my shoes with sand. The air was incredibly clean and fresh. I'd never smelled the desert before and, standing on top of the first dune looking north, it felt like I was on another planet.

We were headed for San Diego. I had never seen a palm tree before and had never seen the ocean. Lake Michigan seemed pretty big, but I could not imagine huge waves that rolled in forever any more than I could imagine a place where it doesn't snow. My name is Calvin.

A quick way to meet your new neighbors is to try and disassemble a bomb in your back yard. That wasn't my intention, but that's how it worked out.

Our house was on its own lot. North of us, on the other side of the three-foot chain link fence, were three smaller houses, all of them with their front doors facing into our yard. South of us was a five-foot high board fence on the back end of the lot, falling apart, that connected into a three-foot white picket fence that continued up to the sidewalk in front, also falling apart.

I say all of this because after the police and bomb squad cleared the area, most of the fence perimeter, the back half anyway, was lined with neighbors. The only ones allowed in our yard was the bomb squad, wearing their protective suits, carrying long tongs and some kind of steel box to put the bomb in, a reporter from a local TV station and his camera man, the police and me.

They got video of the bomb squad placing the device into some kind of reinforced steel trunk and hauling it out of our yard, a few seconds of the cop waving his finger and lecturing me, leading me to believe that I was going to make the news at six. But my television fame was cut short because somebody's cesspool opened up and swallowed somebody.

After that, it was easy to make friends. Everyone wanted to know where I found it, Imperial Beach, half buried in the sand.

I was told by one of the beer drinking adults sitting around the campfire that night, that it was a spent water flare used by the navy. There were markings on the side that confirmed that it came from the navy.

Already spent? Why not take it home and see how they made it? I threw it in the back of the pickup and hauled it out to the back yard, anxious for the morning to arrive. I had a hammer, screwdriver and a pair of pliers.

I was baffled as to why, when it began smoking, that

the flame grew larger when I sprayed water on it. Water should put out fire, right? More water, more fire. This goes against my fourteen-year old logic. Spent? Maybe not.

The main lesson I've learned from this is to leave those kinds of things alone. Report it, so that if someone else comes along with as little common sense as me, they can't take it home and do something like what I just did.

When I think about it, what kind of thing gets excited, explosive even, when it comes in contact with water? I could've been killed or, worse maybe, horribly burned.

My mind is curious, common sense lacking. I'm fourteen. What do you expect?

We moved into the house in the middle of summer vacation. Wanting to have someone to walk to school with on the first day, I tried to make a lot of friends my age. But I learned that they were either going to Saints, or that they were a year older and going to Crawford or Hoover High School. I was going to Horace Mann Junior High.

There were several ways to get to Horace Mann from my house, all of them up. If it seemed like going to school was an uphill battle, that's because it was.

I was into all of the sports back in Chicago and fully intended to get into intra murals here. Back there, playing football, I'd have been given the ball and would have scored at least one, more like two touchdowns. Here, being the new kid in school, I was assigned left guard.

Right. That's what I am, all one hundred and thirty pounds. I can run. And I can catch. Make me a receiver, give me the ball however you can and I'll get you yardage.

"Don't you get it, kid?" Aaron, picked himself up and brushed off the dirt. "You're a guard! I thought you said you knew how to play."

"I can play. But I'm not a guard. I'm a receiver. Give me the ball and I'll get you points."

"Right. Look at you, skinny ass. You gotta prove yourself. Now, block that guy!"

"That guy" was John, six inches taller than me and thirty pounds heavier. He had a big smile and he loved to play the game. "You're gonna try again? Give it up, kid."

"I'm not a quitter. I'm taking you out, little boy."

John laughed. "Riiight. Hang on to your shorts."

When the ball was snapped, I threw my weight, shoulder first, down into John's legs, hoping to take out his feet. John pushed me down, planted my face into the grass, jumped over me and went straight to Aaron. Another loss.

"Jesus!" Aaron glared at me. "Can't you at least slow him down?"

3

"I can make it up. Give me the ball and...,"

"Shut up. Brad, go out five, cut left, and then go long. Sonny, I want you to come right across the middle. It'll be open since they're all gonna be on Brad. And you, kid...,"

"My name's Calvin."

"It's gonna be worse if you don't stop that guy."

Back at the line, John grinned. "They're not giving you any help?"

"Don't need any." I managed a smile. "You're going down."

When the ball was snapped, I lunged at John, driving my shoulder into his gut and wrapped my arms around his legs. He grabbed me by the shoulders and swung me out of the way, but I refused to let go. I climbed onto his back and together we went over and took Aaron for another loss.

By the end of the hour, I was black and blue all over, limping, and the friends that I'd hoped to make now thought of me as just a big wuss. At the end of the game, John came over and shook my hand.

"Gotta hand it to you, kid. You don't give up."

Afterward, I was famished. Conveniently located across the street, on the corner of Fifty-fourth and El Cajon Blvd. was a Heavenly's Donut Shop. Sugar was calling my name. I handed a dollar to the kid behind the counter and pulled a couple of napkins out of the holder while waiting for my change. *Louie, Louie* was playing in the background and, while I liked the song and normally would have stayed to hear it through, today I just wanted to get home.

Change in pocket, I picked up the two donuts, a glazed and a maple bar, stepped out on the sidewalk and headed west on El Cajon Blvd. I had only gone a few steps when I heard a familiar voice.

"Hey, kid."

Turning, I spotted John standing in the shade next to Heavenly's. Grinning, he motioned for me to join him.

"You make a terrible guard."

4

I shrugged, taking a bite from my glazed. "I should be a receiver."

"Where you from?"

"Chicago."

"What's it like back there?"

"Cold. Freezing cold."

"You ever been out here before?"

"No."

"Reason I called you over." John pointed to three boys approaching us.

"Yea. So?"

"They were on the other side of the street until they saw you. Didn't you see them run across traffic?"

"Yeah. So?"

"They were coming after you. They'll pop you once or twice, take your money and eat your donuts. Don't you notice stuff like that?"

"Never thought about it. Why would they do that?"

"Because you're a new kid. You're an easy target. Stand here with me until they go by."

"Why you want to protect me?"

"You're a terrible guard, not a bad person. I beat you up for over an hour. You don't want them to finish it off, do you?"

We stood in the shade of the donut shop eating our donuts as they passed by. John nodded to the one in the middle. "Hey, Carlo. What's up?"

Carlo nodded and then studied me. "He a friend of yours?"

"He's cool."

I had this sudden fear that they were about to jump us, Carlo sizing me up, his two friends looking like they were ready for a fight. The big guy on Carlo's left cracked his knuckles with a smile. But then, Carlo just nodded and motioned for his friends to follow. "Adios."

After they were gone, I realized that my heart was pounding. I bit into my donut and chewed without tasting the glaze. "Thought they were going to jump us."

"They won't. I saved Carlo's butt one time. I'm a friend.

You're probably safe now, too. But don't push it. You can nod to him if you cross paths again, but don't talk unless he talks to you first." John stepped out into the sun and started down El Cajon Blvd. "You were headed this way. How far are you going?"

"Fiftieth."

"I'm going as far as Winona. You going back for more football next week?"

"Not if I have to be a guard."

"Can you run? You look like you can."

"Like a deer. Give me the ball and I can score touchdowns."

"I believe you. Can you catch a hard pass?

"Yeah."

"I'll talk to Lenny, our quarterback. Maybe you could try out. Would you like to get revenge?"

"You bet. How'd you save him?"

"Who?"

"Carlo."

"Guess he was messing around with another guy's sister. Her brother and a friend cornered Carlo outside State Theater. He was gonna get his butt whipped. I came up and acted like Carlo's friend. He does go to our school, you know."

"Didn't know that."

"Anyway, the fight didn't happen. Since then, Carlo's been cool with me."

"Why'd you do that? He wasn't your friend."

"Don't want to see anyone get their butt whipped." John laughed. "Especially as bad as yours got whipped today."

"It's not funny, John,"

"Yeah, it is."

Back in Chicago, had I returned to classes after Christmas break, my science project, a third of my grade, was due. I was going to prove that, without air, sound cannot travel, a simple project, an alarm clock sounding off inside a bell jar in which all of the air has been removed.

In theory, that should work because sound waves travel through air by compressing and decompressing the air molecules. Remove the air and sound is gone. The bell jar is small, so it shouldn't be too hard, I was thinking, to get all of the air out before the alarm goes off. Do that and I've got an A.

The bell jar had a pump attached to the base, looking like a sturdy bicycle pump, a very simple process. All I had to do was set the alarm, put the clock on the base, put the jar over it and pump out the air. My Science class went from nine to nine forty-five. I set the alarm for nine-thirty, placed the bell jar over the base and started pumping.

What I discovered was that the more air I pumped out, the harder it became to pump. Before long, I could hardly move the handle at all. Hot and sweaty, breathing hard, I saw the minute hand hit the six, motioned for the class to be quiet and the alarm went off. Everybody heard it.

Until I could run the experiment again, comments from friends in the hallway...,

"I hear bells!"

"Ding-dong."

"Ring-a-ding!"

"What's that I hear? A failed experiment?"

"Ding-a-ling."

It was funny for a while. I couldn't wait for the lab to open. I had something to prove but I never learned the results of my second attempt because we had a fire drill during the time my alarm was going to go off. Standing outside, waiting for permission to go back in...,

"This isn't a real fire drill. That was Calvin's alarm

clock."

"Hey, Calvin. You must be pumping air in. You're turning it into a speaker!

Thinking that maybe the bell jar was not sealing properly, I smeared Vaseline along the base and on the bottom of the glass. Do not do this. It will make your Science teacher very mad.

What I've learned here, is that theories help us to understand why things do what they do. Proving them is much harder. And, no. I was never successful with that experiment.

Everyone called him Mr. D to his face and Mr. Dazzle behind his back. I was told that his teeth glistened when he talked, moonbeams came out of his eyes, his breath smelled like Magnolia flowers and it was impossible to scuff his well-polished shoes, that not even a stiff wind could blow a single hair out of place, that dust avoided him.

That's a lot to take in before you meet that someone. I didn't know whether I was going to be impressed or disappointed. I would have to wait until fourth period. Mr. Dazzle was my Science teacher.

He would be tall if he didn't slouch. Actually, it wasn't a slouch. He had a humped back, the result of that being that his head and long neck were thrust forward. Adding to that, with his long, narrow jaw and perpetually toothy smile, he reminded me of a crocodile, a friendly one. He smelled like a chain smoker and wore cowboy boots.

After taking role, he put his clipboard down, sat on the edge of his desk and looked over his class, recognizing a face here and there. Noticing me, he paused. "I haven't seen you before. Are you new here?"

I was sitting closest to the door, second chair back from the front row, close enough to see if anything interesting happened and close enough that I wouldn't fall asleep if nothing did. I hated being singled out. "Yes."

"Where from?"

"Chicago."

"The Windy City, right? And mosquitoes. I used to live there. How do you like California?"

"Amazing."

"Have you seen the ocean yet?"

I nodded, not liking the attention, thinking about the water flare, wondering if I should tell them about that.

"Chicago is interesting," said Mr. D. "It sits next to Lake Michigan. When you have a large body of water surrounded by land, you have a situation where land, whose temperature rises and falls with the heat from the day, is next to a large body of water who's temperature pretty much remains the same. What happens when the temperature differences increase?"

It was the first day of class. Did he really expect anyone to raise their hand? He picked up his clipboard, looked at the seating chart and then over at me. "Calvin. Tell them what happens."

"It gets windy."

"Right. Hot air rises. Cold air comes in to take its place. Daytime, it goes one way across the lake, nighttime, the other. And yet, water is an excellent conductor of heat. Easy question. Why doesn't the water absorb the heat and keep temperatures the same? Anyone?"

It was going to be a long day for Mr. Dazzle.

He sighed. "OK, let's go back to basics. What happens if you put a lit match to paper?"

Silence.

"Calvin, please tell these folks what will happen. I think their summer vacation has been too long. They're still dreaming of the beach, having fun, swimming in the pool, being anyplace but here. What happens when you put a match to paper?"

I shrugged, not liking the spotlight at all. "It burns."

"Excellent. But if I make a container out of plain old notebook paper and fill it with water and put a flame under it, what do you think would happen?

"I shrugged. "You're going to make a big mess."

That got me some laughter.

"That's beside the point. Will the paper burn? Or will the water boil?"

Somehow, I got into the middle of this conversation and he wasn't letting go. Does the paper burn? Of course, the paper burns. But wait. This could be a trick question. He's talking about water and temperature and didn't he say it absorbed heat? It is a trick question.

"Calvin?"

"The paper burns. The water spills, puts out the fire and then you've got a big mess."

Pleased with my answer, Mr. Dazzle waved to the room. "How many of you agree with Calvin? Raise your hands."

A few hesitant hands, a pause, a few more, everybody looking at everybody else to see if they agree. In the end, about half agreed.

"OK. Hands down. How many think the water will boil? Raise your hands."

I started thinking that Mr. Dazzle was pretty good. Ten minutes into the class and he already had everybody involved. No matter your opinion, you had to think about it. Most of the other half raised their hands.

"OK. Hands down. We seem to have a dilemma. How are we going to resolve it?"

Silence.

"Calvin. Back in Chicago, what do they do?"

"Same as anywhere. Experiment."

Mr. Dazzle nodded. "Of course. How else could you know for sure? Tell me, Calvin. Are you adept at building things?"

I thought of my failed experiment with sound. How to answer that question? I nodded, hesitantly.

"Would you do us a favor and do that experiment?"

"What? In the lab?"

"No. We don't have a lab. Isn't that sad? Did you have one back in Chicago?"

"Yeah. We did."

"Could you do us a favor?"

"I guess."

"You'll be given extra credit." He turned his attention to the rest of the class. "Who thinks the water will boil?"

A few hands went up. Mr. Dazzle pointed to a girl on the other side of the room, short brown hair, freckles, glasses. "I remember you from last year. Penny, right?"

She nodded.

"Would you do the same experiment? It will be interesting to see if your results are the same. Will both of you report back to class on Wednesday and tell us what happened?"

11

Penny and I exchanged glances. I shrugged, thinking this might be interesting and in any case, I was going to be able to meet up with Penny.

"This experiment," said Mr. Dazzle, will help us answer the original question. Does anyone remember what that was?"

Silence.

"Why don't the temperature differences between land and water even out? If the water in this experiment absorbs the heat fast enough to keep the paper from burning, why doesn't Lake Michigan do the same? Write it down. After Calvin and Penny give us their results on Wednesday, I'll expect a report from each of you on Friday answering that question. Meanwhile, read pages...,"

After class, Penny caught up to me, laughing. "I think they call that a goat-roping."

I shrugged. "He got you, too."

"He knows me. I had him last year."

"How was he?"

"He's fun, gets everybody involved. I have an idea. Why don't we do the experiment together? That way we have the same answer..., even though you're wrong."

"You put a flame to paper, it burns."

Penny smiled.

"Whose house, yours or mine?"

"Where do you live?"

"Fiftieth Street."

"When are you going to do the experiment?"

"Soon as I get home."

"Can I tag along? When we're done, I'll call my Dad to come get me."

"Sure."

"Out front after class?"

"Sure."

Back at my house...,

Penny pulled a sheet of paper out of her notebook and cut away the three holes. "How do you want to fold it?"

"I don't know. Single layer, right?"

"OK. How about if I fold it like this?"

12

She did a fancy fold that did not require any cuts to the paper, nothing like what I was going to do. I was impressed. "Looks good."

We scotch taped the corners, placed the container on the stove and filled a glass with water.

Penny looked at it doubtfully. "We can't turn on the flame until we pour in the water."

"What happens when we pour in the water?"

"Pour in a little. A teaspoon?"

"Sure."

Almost immediately, the paper began to crinkle, little waves of white paper soaking up the thin blue lines, turning them into a blur. Drips began to form on the bottom of our container.

"I think whatever we do," said Penny, "it's all going to happen very fast."

"Right. You pour in the water, I'll turn on the flame."

Penny started laughing. "All of it?"

"The more water we pour in, the bigger the mess when the paper burns."

"It's not going to burn. The water's going to boil."

"Pour in a half inch. We'll know by then what's going to happen."

"Ready?"

"Do it."

Seeing the water already seeping through, I turned up the flame higher than I should. All of the paper that was not touching water burned up in a short, but brilliant burst of flames, black, glowing sheets of burnt paper drifting up into the air, smoke filling the kitchen. Dry paper gone, the water line was at the top, wanting to spill over.

I started laughing. "How are we going to stop it?"

"Water's starting to boil."

"It's not boiling."

"It's a hard simmer."

"Still not boiling."

"Paper's not burning."

"So far."

But water was bubbling over the sides and spilling into the flame.

"Your water is killing my fire."

"Don't turn it up. That'll only make it worse."

"But if I turn it off, all of the water's going to come through."

"It's boiling? You agree?"

"You know what's going to happen? The water's going to boil away and then the paper's going to burn up."

"So..., we agree? The paper didn't burn up until the water was gone. Right?"

"So far. How do we stop this?"

"Turn off the flame."

"All of the water will run out. Maybe, if I turn it down."

"Water's coming through. It's steaming more."

"OK. I'll turn it up. Maybe we can make it steam faster."

"Glad it's your house."

"So," said Penny, while waiting for her dad to come pick her up. "Why doesn't Lake Michigan soak up the heat? That was the question, right?"

"Heat rises. It's not going to go down into the water."

"Maybe..., evaporation. The water gets hot on top, evaporates and cools the air."

"If the heat came from the bottom of the lake, all of the water would start to get warmer. It has to do with where the heat comes from...,"

"Here's my dad. See you at school tomorrow."

I didn't mind if my answer was right or wrong. I got to meet Penny and I was thinking that she was a pretty cool girl.

14

Lenny reluctantly agreed to make me a receiver. John pleaded my case and reminded him several times how determined I was, although unsuccessfully, attempting to block him. Lenny looked at me doubtfully.

"You're not tall enough. Look at their defenders. They've got six inches on you."

"That's their problem," I replied. "They're not going to be able to keep up."

"You don't have any meat on your bones. You're going down soon as they get a hand on you."

"They've gotta catch me first."

"Jesus. OK. We'll give it a shot. Line up on the right side."

John patted me on the head. "OK, Calvin. You gotta give us a show."

"Nobody's seen me run."

Out on the field, in the huddle, Lenny looked over at me. "Can you catch a long pass?"

"Yep."

"You say you can outrun them?"

"Yes."

"OK. I'll put one out there. Go up the sideline till you get to the defender, fake in and then keep going long."

"Right."

It was too easy. They didn't take me seriously. I ran up the right side, faked left and then ran right past him. A long lob from Lenny was an easy catch and there was no one even close. Touchdown.

Coming back to the bench, glancing out of the corner of my eye, I saw Aaron studying me and talking to Brad. That felt good. But at the same time I knew that the next attempt was not going to be so easy.

When it was our ball again, Lenny looked at me with a grin. "They're going to be watching you this time. They're going to play you deeper. Let's do the same thing except this time cut left. I'll hit you mid-field."

The defender started back peddling, ready to run with me, was not convinced with my fake left and was flat-footed when I actually went that way. Lenny hit me in the open. Touchdown. The rest of the day was tougher. I was blocked at the line, tripped, held and took a few "accidental" hits. We beat them by twenty-one points.

I thought this was going to be a big feather in my cap and it was with my teammates. It didn't go over so well with Aaron, Brad and Sonny.

When I crossed paths with any of them in the hallway, I noticed that they went out of their way to bump me when they passed by. At first, they made it look like an accident, like they weren't paying attention to where they were going.

But if they knew no one was looking, they hit harder. From that, I learned to act like I was not paying attention to where I was going and just when I knew the blow was coming, I'd turn my shoulder away. The first few times they almost tripped over themselves. I also learned to keep an eye on my backside. I got bumped into and somehow all of my books got knocked to the floor.

Not wanting to get caught alone after school, I started walking home with John. Whatever route he was going to take, I was with him. Neither one of us could afford to buy a donut daily and it was torture to walk past Heavenly's and have to ignore the smell of fresh donuts, which I'm sure they did on purpose.

We usually walked west on Trojan until we got to Fiftieth St. and then headed down the hill to my house. John never stopped in on the way home. On the way to school he stopped in from time to time if I wasn't already standing on the corner waiting. Going to and from school was safe as long as I was with John.

I later learned that Aaron, Brad and Sonny lived in El Cerrito, the opposite direction from the school. Hearing that, I didn't think they would bother with me after school anymore.

16

As the semester wore on, Mr. Dazzle continued to impress upon us the need to understand our environment. I continued to be his go-to target on the days when the class was silent. I wasn't brilliant in Science, but one day I just could not buy into what he was saying...,

"Nothing can go faster than the speed of light."

I raised my hand.

"Yes, Calvin?"

"If I'm travelling at the speed of light and I turn on my flashlight and shine it in the direction that I'm going, won't that beam of light be going at twice the speed of light?"

"You would think so. But, no."

"Why not?

"Because nothing can go faster than the speed of light."

"So..., what's the speed of the light leaving my flashlight?"

Mr. Dazzle smiled. "Depends on who's looking. If you measure from your perspective, it'll be the speed of light. If someone is watching you travel at the speed of light and they see you turn on the light, they will measure both you and the light from your flashlight traveling at the speed of light."

"That just doesn't make sense."

Mr. Dazzle motioned to the class. "If Calvin turns around and shines his light in the opposite direction, how fast would the light beam be going? Anyone?"

Penny raised her hand. "The speed of light."

Mr. Dazzle sat on the edge of his desk, enjoying the moment. "Is she right or wrong?"

I raised my hand. "Will the light even leave the flashlight? If I'm travelling at the speed of light in the opposite direction, won't the two equal out?"

"Are you saying that the light will never turn on?"

"If I measure from my perspective, that I'm already

17

going in one direction at the speed of light and I turn on my flashlight and point it in the opposite direction, the light will never come out. That's my opinion."

"Penny?"

"Sorry to say you're wrong, Calvin. They'll measure it at the speed of light."

"What equation says that?"

Mr. Dazzle was off his desk and over to the blackboard almost before I noticed that he was standing. His motions, mannerisms all seemed to be driven by some high octane impulsive drive from inside.

He put Einstein's famous equation up on the board, E=MC squared, and spent another fifteen minutes explaining it. Afterward, brushing the chalk dust from his hands and then rubbing them on his pants, he turned back to face us. "Today, we're going to talk about the speed of light versus the speed of sound. The speed of sound can vary depending on what medium it's travelling through while the speed of light does not vary at all. Why?"

Returning to the board, "If lightning strikes a mile away, will I hear the thunder before the light from that strike goes to the moon and back, if there was a mirror up there? This question, we'll solve in class today. On your way out, grab a copy of the questionnaire and be ready to hand it in next class. To answer those questions, you're going to have to read through pages...,"

Penny was signaling that we study together at my house after class. I nodded, yes.

John and Penny were both waiting for me when school let out, John by the flagpole, Penny by the steps. I introduced them and the three of us walked to my house together. For the first time ever, John stopped in and hung around for a while.

I got myself a paper route, but didn't have a bike. Before I could buy one, I had to pay the previous owner of the route for his customers, ninety-two of them. And he didn't want to sell his bike. I could own the route after one month if I gave him all of my profits. He agreed to let me extend the payment over two months.

Collecting would be easy if all of my customers paid on time. In principle, you've already given them their paper for a month and, in theory, you should be able to knock on their door, get your money and leave. That was my belief.

What really happens is some, but not very many people happily pay on the first visit and even give a small tip. Others act like they're not home, even if you saw them go in. Others say come back when the person with the money is there and some don't pay at all. Going back to the same houses over and over, walking to collect, was irritating and tiresome.

My route was all hills. It extended north from Orange Avenue up to Trojan Avenue, the road that runs along the top of the hill, and included all cross streets from Forty-ninth on the west all the way over to Fifty-second to the east with other streets in between, most all of them hills.

I was given a canvas carrying bag that would either fit over my head for shoulder carrying or over the tandem of a bike. Mondays through Saturdays, the bag was big enough to hold all of the papers. I had the Evening Tribune route so I delivered in the afternoon, after school. Sundays were a morning delivery and the papers were easily twice as thick. I couldn't fit all of them into the bag so two trips from my house were necessary.

Walking the route uphill with ninety-two papers was a struggle. I picked the street that had the most customers and delivered there first, even though it was the one with the most dogs.

Taking that route also meant that I'd have to cross over

19

the streets that I'd already delivered to get to the ones on the other side, basically adding another few blocks of walking to my route. I dreamed of having a bike. I could easily get the delivery done in half the time and effort if I only had a bike.

Somehow, I came across a pair of old roller skates with metal wheels. The axles were not wide enough to fit under a two by six piece of wood but with a bit of ingenuity, I was able to attach them to a two by four that was about two feet long.

Wheels! One of the greatest inventions of mankind, one of the greatest threats to teenagers that have no common sense. Did I really think they would help with my quest to ease the burden of delivering papers? Yes!

Going uphill, the skateboard was useless. It became one extra thing I had to carry, heavy and cumbersome, but good for keeping the dogs away.

I had no idea how fast I would accelerate going downhill with the extra weight of the papers. My plan was to go down the middle of the street and throw papers to my customers on either side. Moving cars did not enter into my calculations.

As my speed picked up, I couldn't retrieve the papers out of my bag fast enough. I missed several houses and had to walk back up the hill to deliver. Also, the faster I went, the sooner I had to release the papers.

Learning quickly, as only a teenager can, I pre-counted the number of customers on each downhill run and stacked them in my arms outside the bag. It's the little things.

Slowing down was beyond tricky. Zigzagging down the street helped but with such a narrow wheel base and the extra weight of the papers, it was easy to lose control. If necessary, I could drag the back of the board on the concrete, but that almost always flipped the board up and me down.

Lacking loyalty, it usually rolled on, worst case, across Orange Avenue below. Mostly, it just hit a curb or tire and I didn't have to go too far to get it. But I had to keep an eye on it. If it started to roll again after it hit something, and that seemed to happen more often than I thought it should, it could easily take off and roll out of view.

Seeing that, I was forced into either letting it go and watching its trajectory while I delivered my papers or, seeing that it might go all the way down, run after it.

One day, having decided to let it go, it disappeared completely. I looked everywhere and even walked back up the hill a second time. Nothing. Crossing over Orange Avenue and searching the street on the south side, the skateboard was not to be found.

Good riddance, I was thinking. More trouble than it was worth. All I got from that thing was experience and bruises, although I did learn how to ride a skateboard.

There is a problem with this. If I had seen it cross over Orange Avenue and get hit by a passing car, squashed beyond repair, I could live with that. It was a piece of junk, trouble on wheels that shouldn't have been built in the first place.

Still, for weeks afterward, I always kept my eye out for it whenever I was on that street. I checked out the bushes, hedges, anything that could hold and hide my skateboard. I always looked for it beneath parked cars when I walked by, expecting to see it wedged between the curb and tire.

Gone without any explanation? Did someone see it roll by, run out into the street and confiscate it? Are they laughing at my loss every time I walk by their house? Did it hit something that caused it to deviate from its normal course and is now beneath the weeds in one of the many canyons that pepper the area? Not knowing leaves a vacuum. The last piece of the puzzle won't fit because it's missing.

It wasn't so much that I wanted to drive it. Of course, I did. But that was out of my realm of expectations. What I really wanted to do was clean it. It bothered me to see such a fine piece of equipment covered in dirt.

It didn't have a body, just a frame, sheet metal floorboard, two seats behind a dashboard that used to have a windshield. It did have an engine, pedals, four tires, all of which were holding air.

It looked like some doves attempted to make a nest beneath one of the seats but got discouraged when something came along and ate their babies, down feathers scattered everywhere.

The seats were cracked, faded, covered in a year of dust and bird poop. Looking at the engine, I didn't know what most of the parts were, but I knew that I wanted to sand the rust off and repaint everything. Bottom line, I wanted to be able to work on it.

The owners lived next door to one of my customers and the dune buggy was parked in the dirt lot next to their driveway. I'd never heard it run and it just seemed to sit there forever, neglected, begging for attention.

One day the owner was getting out of his car when I came by to deliver the paper. I took the opportunity to introduce myself. His name was Charles.

Charles was, I later learned, a beatnik. He had a goatee, wore sandals, had holes in his jeans and was wearing a gray sweatshirt that had the arms cut off. The glass in his sunglasses was blue. I asked him what was wrong with the dune buggy.

"Nothing."

"Does it run?"

"It would if it had a battery."

"Dead?"

"Missing."

"Oh. Where is it supposed to go?"

He pointed to a metal plate, covered in rust, near the

front of the engine and then pointed to the two cables sitting on top of it.

"They didn't even bother to disconnect the cables. They just cut em."

"Oh. Can't you buy new ones?"

"Why? Putting in a new battery and cables is a calling card to come back."

"But now you can't use it either."

"I had my fun with it. I'm building a sailboat now."

"What are you going to do with this?"

"I don't know. Junk it. I'll get fifty bucks."

"That's all?"

"It's worth more. It's a stripped down Willys Jeep. It's got the Go Devil Engine."

"What does that mean?

"It's a sixty-horsepower engine. This thing will fly over the ground."

"How much does a battery cost?"

"You'd have to replace the cables, too."

I'm not quite sure when this happened. But before long we were calculating how much it was going to cost me to fix everything.

"The spark plug wires are cracked. You'd probably have to replace those as well."

"Where are they?"

Charles pointed to the four wires attached to the spark plugs on top of the engine. "And you might as well replace the coil wire at the same time. They're all cracked, sitting out in the sun like that."

"Did it used to have a hood?"

"Yeah. But that was extra weight."

"If you would've had the hood on maybe the battery never would've been stolen."

"Oh. I've still got the hood. It's out back. There's nothing to attach it to, though. Body's gone."

I went home and started to total everything up. Charles agreed to sell me the dune buggy for fifty bucks if my parents said OK. I knew I could convince them. Our back yard was fenced, of sorts, and I could keep it by the gate and behind the tree so they wouldn't have to look at it.

I saw this as an opportunity to learn about engines and, in the back of my mind was seeing it as a possible way to deliver my paper route.

Wouldn't that be something if I could deliver from behind the wheel? I could replace the passenger seat with a box to hold the papers and deliver the whole route in about fifteen minutes.

Go Devil Engine. I liked the sound of it.

Sometime around mid-semester, Owen started hanging around after school. We shared a table in Art and I was amazed at his ability to draw, mostly in pencil, whatever objects the instructor set out for us to sketch.

While I busied myself with just making the object identifiable, he created masterpieces. He had light sources, highlighting, shadows, sketches that almost appeared more realistic than the objects themselves.

While the classroom had fluorescent lights overhead, a rather boring perspective, Owen assigned a light source from an angle that vastly improved the nooks and crannies of the object and, after shadowing in the desired areas, made the object better than it really was. I was in awe of his talent.

He didn't look like an artist. I suppose I was thinking they should wear a beret and have a brush in one hand and a pallet in the other. I envisioned different colored splashes of oil paints on their clothes, places on their pants where they wiped their hands and maybe even some spilled paint on their shoes.

Owen had none of that. He wore cuffed slacks, ivy league button down shirts, black, well-shined shoes and kept his hair cut short. He was shorter than most of his peers, me included, and with his frail frame, perpetual smile, contagious laugh, he was an easy person to like.

When he did hang around at the house, he busied himself with drawing Penny or John or me or whatever thing we put out for him to draw. He also lived to tell jokes and unless we told him to shut up because it was interfering with our studies, he was nonstop. Owen was a natural high, a comedian and artist all rolled into one. How cool was that?

The next person to join our group I met one Saturday when I decided to walk up to Hoover High School where I'd be going in the fall. On my way, I passed by someone sitting on the steps of his house, whittling. He was about my age. I nodded as I walked by, impossible not to since the steps were only a few feet from the sidewalk. He held up his project, a half-carved piece of wood about four inches long, looking like a lopsided ice cream cone.

"What do you think it is?"

"You want me to tell you?"

"Yeah."

"No idea. I think it needs more work."

"It's going to be a pipe. Can't you tell?"

"Not yet. Don't you have to drill the holes first?"

"I'm going to carve them out."

It looked like he was carving with a plain old pocket knife, the typical kind, two blades, one big, one small. I didn't see any other tools. "With that knife?"

"It's got a punch." He put the pipe down and struggled to get enough of his chewed nail into the tiny slot to unfold the punch. Finally, he held it up.

"Isn't that for leather?"

"I think it'll work on wood."

I noticed that the length of the punch was shorter than the pipe. "It's not long enough."

"I'm going to carve in from both sides."

"Then you've got a leak."

"I'll just hold my finger over it. That, or I'll stuff some wood into the hole."

"You can get a corn cob pipe at Thrifty's for twenty-nine cents."

"Where's the fun in that?"

"You've got a point."

He held out his hand. "Jimbo."

"Calvin."

"Where you headed?"

"Hoover. I'm going there in the fall."

"Me, too. What grade?"

"Tenth."

"Me, too." He folded his knife closed and stuffed it and his pipe into his pockets. "I'll go with you."

Standing, I noticed that Jimbo was about an inch taller than me with muscular build and he had a look about him like he wanted to fight, jaw set hard, narrowed eyes. I found this disturbing, a sharp contrast to how our conversation was going.

Still, the more people that I could meet and possibly know before school started, the better I liked it. Decreased first day trauma.

I discovered that Jimbo had the paper route next to mine and, like me, delivered in the afternoon. The reason we never saw each other was because he did the adjoining street first, had less hills and he had a bike. He was done about the time I got to that section of the route and I wasn't even half done at that point.

We walked through the Hoover courtyard and around the perimeters of the buildings, noting the room numbers and where the auditorium was, the most important thing because that's where we were supposed to go on the first day.

On the way back to his house, we stopped for a Coke.

"Where do you live?"

"Fiftieth Street."

"You've got the shitty route. It's all hills."

"Don't I know it."

"You got a bike?"

"Not yet. I'm saving up."

"Man, that must be tough. You gotta *walk* it?"

"Yeah. It sucks."

"When we get back to my house, I'll give you a ride home."

"Thanks. What are you gonna smoke in your pipe?"

"My mom doesn't smoke her cigarettes all the way down. I'll take what she leaves."

"Why don't you just smoke her cigarettes?"

"She counts them."

"Why?"

"She doesn't let herself smoke more than five a day. If I take one, she'd know."

"Take five. Then she'll just think she forgot to count a day."

"Hmm. I like that. Wonder if it'll work."

"Why you want to smoke?"

"It's cool, man. You ought to try it."

"I don't think so."

Katie, Jimbo's sister, met us on the front steps when we got back to his house.

"Mom wants you to clean up your mess."

"What mess?"

"All these wood shavings."

"I'm not done carving."

"Go talk to her. She told me to tell you."

Jimbo went inside while Katie and I sized each other up. There had been no introductions. I held out my hand.

"Calvin."

She appeared reluctant to shake it, as if I was poison or something. If you can imagine shaking hands with the least amount of contact possible, that's what she gave me, a limp hand. I was not impressed and I'm pretty sure that she wasn't either.

Coming from inside, we heard a lot of yelling. Katie just shrugged, rolled her eyes and went back inside, leaving me to wonder if I should just continue on home or wait. I didn't want to be a witness to a fight and I didn't feel welcome. I started to leave when he came back out with a broom and dustpan.

"Hang on. I'll be done in a minute."

Jimbo gave me a ride home and that's when I discovered that my afternoon stack of papers had been delivered. He helped me fold them and then took off to do his own route. When he was done, he came back and helped me finish mine. Nice to have some help.

Lunch hour was over. I was in a hurry to dry my hands and get to class. The bell was going to ring any second and most everybody else had already left the courtyard. I grabbed my books, flung the bathroom door open and ran straight into Aaron, who was coming in. He shoved me out of the way.

"Watch where you're going, wimp."

I was so surprised by this that I was basically speechless. I mumbled, "Sorry," and attempted to leave. Aaron's friend, Brad, grabbed my collar and shoved me up against the outside wall.

"I think he needs a lesson in manners. What do you think, Aaron?"

"It wouldn't hurt." Aaron laughed. "Not me anyway."

Holding me against the wall with his forearm, Brad twisted around, checking for witnesses. Seeing none, he punched me in the stomach. I doubled over, trying to catch my breath, dropped my books, covered my ears with my forearms and clasped my hands on the back of my head.

It didn't make sense to me that I had somehow become the bad guy in all of this. I came out to play football, was not given the opportunity to show what I could do, switched teams and was successful. Why should I be the one that takes the hit?

I don't think Aaron and friends wanted to think anything through. If they did, they would see that all of this animosity was due to them. They preferred the role of being the school jocks, loud, confidant, respected within their circle and, outside of that, basically not thought of at all.

Before the next blow landed, I heard someone yell, "Let him go!"

Brad released me. Standing, I saw Carlo and two of his friends approaching. Aaron had been holding the bathroom door open. He let it close and turned to face them. "It's none of your business what we do. Get the fuck out of here."

Carlo stood his ground. "He's a friend. You fuck with him, you fuck with us."

Aaron and Brad appeared ready to take them on. They forgot about me entirely and started toward Carlo.

Because they were between me and Carlo, I couldn't see what was happening, but I heard the unmistakable sound of a switchblade snapping open, and another.

A standoff. I can only imagine what happened between them. There weren't very many words, spoken quietly but filled with threats, then the sudden departure of Aaron and Brad. All of this happened in about one minute.

I was left facing Carlo. I picked up my books and started toward them, wanting to shake hands. "Thanks. I...,"

Carlo motioned for me to stay where I was. "It's got nothing to do with you."

The bell sounded and all of us hurried to our classes.

Jimbo sat on the edge of the steps at my house and carved his pipe over the dirt, the shavings spilling into the branches of a juniper growing alongside. No cleanup there. Tap the branches a bit and all of the shavings fall and disappear down into the dirt somewhere.

The pipe was actually beginning to look like a pipe. Jimbo made the discovery that if you carve against the grain, the blade goes down and you'll have a really hard time keeping a straight line. He'd carved the bowl at the wrong end and now he was going to have to fight it until he was done.

"Why don't you start over?" I asked after he showed me the problem. "Have you got any more of that wood?"

"Yeah. There's a long stick of it out in my back yard."

"Start over. Now you know how to do it."

"Naw. I've got too much work in this one now."

"It's never gonna be easy."

Jimbo folded the blade shut, opened the leather punch and began digging into the long end of the wood. It appeared that he'd carved out a small hole about an inch deep.

"How long did it take you to get that far?"

"Bout two hours."

"You gonna use that to dig out the bowl?"

"Naw, I'll use the blade for that."

"If you had a drill, you could be done by now. Maybe take it into wood shop and...,"

"He'd want to know why I'm making a pipe. And then he'd call my house. You know how that'll go over?"

"Yeah. I get it."

"Besides, if I finish this, I'd have to go find something else to do."

"Don't you ever have homework?"

"I do it in class."

"Man, it's not that easy for me. What kind of grades do you get?"

31

Jimbo didn't answer, instead turning his attention to digging aggressively into the pipe. Suddenly the punch collapsed, trapping his fingers between the handle and cutting edge.

"Shit!"

He pulled the blade open, threw the knife down and held his hand over his head. Blood trickled down the back of his hand, heading for his elbow.

Standing, I headed for the door. "I'll get a rag and some band aids. "

"That'd be cool. Thanks."

It was hard to read Jimbo. Sitting there on the porch, bleeding like that, I knew he was in pain. But his expression never changed. He still had his hard-set jaw and narrowed eyes. That seemed to never change, even when he was having a good time. I wondered about what happened earlier in his life to make him be like that.

Going inside, Penny was helping John work through some math problems. What used to be her and I studying together was now turning into her helping John. Our dining room table was round and John sat close. He looked over with a grin.

"I have to see the numbers right side up."

"Right."

"She's really good at this."

I didn't comment, instead choosing to raid the bathroom cabinet for band-aids, hydrogen peroxide and several squares of toilet paper.

One day, both John and Penny were absent from school. To my knowledge, neither of them had ever missed a day so I thought it odd, but thought no more of it.

I didn't take Trojan Avenue home the way I normally would, if I was walking with John. I was sick of walking that way and instead walked down to Orange Avenue and then headed west.

Walking behind me was a girl I'd seen at school, but had never met. I stopped, turned and waited for her to catch up. "Walk together?"

"Sure."

"I'm Calvin."

"Darla."

"You always come this way?"

"Yeah"

"Where do you live?"

"Fifty-first"

"Oh. North or south of Orange?"

"Huh?"

"What side of Orange do you live on?"

"I just turn left."

"Oh, south then."

"I guess."

"What classes are you taking?"

"I don't know. A few."

"Math?"

"I guess."

"Who's your teacher?"

"I don't know. Some guy."

"Mr. Dazzle?"

"No. I don't think so."

"Oh. What else are you taking?"

"Um, stuff."

Not only was she slow with words, she was an even slower walker. Resuming my normal pace, she lagged behind. I forced myself to slow down. Try as I might, I could not get her to say anything that went beyond a few syllables. I felt like I was talking into a pillow. Nothing bounced back. Soon, I was regretting our walk together.

On the other hand, she was very pretty, dimples in her cheeks when she smiled, which happened at the beginning of any utterance along with a slight giggle, which I didn't understand. She had a dynamite body and I was interested, but didn't know how to approach her.

We walked in silence, her just staring down at the sidewalk and me scrambling to find other subjects to talk about. But at her street she just said good-by and turned left on Fifty-first, south.

I concluded that she had a clean slate for her mind. Nothing was sticking as far as I could see. That, or she just didn't want to talk to me. Would I walk with her again should the opportunity arise?

Continuing on to my house, I fretted over that question. Maybe she was just shy, a definite possibility. Still, everyone knows the names of their teachers and what classes they're taking. Everyone has things they like to do and subjects they like to talk about. The fact that she had none was disconcerting.

I finally came to the conclusion that she just didn't want to share anything with me. That conclusion answered my question. No. I would not walk home with her again. I would give her a friendly wave and continue on at my speed.

Walking with her made me late delivering my papers.

My house was becoming the meeting place for kids after school. Everyone knew that I had to deliver papers first so they helped me fold them and waited on the front porch until I came back. At least that's what I think they did. We never locked our front door. I don't think we even had a key and, in any case, the back door was always unlocked.

Did they go inside while I was gone? I'm not sure. John was the guy in charge until I got back and he always assured me that no one had gone inside. I wondered if the home life for these kids was so bad that they had to come here or if they just wanted a place where they could hang out.

They brought snacks, cookies, pretzels, chips, uneaten apples left over from lunch, oranges, sodas, all kinds of things that either left crumbs on the floor, scattered across the couch, left in the sink or, in some rare cases, actually made it into the trash.

I had to be very careful about this. Everyone had to leave by five thirty because my parents would be home by six and their coming home to a room full of teenagers would not go over very well at all.

That left me half an hour to get out the vacuum, rush through the house sucking up little messes here and there, picking up wrappers, papers, orange peel, whatever teenagers leave behind when they're done with something. Studying was impossible, the last thing anybody wanted to do after being in school all day. The radio was on as soon as we came through the door.

Mama Said.

"Hey, Calvin. Where are the ash trays?"

"No smoking in the house."

"You don't have any ash trays?"

"Smoke outside."

That led to the inside contingent and the outside contingent and added to my cleanup duties between five

35

thirty and six. I secured a coffee can and filled it with sand and told everybody to put their butts in the can.

That helped control the mess but I still found butts out in the grass, once in a while still smoking, and cigarettes squashed on the sidewalk alongside the house, which left black stains. The hose became my friend.

Mom was happy because it looked like I was taking an interest in the yard. It's the little things.

Before I could scrape up the money for a battery and cables for the dune buggy, an opportunity of a lifetime came along. Next door, living in the third house furthest from the street and next to the alley, was a heavy-set man who was always tinkering in his tiny garage.

Inside, with the hood removed and engine parts scattered across the floor and piled up on top of the wobbly wooden bench, was a nineteen forty Dodge coup.

The car did not have the beautiful lines of a nineteen thirty-two or thirty-six Ford. I didn't care for the elongated trunk. But the body was not rusted, the windows were all intact, rolled up and down, the tires held air and, with a bit of scrubbing and a couple coats of wax, the car would look pretty good.

Glen, the owner, the unshaven, balding, ruddy faced man that I always waved to as I passed by when coming or going through the alley, called me over.

"Hey, Calvin. Interested in buying a car?"

"I've already got a dune buggy that I can't afford."

"It's a good deal. You can't afford not to."

"That car? What are you asking?"

"Fifteen dollars."

"That's all?"

"Well, the engine is in a basket, so to speak."

"Why are you selling it?"

"Got a chance to buy a nineteen thirty-four Packard V twelve."

"What's that mean?"

"The engine's got twelve cylinders."

"What's this one got?"

"Six. But these are good little engines. They got lots of spunk."

"If it was all put together."

"Right. I can show you where everything goes. I just bought new rings and bearings for it."

"I don't know what that means."

37

"A rod was knocking. You can hear it when the engine's running. Sounds like knock, knock, knock. That means that the bearings are worn and the pistons are getting too close to the head. You have to replace the bearings."

"They're thicker?"

"Riiight. You got it. See? You got a mind for that."

"Yeah. But I don't have the money."

"You put this thing back together, you can sell it for two or three hundred."

I strolled through the garage, stepping over scattered parts here and there, boxes of things unknown, greasy rags, old beer cans. It seemed like there were an awful lot of parts that needed to go back together somewhere. Still, hook everything up and make a couple of hundred?

"Can I pay you over two months?"

"Naw. I gotta have the money today or tomorrow or he's gonna sell it. He's already got another buyer if I don't take it."

"How much you paying for it?"

"Couple a hundred."

I did have fifteen dollars. But that was intended for my bike. I'd have to wait another month to buy it and the prospect of walking the route for another month seemed daunting. However, the prospect of making two hundred dollars just for putting this thing together and cleaning it up seemed like a pretty good deal.

"Do I have to buy more parts?"

"Well, you'll need to buy a gasket set."

"What's that for?"

"You gotta have some kind of seal between the outside of the engine and the inside. Otherwise all the oil leaks out. It's called a gasket. You need one for the oil pan, one for the manifold, one for the carburetor...,"

"That sounds like a lot."

"The whole set is about ten bucks."

"And you're going to help me put it back together?"

"Sure. I'm gonna be here working on the Packard."

"I don't have any tools."

"You can borrow mine. I know you'll bring them back. I

been watching you work on your buggy. You like things to be neat and tidy and this car needs someone like you to take care of her."

"I'm not sure my parents would let me. They already don't like the dune buggy back there."

"You can keep it in the garage for the next week. After that I'll be bringing the Packard over. We could probably even get it back together by then."

Other than my parent's objections, I couldn't think of any reason not to buy the car. If he was going to help me and I could use his tools, what was there to stop me? My parents didn't come out in to the back yard that often. I could probably sell it before they even knew I had it.

"OK, Glen. Fifteen bucks. It's a deal. But you have to help me put it together."

"You know I will.

I bought the car. Glen said he'd come right back as soon as he gave the man the money. I never saw him again. The garage was unlocked so, going in, I noticed that all of his tools were gone. A week later, Mr. Morrow knocked on our front door and asked if I owned the car in the garage. Fortunately, my parents were not around for this conversation.

"Yeah, I own it. Glen said I could keep it there until he brought the Packard back."

"Well, Glen doesn't live there anymore. He was behind in his rent. I'm cleaning the place up so I can rent it again. It comes with the garage, so you'll have to get your stuff out of there."

"He's gone? Where did he go?"

"Arizona, I guess."

Going through the garage more thoroughly, I was hoping that he'd left some tools behind. All I found was a crescent wrench. At least it was big enough that it could grip all of the nuts and bolts that I saw. I had no idea what a socket set looked like.

Getting Jimbo to help me, we moved the dune buggy closer to the tree and pushed the Dodge up close to it on the alley side, pretty much out of view from the house. I cleaned all of the parts using hot water, detergent and a bunch of old clothes that I knew I'd never wear. I never thought about rust or how I should coat everything in oil. All of the spare parts were placed in the trunk.

Proud of my purchase, I showed the car to John and Penny one afternoon. John nodded approvingly. Penny was a bit more skeptical. She walked around the car a couple of times without saying anything and then opened the door on the passenger side and checked the glove box.

"Where's the pink slip?"

"What's that?"

"That's what says that you own it."

"I've got a sales receipt."

"Let me see."

I handed her all the paperwork that I had. "All this says is that you paid fifteen dollars for the car."

"What's wrong with that?"

"Nothing, except this guy's name is not the same as the one on the registration. This car might be stolen."

"How would I find that out?"

"Call the police and ask."

I didn't want to do that. If it was, I'd lose everything. Better to fix the car up and sell it. I called the landlord and asked if he had a phone number for Glen in Arizona.

"Nope. If you find out where he is let me know. He still owes me money."

"Right."

"Did you clean out the garage?"

"Yeah. I'm out of there."

Checking the license plates, I noticed that the last time the car was registered was three years earlier. I couldn't find any phone numbers for the old registered owner, but I did talk to a relative who knew him and she said that he'd died. When I explained my situation, she said she'd look around for a pink slip and give me a call back. Two days later, I called her.

"Somehow I lost your number. I was hoping you'd call."

"Did you find the pink slip?"

"No. I looked around. We burned most of his papers in the fireplace two years ago, used them to start the fire. You know, when it got so cold?"

"I wasn't here two years ago."

"Oh. Where are you from?"

"Chicago."

"It gets really cold back there, doesn't it? I can't imagine."

"Yes. This is paradise. Listen. If I need to get a note from you saying that I own the car, could you do that?"

"I didn't know that he sold it."

"Oh. Well, I just bought it from my neighbor. I've got the receipt, but not the pink slip."

"Who did you buy it from?"

"My neighbor, Glen..., wait. Let me look at the receipt." I studied the scribbling.

"Glen Kitenten?"

"That might be it."

"That scoundrel! He was hanging around before Amos died. I've always wondered if he didn't have something to do with that."

"Amos?"

"The owner who died. He was fixing that car to sell. Glen was there with him, drinking beer..., even in the morning. They said it was a heart attack, but Amos seemed pretty healthy to me. Where is Glen now?"

"Arizona, I guess."

"What condition is the car in?"

"The car's OK. The engine's in a million pieces."

"Well, I certainly don't want it. But I can't imagine that a note from me will do any good. I never owned it."

"But couldn't you say that the owner died and the pink slip was accidently destroyed?"

"The one person that might have inherited the car would be Charlie, his son."

"Oh. OK. Do you have his number?"

"He doesn't have a number. He moved up to Alaska over a year ago. We haven't heard anything since. No address, nothing."

41

"If you do, can you give him my number?"

"If he calls. But I doubt that he will. We never had a good relationship with him. He was trouble, always getting in fights, had a short temper. What's your number again?"

None of this was very promising. If she already lost the number once after two days, I couldn't imagine her hanging onto it until Charles called from Alaska. I gave her my number, thanked her and hung up.

Bottom line, even if I got the car running I couldn't sell it until I could prove that I was the owner. I couldn't even renew the registration. I was not very happy about any of this.

Friday night. Jimbo and I had just finished playing a game of chess and were trying to figure out what to do next when the phone rang.

"John? What's up?

"Got a six-pack here and we need a third hand for poker. You in?"

"Where'd you get the beer?"

"Don't ask questions like that. You in, or not?"

"Jimbo's here."

"That cuts down on our beer. You guys have money?"

"You're going to charge us for the beer?"

"No. I'm going to win it from you in poker."

"Riiight. Hang on. Jimbo? You want to go drink beer and take John's money in poker?"

Jimbo burped the last of his Pepsi. "Sure. Why not?"

"John. You heard that?"

"I heard it. We're over on Rolando. Here's the address. Bring lots of money."

Heading out the front door, Jimbo paused at the bottom of the steps. "Where are your parents tonight?"

"Some meeting over in Balboa Park. Why?"

"How'd they get there?"

"Some friends picked them up. They were going to a party afterward. Why?"

Jimbo was looking at our family car. "Didn't I see the keys on the dining room table?"

"No. We're not taking the car."

"It's a long walk over to Rolando. That's on the other side of College."

"We're taking your bike, right?"

"What time does their meeting end?"

"No, Jimbo."

"Just answer, what time?"

"Nine."

"It's only seven, right now. Five minutes to get there. Play for an hour. Five minutes back. We could be back by eight-fifteen."

I drove east on Trojan Avenue until we ran into Fifty-fourth, turned north and headed up toward El Cajon Blvd. But before I got there, I turned right onto a side street. Jimbo was riding shotgun.

"What are you doing? Go straight!"

"I don't want to drive on El Cajon Blvd. It's too busy."

"Does this road go through?"

"No idea. Fifty-fourth and Rolando are both major streets. There's got to be a way through the middle."

Fifteen minutes later...,

Jimbo leaned forward, squinting through the windshield at the road sign ahead. "There! Rolando. We got it!"

"Man. What a maze! We're not coming back this way. Left, or right?"

Nine-fifteen, we left John's house. I lost eight bucks, Jimbo five. Forty-five minutes to get home before my parents and I was beginning to feel the pressure. We stepped out into pea-soup fog. I could hardly see the car.

Jimbo got in the passenger side. "I hope your windshield wipers work."

"I've never seen it so thick. I can't even see the road."

"Are you going to take El Cajon Blvd.?"

"No way."

"University? It's not so crowded."

"No. I'm going back the way we came. I don't want to take any chances getting in an accident."

"So..., take a busy street that has lots of light."

I turned back into the maze. "There aren't any cars, going this way."

"You better hope not."

The light from my high beams came right back at me. I couldn't see the road, the curbs or any other parked cars. I discovered that low beams worked better and if I used them while sticking my head out of the window, I could see the tires and the road, but I could not see ten feet beyond the hood of the car. Time..., nine-thirty.

"I am screwed, Jimbo. They're going to skin me alive."

"You're not caught, yet."

44

"Yeah. But we're only going two miles an hour. I can walk faster than this."

"Move over. I'll drive."

"No. If we hit something, I want it to be me driving."

"Maybe you could tell your parents that John needed emergency medication and you were just trying to help."

"They won't buy that."

"How about his dog got hit and you...,"

"Just shut up, will you?"

"You've got to have a story, just in case."

"You know what would help? You get out and walk alongside the car and tell me where the road is."

"That's not going to help."

"You're right. Jog alongside the car and tell me where the road is."

"What? You want me to run back to your house?"

"Not run, jog."

"You're crazy. I'm not jogging all the way back."

"You're the one that talked me into this."

"You didn't *have* to take the car."

"I wasn't going to. Come on, Jimbo. You gotta help save me here."

Going through the maze once in the opposite direction does not necessarily mean that you know the route going back, even without the fog. By ten, we were back on Trojan Avenue. I turned left on Fiftieth and slowly went down the hill.

My stomach was mush and I was feeling light-headed. But if I had a sickening feeling in my gut before, it only got worse when I noticed that someone had parked in my parent's spot out on the street.

"That's not good," said Jimbo as we idled past. "Who owns it?"

"No idea. I hope it's not my parent's friends."

"I'll just get my bike and get the hell out of here."

"A rat deserting a sinking ship."

"I'm not the captain. Pull over, will you?"

I had to park three houses down with the car pointed in the opposite direction. Jimbo quietly retrieved his bike

45

from the side of the house. "Good luck."

Going inside, much to my relief, I discovered that there was no one home. But that just added to the mystery. Sitting at the front window, waiting for that car to move, I pondered all of this for the next several hours.

Not knowing and being culpable is a bad combination that inspires the imagination into new realms. I wasn't off the hook. It was a race to see if I could get the car back to its spot before my parents got home.

Unless that car belonged to my parent's friends. Why didn't I look to see who they were and what they were driving? Maybe they parked there on purpose, went to a neighbor's house and are having a party over there, in which case I'm still screwed.

It all depends on the car parked out front. No going to bed until this situation is resolved. I tried to imagine who owned the car, what kind of person they were to buy such a thing? Are they passed out in someone's house and won't get up until ten tomorrow morning?

I squirmed like a worm on a hook until sometime around two when a car door closing woke me up. I didn't see who it was, but it had its lights on and the car was moving! As soon as it was gone, I parked our car there, along with a big sigh of relief.

My parents never knew. I escaped unscathed, but paid the price, sitting alone in the dark for those few hours, waiting to see what my fate was going to be.

I found the old pan gasket for the engine in a beat-up metal trash can outside the garage, but it was broken in two places and, after piecing it together, I discovered that a section was missing. I didn't have the money for a gasket set, but I found a nice piece of thin carpet in a customer's trash can while delivering my route. I wondered if that might do the job.

Glen left the engine bolted to the frame of the car so I didn't have to deal with any of that. The hoses going from the radiator to the engine were still connected and, opening the radiator cap, I discovered that the water was low. When I added water, it poured out from several different places on the engine. Studying where it all came from, I decided that I still had a lot of work to do.

Fortunately, Glen did not throw out the old gaskets. I matched them up to the corresponding holes in the engine block and searched through the parts in the trunk until I found one with a matching footprint. I bought a tube of Form-a-Gasket and coated both sides of all the old gaskets before I installed the parts back onto the engine. I had no idea about the wiring, but discovered that the wires kind of knew where to go once I got the piece bolted back into place.

It took me a while to figure out how to get the rings on the pistons. Each ring is slightly larger than the piston and has a break in the circle that is used to begin the process of fitting it into the narrow slot provided around the piston. It's a springy, high tensile steel and it fought me all the way. The edges are sharp and they cut.

That, I discovered, was the easy part. Once the rings were on the pistons I couldn't get them to fit into the cylinders. I resolved that by tapping a tiny section of the ring into the slot in the piston with my hammer and a screwdriver while I patiently (and many times not so patiently) tapped the top of the cylinder with a piece of wood and the hammer, hoping to nudge the piston

47

further into the cylinder. Sometimes it popped back out altogether. It is not fun. This process took me three days.

Cylinders in, I tapped the pistons down toward where they would connect to the crankshaft at the bottom of the engine and then discovered that I should have attached the rods first, the things that connect the piston to the crankshaft. It is not an easy process to connect them once the pistons are inside the cylinders.

I was not about to take the pistons out and start all over. In a short moment of brilliance, I thought I could tap the pistons down to the bottom of the cylinder and see if the connecting place would pop into view without the rings popping out.

Worrying about that very thing caused me many trips between the bottom of the car, crawling through the dirt, to hovering over the fender with the hammer in my hand. Between that and delivering papers on foot, I was getting a good workout. It took me a week to connect all six rods to the pistons and crankshaft. I was rather proud of that.

Then came the decision about what to do with the pan gasket, the place where all of the oil is kept. Surely a piece of carpet would do as well as the rest of the gasket if it was the same thickness, wouldn't it? I scraped off as much of the fiber from the carpet as I could, cut it fill the gap left by the missing piece, bolted the pan onto the engine, walked up to Thrifty's on Fifty-fourth and El Cajon and bought two gallons of the cheapest oil I could find.

Finally, the engine was back together. All of the wires went somewhere, but I wasn't sure if all of them were correct. It looked good. I kept the hood off so that I could see what was going to happen when I turned the key.

When I did, the engine turned over slowly, ka-wump, ka-wump, and then a fireball came out of the carburetor along with a big puff of black smoke. A bit disturbing, but I thought it was because everything was new and it was just getting warmed up. I turned the key again.

An even bigger fireball exploded out of the carburetor with more smoke and a loud BOOM. I decided that was enough for the day and moved onto other things.

Help came in the form of Stan, who worked at a local gas station. Jimbo and I strapped the Dodge's dead battery onto the tandem of his bike, hauled it over to Stan and in exchange for a dozen donuts, he charged the battery, showed us a picture of the engine, named the different parts and pointed out the distributor in particular.

"That's what sends the spark out to the spark plugs. If that's not right, your car will never run."

"How do I know when it's right?"

He flipped to the next page. He had a whole row of these books, all blue, hard-bound up on a shelf above the work bench, tools down beneath the counter. It looked like he had information on almost every kind of car. Impressive.

"Inside is a thing called a rotor. It's got to point to the number one cylinder when the number one piston is in its compression stroke."

"How do I know that?"

"You know the valve cover, right?"

"Right."

"Take it off and watch when you turn the engine over. Those little arms, they're called rocker arms, go up and down and push the valves open and closed. Take out the coil wire so's the engine won't start. Sometimes one arm is up while the other's down. When they're both up, the valves are closed and the gas can't escape. That's when you want that spark to get there."

"Where's the number one cylinder?"

Stan laughed. He had a gold tooth about three teeth back from the front He pointed to a picture in the book. "Yeah. You gotta know that. It's right there."

Made sense to me. Send the spark to the right spot at the right time. Otherwise you get what I got, fireballs. It's the little things.

We ate the whole box of donuts and became pretty good friends. Stan told us to stop by with the car when we got it running and he'd show us how to tune it up.

Does all of this sound like more trouble brewing?

On the days that John did not stop by after school, Penny and I got our studies done quickly and we always had good talks. We laughed a lot together when it was just the two of us and I thought that she liked me. I hadn't attempted to kiss her or anything like that because it just didn't feel like the moment ever presented itself.

Whenever John was around, everything changed. At first, I thought that Penny was just being nice, but there was too much joking going on between them, a little snicker here or there in the conversation, bantering.

I finally came to the conclusion that they had a thing for each other. I didn't like it, but there was nothing for me to do about it. Since they were both my friends I wasn't going to alienate either of them by bringing it up. Basically, it was not my business.

I had other problems. Between my paper route, fixing up the dodge and the dune buggy, I was very busy. I longed for a good set of tools. Putting a car together with a pair of pliers, crescent wrench, screwdriver and hammer was greatly limiting.

Not to mention a bike. If I hadn't bought the Dodge I'd have the bike and a tandem to put the bags on. I could get the route done in thirty minutes instead of an hour and a half.

Basically, what I learned from this is don't take anyone for their word. Had Glen been on the up and up, the Dodge problem (I'm now calling it a problem rather than an asset) would be over. I'd have the profit for my labor on the car. I'd be able to deliver my route on my bike and have more time and money to work on the dune buggy.

I had to quit football. It wasn't that much fun anyway and I no longer had the time. I had no solution for the Dodge registration and ownership. The dune buggy sat in the back yard unattended. Out of all of this bad news came one good piece of news and one that had obvious benefits although it was illegal.

50

Jimbo showed up one day with a current registration sticker in hand. It looked a little beat up, certainly not new, but there was enough sticky surface on the back that it stayed stuck to my license plate.

"Where did you find it?"

"What does it matter? Now you've got wheels."

"What's the penalty for driving with no registration?"

Jimbo laughed. "No registration, no insurance, no driver's license. The car might be stolen and you're not even old enough to get your learners permit. They're gonna throw away the key."

"I don't know. Maybe I should just call the junk yard and have them come get it. I'd be out my money but...,"

"You're not caught yet. You should at least try driving it around the block a few times just to see how it runs."

I was curious about that. The engine started, coughed a lot when I stepped on the gas and wanted to keep running after I turned off the key. Running, it sounded like both a tractor and a ringer washing machine, pop, pop, pop, chug, chug, pop, pop. Something like that.

I didn't know how to shift gears, but with a little practice I learned first and reverse and thought I knew second and third. I'd figure that out once we were on the street. We backed the coughing and sputtering car out of the alley and onto Orange Avenue.

After lots of grinding the gears (I kept forgetting to push in the clutch), I finally got the car into second gear and that's the one we stayed in on our way up to Heavenly's to buy donuts. We took only the back streets.

Stan got the car running pretty well. I accidently burned rubber leaving his station. Glen was right. The car had lots of spunk. Under normal circumstances, that would be a good thing.

Driving the car was a natural high. I started taking it to school, always staying on the back streets and parking a couple of blocks away. What I wanted most was to avoid having to walk the hill. I also found many other reasons to drive somewhere rather than walk.

There were a couple of problems with all of this, keeping

51

gas in the tank and for some reason the car was using a lot of oil.

Buying those two things kept me perpetually broke. Wondering where all the oil was going, I looked under the engine one day and was surprised to discover that the oil pan was not only covered in oil, but dripping oil even when the engine was not running. Definitely the carpet gasket was not working.

I couldn't afford the gasket and decided to leave the car alone for a while. I put a coffee can beneath the oil pan to catch the drip and every now and then poured it back into the top. Obviously, this was not a fix.

I resumed walking everywhere. Crossing over the streets, I noticed that there was a long stream of oil going off in one direction or another, places where I normally drove. My guess was that I was losing about a half quart of oil every two or three trips to and from school.

I was sitting on a concrete wall away from everybody during lunch when this girl sat down next to me, retrieved her sandwich from the neatly folded brown paper bag, opened it and took a bite.

I had been reading my physics book, preparing for a test in Mr. Dazzle's class. There were several other places where she could sit. OK. I'll bite.

I held out my hand. "Calvin."

She folded the cellophane back over her sandwich and shook my hand, a firm shake. "I know. Letti."

"How do you know?"

"I watched you play football."

"Oh. Well..., thanks. But that's all over now."

"You weren't meant for it anyway."

"What?"

"You're too small. You were getting beat up."

"I can take the hits."

"Why? Do something where you can use your talent and not get hurt."

"Like, what?"

"Track. You could do the fifty, one hundred and maybe the two hundred. I think you'd be pretty good."

I laughed. "Right. I could do the fifty and maybe the one hundred. I don't have enough air for two hundred."

"It's how you breathe. You gotta pace yourself."

"How do you know so much?"

"I'm on the women's track team."

"I didn't know we had one."

"Your loss." She said it with a smile. She had pearly, white teeth, a nice contrast to her olive skin and dark hair, kept it a short ponytail.

"What's your event?"

"The two hundred, four hundred and the four hundred relay."

"That's tough. You winning anything?"

"Runner-up to state championships last year."

"Amazing. So, what made you decide to come sit with me?"

"The men's team needs some spark."

"Maybe..., if I had time."

"You going to Crawford next year?"

"Hoover."

"Oh." She sounded disappointed. "I thought you were going to Crawford."

"I have a choice. I live in some kind of neutral zone. I can go to either one."

"And you chose Hoover?"

"It was assigned. I've been told that if I don't like it, I can change."

"You've got all summer to think about it."

I was already thinking about it, two months total freedom, except for my paper route. "Can't wait. What are you doing for the summer?"

"Go to the beach, visit family. I might try and work at the zoo."

"They pay you?"

"No. Volunteer. But you get to know people and that might lead to a job."

"Do you practice over the summer?"

"Every day."

"What do you do?"

"Different things. Sprints sometimes, weight training. I'm always working on my breathing."

"You're dedicated."

"I've gotta be."

"You really practice every day?"

She smiled. "No. But I'm trying to inspire you."

"I never tried track."

"You should."

"I'm not good at running in a straight line. It's the zigzagging that I like. I'd be bored with track."

"Suit yourself. You're going to Hoover anyway."

"Are you going to try out for women's track?"

"Well, duh."

I laughed. "Make you a deal."

"What?"

"If I go to Crawford, I'll try out for the track team."

She smiled. "Maybe I'll see you out there."

We ate quietly for a while. I didn't know about her, but I was busy contemplating all of these new avenues. I hardly tasted my sandwich, white soft bread, wilted lettuce, warm bologna and mayonnaise. She offered me one of her slices of apple.

"Thanks."

The bell rang. Seemed like the lunch hour was over way too soon. I closed my book and began to gather up my things. We smiled a good-bye and went our separate ways.

Letti. I'll remember that name.

Do you love me?

Kenny was one of those guys that seemed to have it all. He had straight, white teeth, deep, blue eyes that the girls loved and his blonde hair combed in perfect waves to the back of his head. His laugh was contagious and he found many things to laugh about. While the girls loved him, most of us guys were somewhat jealous, although we never talked about it.

Kenny had been going steady with Gwen, a girl that every guy wanted to date because she was bubbly, had a great, curvy body and big breasts. She was stuck on Kenny and nothing was going to change her mind about that. Their relationship was a, I'm great and you're great, so we'll be even greater together, kind of thing.

But one day after school, Jimbo's sister, Katie, tagged along on his visit to my house, just to see what the attraction was. Coming through the front door, she literally tripped over Kenny's feet. As usual, he was sitting on the couch next to the front door making out with Gwen.

Apologizing as he kneeled to help her up, a couple of us noticed that in doing so, placing his hands under her arms, he also got a feel for more than her armpits.

Accident or planned? Who knows? I was sure that he didn't mean to trip her. Busy giving Gwen a hickey, leaving his legs stretched out, he wasn't even aware that she'd come through the door.

Coming face to face with Kenny, Katie's eyes lit up as if she was being held by James Dean. She put her hand on his shoulder, smiled a smoldering smile.

"Thanks. You are...?"

"Kenny. You're sure you're OK?"

"I'm fine."

"Looks like you skinned your knee."

"It won't be the first time, or the last."

Standing there, eye to eye, Kenny struck the perfect

tone. "Let's go put some Iodine on it. The bathroom's over here."

Holding the underside of her elbow with one hand and putting his other hand over hers, Kenny led Katie into the bathroom, sat her down on the toilet seat and rummaged through our medicine cabinet for some Iodine.

Glancing over at Gwen, who was now sitting upright and staring at the floor, I could just about see smoke coming out of her ears. She waited a minute or two longer and then got up and stomped her way to the bathroom.

Kenny was on his knees, sitting in front of Katie and applying the Iodine when Gwen burst into the room.

"It's just a scratch! Leave her alone!"

"Gwen. I'm just trying to help...,"

"She's fine. Aren't you, Missy? What's your name?"

Katie took on a demeanor much like her older brother, Jimbo, like she could easily explode. "What's yours? Who are you to be questioning me?"

"I'm his girlfriend!"

"I'm so impressed."

Kenny was trying to make himself little. He backed away from Katie and leaned against the bathtub, but before he could stand, Gwen hit him with her purse, a big, black thing that held all of God's creations, for cosmetics anyway.

Katie stood. "Leave him alone. He was just trying to help."

"Stay out of it. You don't know nothin' from nothin'."

"I know a bitch when I see one."

Jimbo heard all of the commotion while he was in the kitchen searching for a soft drink. He joined the rest of us standing in the hallway and when he heard that Kenny was putting the make on his little sister, he pushed everyone aside, stood over Kenny, who had yet to stand up, and nailed him with a brutal punch that caught Kenny on his left cheek.

"You fuck with my sister, you fuck with me!"

Katie shoved Jimbo back toward the door. "Leave him alone! You're not my protector!"

"This guy's a creep!"

"No, I'm not! I was just trying to help." Kenny stood, went to the mirror and inspected his swelling cheek. "Crap! I'm going to have a black eye."

"You deserve it," said Gwen.

Katie pushed through the crowd and made her way back out into the living room. "I don't believe it! He got beat up for being *nice*?"

"It was more than nice," Gwen said, coldly.

"I didn't get beat up. I was hit for no reason. Step outside, Jimbo. Let's have it out."

"Don't push it, Kenny. I can kick your ass."

"Outside! Right now! Come on!"

I stepped in between the two and pushed them apart. "Hey, guys. It was a misunderstanding. Let it go."

"I've got a black eye! I'm going to break his nose!"

My heart was pounding. "You're in my house! We don't fight here. Let it go."

I didn't think Kenny could kick Jimbo's ass anyway. While he was built slight and pretty, Jimbo was more muscular, an inch or two taller and at least ten pounds heavier. Kenny was going to get the worst of it.

John, my offensive lineman friend, got up from the living room table and joined us. "Calvin's right. It's his house and all of us need to respect that. If you can't, then it's time to leave."

Kenny sat down in the big, overstuffed recliner and felt his swelling eye. Gwen wasn't done. She pulled a knife out of her humongous purse and lunged at Kenny, who ducked sideways as the knife cut into the upholstery.

"You bastard!"

I didn't think she wanted to kill him because she telegraphed the move. Still, a crime scene in my house? My parents would kill me! Gwen threw the knife back into her purse and headed for the front door. No one tried to stop her. But when it was apparent that she wasn't coming back, Kenny quietly followed.

"Sorry about the chair, Calvin. I gotta go find her."

The cut into the chair was a vertical rip a little longer

than an inch. If the fabric was cloth, I could have sewn it back together, maybe. But this was fake leather, dark brown, almost black, with a white cloth backing. While I rummaged through the drawers looking for some kind of a fix, everybody started to leave, saying their good-byes and filtering out the door. I turned off the radio.

Masking tape. Good old, extra-sticky, cloth-backed masking tape. I cut a piece about two inches long, placed it inside the cover, sticky side facing me (this was not an easy thing to do at all) and stuck the two sides together.

The result was a narrow, white strip of the backing showing through along with a few white threads hanging in front of the puncture. I cut the threads and a little work with a black ball point pen solved the white problem. My hope is that I can move out before my parents notice.

Owen heard that Jimbo and I were going to watch *The Manchurian Candidate* up at the State Theatre on Friday night and asked if he could tag along. We were standing on the corner of Forty-eighth and El Cajon Blvd. waiting for the traffic to clear and, as usual, Owen was talking.

"What's black and white and red all over?"

I shrugged. "No idea."

Jimbo made an attempt. "A zebra that fell into a vat of red paint?"

Owen shook his head. "A newspaper."

Jimbo moaned, "Oh, man."

"Pretty good," I admitted.

"Railroad crossing, railroad cars, how do you spell it without any r's?"

Jimbo shook his head doubtfully. "You can't."

"I've already heard this one."

Owen laughed. "I - T. How do you spell "it" without any r's?"

Jimbo moaned. "OK. You've gotta stop now."

When the traffic cleared, as we were stepping off of the curb, another group stepped in front of us, taking the lead in crossing the street.

"I have this boomerang," said Owen, keeping his eyes on the pavement. "I keep throwing it away, but it keeps coming back."

Someone from the group in front of us turned around and decked Owen. None of us saw it coming. Owen went down like he'd been hit with a baseball bat.

We heard their laughter as we tried to help Owen to his feet. They were already across the street and running into the night. We did not get a good look at who they were.

Owen couldn't stand and his eyes were glazed. He kept falling to his knees while Jimbo and I struggled to keep him on his feet. We dragged him back to the curb, up to a storefront where we sat him down and leaned him up against the wall. I stayed with Owen while Jimbo went inside and asked the clerk to call the police.

By the time they arrived and after they'd taken a report, Owen was able to give them his home address. He did not want to go to the hospital, so they took him home. When he left, his eyes were still glazed, his words jumbled and he was unsteady on his feet.

We went back to Jimbo's house, retrieved a tire iron and a long screwdriver and set out walking the streets looking for the perpetrators. After about two hours of searching and finding no one, we decided to let it go. This was a job for the police, not us.

It was fortunate that we didn't find anyone. If we would have, even if they were guilty, they would have denied it and the chances were good that we might be the next ones to get hurt.

Owen missed classes from then on. My Art class didn't seem the same without his magnificent drawings and constant jokes. It was lonely in there without him. When I asked the instructor when he was coming back, I was told that his parents pulled him from school and that they had moved back east somewhere.

We never heard from Owen again. His absence was louder than his words and, as irritating as they were at times, we all missed them.

I could have just as easily been the one that took the hit that night. I, too, was looking down at the pavement, watching my feet as we stepped off of the curb.

A sudden unseen blow to the face? How would that change my life? A broken nose? A dislocated jaw? How long does it take for those things to heal?

In the weeks that followed, I was always on the look-out for anyone who was too loud, angry or sneaky. I didn't like feeling that way.

What compels a person to sucker-punch someone else for no apparent reason? Was this for an initiation into some club or gang? Or, was it just downright stupidity? Probably both.

Standing against the wall in the auditorium, I was already wondering if I'd made a mistake keeping Hoover as my choice for high school. It wasn't my choice actually, more like lazy, too lazy or unconcerned to make a call during the summer and change schools. One simple call and I'd be over at Crawford with John, Penny, Letti, a whole slew of other friends that I'd made over the summer.

I was part of the standing room only spill-over crowd standing up against the wall. I arrived a little late because Jimbo, the one person that I knew that was going to this school, was sick when I stopped by. Sick on the first day?

I didn't know anybody and, even if I had a seat, I wouldn't be comfortable sitting in it with a bunch of strangers who all seemed to know each other.

"I don't know why they're doing this on the first day of school. It's a waste of time, don't you think?"

I glanced over at the person standing beside me, his crooked smile suggesting that I should agree.

"What?"

"Why are they showing us this typewriter guy on the first day of school?"

I shrugged. "Don't know."

"You think they want us to take up typing? Who cares if he can type a hundred words a minute?"

"Is that what they said?"

"I wonder how many mistakes he makes."

I'd never really ever thought about it. A hundred words a minute, a word and a half every second? Wow.

He was making the typewriter sound like a train now. Clackety-clack. Clackety-clack. Holy cow.

My new friend, whoever he was, nudged me with his elbow. "Doesn't that just make you want to sign up?"

He had a point. We should be getting our homeroom assignments, class schedule, books handed out. This typewriter thing might be a fun escape later, but right now I wanted to know what I was in for, where to go, what to do. Typing was at the bottom of my list.

If I could get into Mechanics, that would be good. I could bring my Dodge in and learn what everything was and what it was supposed to do.

But I wasn't old enough to drive yet, so could I really bring it in? Would the teacher have to verify that I had a license, that the registration was up to date? Was my car ever reported stolen? Or, would he turn a blind eye? Hmm.

I noticed that my new acquaintance had never stopped talking. He was fixed on the typewriter guy, analyzing his every accomplishment, talking toward the stage.

"Do the keys get hot because he's typing fast?" He laughs as if it's some kind of trick question. "Or, is it because of the words? Maybe he's typing porno?"

He actually expected an answer, looking at me, waiting. I didn't know how to answer that question, so I changed the subject. "What's your name?"

"Harold."

I held out my hand. "Calvin. Maybe we'll have some classes together."

"Are you in Advanced Math?"

"No. I'm pretty sure I'm not."

"Physics?"

"No."

"Calculus?"

"No."

"Well, maybe we'll have the same lunch hour."

"Maybe."

I could only imagine what kind of conversation we would have over lunch. I began to think that this was going to be a very long year.

For my birthday, I was given a set of tools, not a great set like Craftsman or Snap-on. But it had two ratchet wrenches, half inch and three-eighths inch drives, a couple of extensions and most all of the socket sizes that I needed, not to mention a decent collection of open-end, box-end wrenches, pliers, channel locks and several different sizes of screw drivers. I was in hog heaven.

I was out in the back yard tightening up all of the nuts and bolts that I could find on the dune buggy when Uncle Wally stopped by.

"How are you going to get it to where you can drive it?"

"What?"

"It's got no registration, no fenders, no lights. Not even brake lights. You can't drive it on the street."

Somehow, that hadn't occurred to me yet. "Can't I tow it?"

"I don't think it can be on the street without registration. You'll have to put it on a trailer. How did you get it here?"

"A couple of my friends helped me push it."

"Lucky you didn't get a ticket. Does it run?"

"No battery."

"Looks like the spark plug wires are rotten, too. See how they're all cracked?"

"Yeah. I'm saving up to buy a few things."

"What kind of money you making?"

"Not much. I've got a paper route."

"Yeah. I had one once. Lot of work, not much pay. Would you like to make a little extra?"

"Doing what?"

"I have to move a few jukeboxes and pinball machines back into the shop for repairs. And I've got to move a few others around to take their place. Interested?"

"Sure. Why not?"

"I'll pick you up Saturday morning at eight?"

"Sure. I'll be ready."

I thought he was going to leave, but Wally hung around

a while longer, inspecting one thing or another. I knew that he raced stock cars over at Balboa Stadium from time to time so anything he had to say, I was all ears. And then he looked past the fence and spotted the Dodge parked out in the alley.

"Whose car is that?"

I shrugged, hoping that he'd lose interest. Instead, he opened the gate enough to let himself through. I kept working on the dune buggy. After several minutes he joined me in the back yard.

"It's in pretty good shape. I didn't see any dents or anything like that."

I nodded. "Yeah. I noticed that, too."

"They've got it parked right outside your gate. I think that's illegal."

"Well, we don't use the gate much anyway."

"You don't know who owns it?"

"No."

"Do you know if anyone is driving it?"

"It comes and goes."

"It might be stolen. I think I'll report it."

"Don't do that."

"Why not?"

I wiped off the wrench that I was using and placed it back in the tool box. "Because it's mine."

I think he knew that already. He nodded. "You're not old enough to drive."

"I'm old enough to get my permit."

'Does it run?"

"Yeah."

"How much did you pay for it?"

With a sigh, I explained how I came to buy it, how the engine was in a basket and how I figured out how to put it back together. In the end, he laughed.

"That's amazing! Does your mother know?"

"No. Please don't tell her."

"What are you going to do about the registration?"

"No idea."

"You need to show the receipt to the DMV and explain

that the previous owner has moved out of state without giving you the pink slip. At least that takes you out of the picture in case the car is stolen. If it isn't, they'll issue you a new pink slip and then you can say that the car is yours."

It was very encouraging to finally get some guidance about what to do. Wally was right. Better to take the financial hit doing things right rather than be involved in something that might link me to car theft.

"How did you get the pistons back into the cylinders without a ring compressor?"

"A what?"

"Ring compressor. It compresses the rings into the piston and makes it easy to slide the piston into the cylinder. It's nearly impossible to do without it."

To much laughter, I explained the process that I used and how it took me three days to get them in.

"Normally that would take about fifteen minutes, maybe thirty. Determination. That's what you've got. You did put the rings on the piston in the right order?"

"What?"

"The edges of the rings are shaped differently. You didn't notice that?"

"No."

"Nobody explained it?"

"No."

"The bottom ring distributes oil to lubricate the cylinder. The top rings help create compression. You get them in the wrong order..., well. Bad news."

"What'll happen?"

"It won't run right, bad compression, oil's not getting where it's supposed to be."

"Great." Take out all of the pistons and start over? I put that on the bottom of my list of things to do.

"Tell you what, Calvin. I've got a ring compressor. Let's pick a time and I'll help you pull them out and get everything right. We'll get you a new head gasket and oil pan gasket at the same time."

Where was Wally when all of this was taking place?

66

Having help, good help, was a blessing. "What about Mom. Are you going to tell her?"

"I'll keep quiet."

Later that night, Uncle Wally stopped by and asked if I would like to earn a few bucks while he went out on a service call.

"If I have to move a piece of equipment, I'm going to need some help. Want to ride along?"

It was a chance to get out of the house on a Saturday night and he offered me five bucks even if I didn't need to do anything, plus I got to ride in his new nineteen sixty-three red Chevy Impala. All of this was good.

We drove over to Market Street. I was getting very nervous about being in the dark side of town on a Saturday night. I began to feel like we were in danger. I had butterflies in my stomach.

"Is this where we're stopping?"

"Yep."

"You do this all the time?"

"Only when the jukebox breaks. If it's a pinball machine, I wait until morning."

The bar was loud, smoke-filled and boisterous when we walked through the front door, everybody laughing and drinking. But within the first minute or so, after they spotted us, the place became very quiet, deadly quiet in my mind. I was thinking I was going to get my ass kicked. My heart was pounding.

The bartender was out of the room at the time and when he came back in and saw the situation, he laughed and yelled. "It's OK! They're here to fix the jukebox!"

The place broke into applause, cheers, clinking glasses. I breathed a BIG sigh of relief.

Someone had put a slug into the coin slot and jammed up the works. Wally fixed it and gave them an hour of free music. Suddenly, there was dancing, the game of pool resumed and the place was hopping. It's incredible what music does. Wally motioned for me to follow him to the bar where he ordered a beer and a Coke.

Standing next to me, a gray-bearded man with a nearly

67

toothless smile turned to shake my hand. "Didn't think you were going to make it, did you?"

I obliged, shaking his hand. "What?"

"We all saw the look on your face."

"What look?"

"What's your name?"

"Calvin."

"Mine's, Stitch. I think we're gonna call you, Bolt."

Wally laughed, almost spitting out his beer. "Bolt! I like it."

"How come your name is, Stitch?"

He unbuttoned his shirt and showed me a scar that went from his left shoulder down to his right thigh. "A reminder not to mess around with someone else's girl."

"Wow. Must've hurt."

Stitch laughed. "Hurt? There ain't no word for it. I just wanted to die. Would've, too, hadn't a been for this man here." He put his hand on the shoulder of the man standing next to him. "Boss? This here's, Bolt. This is Boss. He saved my life."

He was a big man, had a deep voice, talked slowly. "Had to. If he'd died, I was going up for murder."

"You cut Stitch?"

"He was messing with my girl."

Stitch sipped his beer. "I didn't press charges."

"Why not?" I looked around to the other side of Boss. "Where is she?"

Stitch burst into laughter. "Ran off with some doctor in Memphis."

"It ain't funny, Stitch."

"Yeah, it is."

Sounds just like me and John. I realized then that we're all not so different once we get past all the bullshit in between.

I was sitting on the bench between the two rows of lockers getting ready for gym when somebody hit me hard on the side of my head. It didn't hurt, but the hit was intentional. I stood to face the perpetrator. There were no words, no cussing, no reason for it, nothing.

Next thing I know is we're throwing punches and I found myself in the center of attention of everyone else in the locker room. Funny. You don't hear who they're rooting for. It's a jumble of noise, like wallpaper, something flat, noisy and alive that surrounds you.

I threw a punch, a right cross aimed for his jaw, but missed. He ducked and returned with a flurry of fast jabs that found their mark but didn't hurt. I backed up, waiting for him to attack and when he did, kicked him between his legs and attacked with another two left jabs and a haymaker right. Missing him, my fist slammed into a locker, causing it to swing open.

Coming out of his crouch, as he stood, his forehead caught the corner of the locker and ripped a gash in his forehead, bleeding down into his eye. I was wearing a white shirt and before long it was ripped and full of blood.

The coach came out of nowhere and shoved us apart. I was thrown up against the wall while my opponent was pinned up against the lockers. Our coach was short and stocky, an ex-marine and a wrestler. No doubt he could easily take both of us out at the same time.

He told everyone to break up, dress up and go run laps until he returned. We were marched down to the principal's office.

We were both suspended for a week even though I explained that I didn't start the fight. I was the victim, not the aggressor. That made no difference.

The day before I was supposed to return, Jimbo stopped by to say that Harvey wanted to fight me after school. That information put a few knots in my stomach. I didn't even know why we were fighting, but I wasn't going to look like the one backing down. Sure, meet on the other side of El Cajon Blvd., after school.

The next day, I was a train wreck. I didn't want to run into him in the hallway and I didn't want to have some kind of encounter during the lunch hour. I didn't want any of this. What happened next took me utterly by surprise.

Harvey was African American. I suspected that he was going to have a huge following after school to cheer him on, while my only back-up was going to be Jimbo and Harold. While Jimbo might jump in to give me a hand, Harold would only be good for predicting the odds against us.

But during the lunch hour, many students that I'd seen around but never knew, came up to tell me that they were on my side and that he had a big mouth and wasn't liked very much anyway. Half of them were black. That made me feel better, a little. When the final bell rang I felt like I was walking in a daze. I put my books in my locker and headed for the exit.

There were about ten people hanging around after classes. I expected a much bigger crowd and was relieved to see the small turnout. Harvey was nowhere to be found. One of his friends informed me that the principle told him that if he fought he would be expelled. There was no fight, much to my relief.

Later that week, Jimbo and I were walking through a deserted hallway and, coming around a corner, ran smack into Harvey, who was all by himself. Jimbo shoved him up against the wall.

Harvey held his hands up. "I don't want to fight, man."

"Then, why'd you hit me?"

"You sat down right where I was going to sit, didn't say excuse me or nothin'. Rude."

"I was just changing clothes. I didn't think anything about it."

"Well that's a problem, ain't it? Who gives you the right to just take over the bench?"

"I was sitting in front of my locker."

70

"Yeah? Well, my locker's right there, too. Right across from yours."

Jimbo was getting impatient. "Just fuck him up, Calvin. That was no reason for him to hit you."

"You know what? He's right."

"What? He got you kicked out of school!"

"No. Harvey's right. I just plopped down and got ready for gym."

Clearly Jimbo did not agree with my decision. Shaking his head, he let Harvey go. I reached out to shake his hand. "Sorry, man. It was a misunderstanding."

Harvey breathed a sigh of relief and shook my hand, grinning. "Sometimes my hands go faster than my brain. I'm sorry, too."

When an enemy turns into a friend, when you can walk around knowing that if you run into that person it's going to be all right, it makes the whole day go by a lot better.

We passed each other in the hallway many times after that, each giving the other a short wave and a smile. We didn't eat lunch together or hang out. We ran in different crowds.

One morning before school, he was hanging out with his girlfriend out front. He waved me over.

"Janine, this is Calvin. Watch out for him. He's a bad ass."

I shook her hand. "Don't know about that. But watch out for this guy. He's got fast hands."

"Don't I know it."

All three of us laughed. It was going to be a good day.

My private place to go after dinner is the driver's seat of my Dodge, parked on the other side of the fence behind my house. I turned on the radio...,

Love Potion Number Nine

Jimbo knocked on the passenger side window. I unlocked the door and let him in. He handed me a paper cup, secured a second one between his legs, opened up a bottle of something. It was too dark for me to read.

"What you got there, Jimbo?"

He didn't answer. Instead, he unscrewed the top and poured some into my cup. "Just try it."

I gagged with my first sip. "What is this?"

"Wine."

"Where'd you get it?"

"Dowd's Liquor."

"They sold it to you?"

"No. He went into the back for a minute. I grabbed the bottle before he came back out."

"You stole it?"

"Well, he wasn't going to sell it to me, was he?"

"This stuff tastes terrible."

"Yeah. But we can get drunk."

I'd never been drunk before. Basically, I didn't like the taste of alcohol. I tried beer and just about gagged. This was not as bad as beer. "What's it called?"

"Thunderbird."

"Oh." Coughing, I took another sip and decided that it was tolerable. "How much alcohol is in this?"

"Fifteen percent."

"How much does beer have?"

"Six, I think."

"Almost three times as much? How drunk are we gonna get?"

"Don't know. I've never been drunk before. One time, after my dad passed out, I finished off his beer. My cheeks got hot and I felt a little woozy. It didn't last long."

"So..., I'm drinking to get woozy?"

"Hey! Can I turn this up?"

"Sure. Who sings that?"

"The Crystals. *He's a Rebel* is one of my favorites."

"Why? You think you're a rebel?"

"Sure. Don't you?"

"Never really thought about it."

"Bull shit. I see you looking at yourself in the mirror."

"That's cause I'm good lookin'."

Pouring more wine into our cups, Jimbo laughed.

"You're full of shit, too."

I was starting to feel flush, heat coming into my cheeks. I rolled down the window, took another sip and listened to *Loco Motion* without talking. When the song was over, I started the engine.

"You gonna drive?"

'No. Just charging the battery."

"We could go, you know, just around the block."

"What am I? Crazy?"

"What's it gonna hurt?"

"For one, I'll lose a whole bunch of oil."

"You're losing it right now, idling."

"No. I've got a can down there to catch it. I just pour it back in the top when it gets full."

"You have to fix that gasket."

"I've got enough money now. I just have to go buy it."

"So..., what's stopping you?"

"It's a long walk to the parts store."

"You need a bike."

"Yeah. But if I get a bike, I won't have enough money for the gasket. And If I get the gasket, I won't need the bike."

"Have some more wine and think about it."

Jimbo refilled both of our cups, placed the bottle on the floorboard, sat back in his seat and started to sing along with the song, *I Like It Like That*.

"You suck at singing."

"No, I don't. I've got a good voice."

"You're flat. You must have a tin ear."

"What does that mean?"

"What note you're singing and what you think you're singing aren't the same. You're flat."

"What does that mean, flat?"

"Not on key. Shut up, will you? You're ruining a good song."

"You getting drunk?'

"I think so. I want some pretzels, peanuts, something."

"Popcorn, salty, buttery popcorn. That's what I want."

"I'm getting hungry."

"I think it's the wine that does that."

"What? Messes up my stomach?"

"Are you gonna run your engine all night?"

"Oops. I forgot."

"Don't turn it off. Let's go for a ride."

"My cheeks are numb. My tongue feels thick."

"Back up. Let's go. Just round the block."

"How much of that bottle have we had?"

"We're past half way. What do you think?"

"My brain is fuzzy."

"Do you like it?"

"I think we need to drink slower."

"How about you let me drive?"

"I'm not that drunk."

"I drove my dad's car."

"That's an automatic. All you have to do is step on the gas."

"There's a lot more to it, than that. I can parallel park."

"I laughed. "Yeah, if there's no other cars around."

"Let me drive."

I turned the ignition off. "I feel like crap."

"I think you're right. We drank too fast."

"Beef jerky. That would be good."

"I've got a couple of bucks. Drive up to Dowd's Liquor. You have to go in, though. He's gonna remember me."

"I'm not driving. Get over it."

Quite suddenly and totally unexpected, my stomach rebelled. I flung the car door open, stumbled down to my hands and knees and heaved my guts out. From inside the car, Jimbo was laughing.

By the time I climbed back in, Jimbo had finished off his glass and pored himself some more. He offered to fill my cup.

"God, no."

"Lightweight."

"How are you getting home?"

"On my bike."

"Really?"

"Yeah. I gotta go, anyway. I've got to study for a test tomorrow."

"Good luck with that."

Jimbo got out of the car, stumbled over to his bike, got on, rode into the gate and crumbled down to the ground. Laughing, I honked the horn and flashed my headlights. He flipped me off and, wobbling precariously, disappeared into the night.

I was under the Dodge tightening up the last of the pan bolts after having replaced the gasket when Jimbo skidded to a halt in my back yard, dismounted and let his bike fall into the dirt.

"Did you hear?"

I crawled out, dusted myself off, wiped down the tools and dropped them into the box. "Hear what?"

"Kennedy's been shot."

"What? *President* Kennedy?"

"Right."

"You're joking."

"I'm not lying. Go turn on the news."

The assassination coverage was on all of the channels and on the radio. We watched the news until it was time for my stack of newspapers to arrive. An hour later, we were still waiting.

Jimbo, sitting with me on the front porch and sipping a Coke, burped. "They're probably rewriting the front page."

"Wonder how long that's gonna take."

"I've got an idea."

"Uh, oh."

"No. This makes sense."

I laughed. "Uh, oh. Uh, oh."

"When he drops off the papers, you use my bike to make your deliveries. He can drop me off at my place with my papers. I'll fold and when you're done, come over and help me deliver."

"What's the rush?"

"This is history in the making."

"So?"

"You know how you get an extra copy with your deliveries?"

"Yeah."

"Keep it. It's gonna be worth a lot of money."

"Maybe in a hundred years."

"It's not just the newspaper. What about Life Magazine?

76

Saturday Evening Post. Look Magazine. They're all gonna have special editions. We need to hit the stores and buy them up."

"They're not gonna be worth anything until I'm an old man. It's too late then. I need the money now."

"Life Magazine goes for fifty cents. You'll be able to sell one for a couple hundred dollars in twenty years."

"In twenty years the silverfish will have eaten them."

"That's why you've gotta put them in special containers. So, the bugs and moisture can't get to them."

"You're serious, aren't you?"

"I know a money deal when I see it."

"Yeah. But you gotta wait twenty years."

"It's not an argument. You don't have to buy any. All I'm saying is I want to get done as soon as we can so I can hit the newsstands. That's all."

We ran into a problem at Thrifty's on Fifty-fourth and El Cajon. Jimbo wanted to buy four each of Life, Look and Saturday Evening Post magazines.

The clerk studied the purchase doubtfully. "I'm sorry. I can't sell you this many."

Not what Jimbo was expecting. "Why, not?"

"That's hoarding."

"It's not hoarding. I just want to buy four of each."

"I'm sorry. I'll sell you two of each. That's it."

"You're selling the magazines, I've got the money to buy. You can't choose who you sell them to. It's the first buyer with the money. That's me."

"We want all of our customers to be able to purchase a copy, if they choose. If collectors come in and buy them all up, that won't happen, will it?"

"I'm buying them for my sick grandmother, my sister who's doing a report, my mom and dad and...,"

"I don't believe you. I'll sell you two of each and that's it."

Jimbo handed me five dollars. "He wants to buy two of each as well. Don't you, Calvin?"

I wanted no part of this conversation. It was not fair for Jimbo to bring me into it. But he was like that, stubborn enough to prove a point. It did not help that he always had this mad look about him, even when he was happy. I looked at the clerk with as pleasant a look as I could muster while putting Jimbo's money on the counter. "I'd like two copies of each, please."

"Sorry. I can't help you. You're with him."

Jimbo's face was getting red. "I want to see the manager."

"I *am* the manager."

I took the five and handed it to Jimbo. "Just buy two."

"That's not the point. He's got to...,"

"Both of you have a good point. Buy two and thank the man. I'll be outside."

I thought Jimbo was going to be furious and braced for whatever when he came out. But he came out laughing and handed me a bag of M & M's.

"What's this?"

"It's from the manager. I did what you said, bought two copies and a bag of these. He gave me an extra, said it was for you."

"That was cool. I should go thank him."

"Later. We've already wasted enough time. Let's get to the next place."

"How many of these are you planning on buying?"

"Maybe..., ten copies each?"

"And then the special editions?"

"Right."

"And then you're gonna lug fifty pounds of paper around for at least twenty years before it's worth anything. Every time you move, there's that box of something that's heavy. You've forgotten what it is, so you open it and go, "Oh, yeah! I forgot about these. I wonder what they're worth now?" Is it worth it?"

Jimbo's eyes had that faraway look, visualizing the future, I think. "You're right. Let's go get a donut."

"Now, you're talking."

Standing inside their living room, I studied the two columns of speakers, one next to me at the front door, the other across the room next to a hallway, both about seven feet high and facing toward the room on my left, which was filled with tambourines, bongo and Congo drums, a guitar, clacking sticks, pillows and chairs, a jam session waiting to happen.

In between the speakers was a long table filled with, starting across the room and working toward me, a stack of records, a turntable, amplifier with the cover off so I could see the glowing vacuum tubes, testers with switches and dials and lights, looking like something out of a Flash Gordon movie. Mounted on the wall above that was a shelf with stacks of books, more records and piles of papers.

Charles reached up and retrieved his sunglasses from the shelf and then handed me a piece of paper with two telephone numbers on it. "We'll be at one of these places."

"What time are you coming back?"

"That depends on the party. Could be midnight. Could be four in the morning."

"OK."

"You're welcome to play the stereo. Don't scratch the records. Don't touch the grooves with your fingers. Put the records back in their jackets when you're done playing them and don't get too loud or you're gonna wake the girls and then all bets are off."

Darlene came into the room doing something with her earrings. "Normally, they'll sleep all night."

"OK. I'll keep it down and not scratch the records. Thanks."

Charles opened the door, patted Darlene on the butt and put on his sunglasses. "Let's go. We're late. Calvin, there's sandwich stuff in the fridge, some sodas and I left you a beer on the top shelf. Be cool."

"Right. Thanks."

I called Jimbo as soon as their car was out of sight.

"We're eating dinner. I'll be down after that."

"Wait till you see these speakers. Oh, man!"

"What's it sound like?"

"Don't know. I haven't turned it on, yet."

"Hang on. What? Oh. Katie wants to tag along. OK?"

My two encounters with her were a limp handshake and an attempted stabbing. I was not enthusiastic.

"Must she?"

"She'll be cool. If not, I'll just take her home."

"OK."

I hung up, went over to the Congo drum and tapped it lightly with my thumb. It had a deep, resonant sound, booom, booom. Hitting it on the edge, bap, bap, bap, crisp and clean. I could have fun with this drum.

Going through the records, I found no rock and roll. I was a bit disappointed, but putting on a Belafonte LP and hearing the wonderful sounds coming out of the speakers, it didn't matter what I played, the sound was beautiful, as clean and pure as if the performers were right there in the room with me. Wow.

A knock on the door. I wasn't paying the music that loud, so I didn't think it could be a mad neighbor and it was too soon for Jimbo to arrive. I turned down the sound and answered the door.

"Harold. What are you doing here?"

"I stopped by your house to pay you back that two bucks I borrowed."

"That could've waited."

"Well, yeah." He laughed. "What do you think the odds are that I'll still have it next time I see you?"

"How did you know I was here?"

"Your mom pointed out the house, said you were baby-sitting."

Looking beyond him, the cul-de-sac was empty except for two cars across the street. Harold wasn't old enough to drive anyway and I didn't see any bicycles. Actually, I couldn't imagine him riding one. My vision of Harold, when I thought of him at all, was of him sitting at a desk or table somewhere with a strong cup of black coffee and working math problems.

"Did you walk?"

"Yeah.

"Oh. Um, come on in, I guess."

"Nice. Look at those speakers!"

"Yeah. Impressive, huh?"

Harold surveyed the room, taking it all in. "This is the whole package. Can you turn it up?"

"A little. I am baby-sitting."

"Who's playing?"

"Belafonte, calypso."

Harold retrieved the guitar, found a seat near the wall and began plucking on the strings, one at time until he started finding the notes. Minutes later, began playing simple chords.

"I didn't know you could play guitar."

"I can't."

"Sounds pretty good."

"I understand the progressions."

I went to the conga drum and, timidly at first, began thumping the center of the skin with the side of my thumb, keeping beat, feeling the song. Put a drum in front of anyone and play calypso and nobody can refrain from beating on it. Between tracks, someone knocking.

"John? Penny? What are you two doing here?"

They were holding hands, John smiling, Penny beaming. She held up the chain and showed me the ring.

"We're going steady."

Not the best news I've ever heard. I feigned a happy look and waved them in. "Congratulations."

John held up a brown paper bag. "Since you're the one that got us together, we wanted to celebrate with you."

"What is it?

Opening the bag, John showed me two bottles of Coke, one of Seven-up and, in a separate paper bag, a small bottle of Seagram's whiskey.

"Where did you get that?"

"From a friend."

"How did you know I was here?"

"Your mom told us. She wants to know if you're throwing a party."

"I better call. Otherwise, she might pop in. We've got to keep it quiet. I'm baby-sitting."

"I don't see any kids," said Penny. "Who are you baby-sitting?"

"Two girls," I said. "Four and six. They're sleeping."

Penny glanced toward the hallway. "We didn't bring any glasses. Can I go get some?"

"Sure. Harold? You want some Coke or Seven-up?"

He looked up. "Sure. Coke. Thanks. Can I flip the record over?"

"No. I've gotta do it. He doesn't want me scratching the records."

"I'll be careful."

"Still, no. I have to do it."

John headed toward the hallway, admiring the speakers along the way. "You have ice?"

"No idea. I haven't been out of this room, yet."

"Hey, Calvin. Are you going to flip the record?"

"Workin' on it."

Another knock on the door. Jimbo and Katie came in like a gust of irritation. Jimbo, immediately down on his knees, thumped the woofers. "Wow. Really deep. Have you turned it up?"

"Can't. I'm baby-sitting and I don't want to wake them up."

Katie went for the records and started flipping through the covers, looking disappointed.

"I don't know any of these. Which knob is for the radio?"

"Don't turn on the radio."

"Why not?"

"Because we're listening to records."

She studied the front of the amplifier. "No, you're not. Is it even on?"

"Yes. It's on. I just haven't had a chance to flip the record."

"Who are you playing?"

"Belafonte."

"Never heard of him. How about those records up on the shelf? What are those?"

"Don't know."

Katie reached for them. If, bull in a China shop didn't describe her presence, then maybe tornado looking for a place to touch down or an accident looking for a time and place to happen, would fit. "Don't take them down."

"Why not?"

"This isn't my stuff. I don't want to mess everything up."

"Then, we should turn on the radio."

"Jimbo, take care of your sister."

"Katie, quit being a pain in the ass."

"I'm just trying to get some good music on."

"You're being a pain."

John came into the room, handed Harold his Coke and me my drink. I'd never had whiskey before.

"Can you believe it?" John asked, amazed. "Not a clean dish in the house."

"I wouldn't know. I haven't been out of this room, yet."

"She's in there washing them!"

"Why? They're not your dirty dishes."

"That's what I said." John headed back to the kitchen. "And she wants me to dry. I *hate* doing dishes."

I laughed. "Welcome to going steady."

Suddenly, Katie was standing next to me. How she got there without my noticing was a mystery.

"What you got there, Calvin?"

This was the first time she'd ever called me by my name. Normally, I'm just the person that she has to walk around. "Coke. Go in and talk to Penny. She's the one pouring."

"Can I taste it?"

"No. Go get your own."

"That's got alcohol in it, doesn't it?"

"Don't know I haven't tried it, yet."

"I'll tell you if it's good, or not."

"Jimbo, take care of your sister."

"I'm not going to tell you again, Katie."

"I'm so scared."

Harold stood and went to the turntable. "I'm just going to flip this."

"Harold, leave it. I'm trying to get to it. Katie, leave me alone."

"Just a sip."

"Get away from me."

Jimbo jumped up, grabbed Katie's wrist and bent her middle finger backwards. "I told you!"

"Ow! What the hell is wrong with you?"

"You're like a fly on shit!"

I set my drink down on the other side of the turntable, away from Katie. "Hey! I resent that!"

Harold laughed. "You resemble that?"

"Not funny." I flipped the record over and carefully set the needle down. Belafonte filled the room.

Harold was content to lose himself in his guitar. I checked to see where he'd set his drink, saw that it was in a safe place and was satisfied that I could leave him alone.

Jimbo dragged Katie, cussing all the way, to the front door and, still bending her finger backward, made her open it. Stepping out onto the front porch, door closed, calm once again settled into the room. I decided to leave the porch light off.

Heading down the hallway toward the kitchen, I opened the door to the girl's bedroom. They were both sprawled out across their beds, completely oblivious to what was going on in the rest of the house.

How would I explain all of these strangers? I'd only met them once, waved several times while delivering my papers so, in some regard, they trusted me. Surely, if these girls woke up and saw what was happening in their house and told their parents, I would be in big trouble. The party had to come to an end.

I thanked Penny for doing the dishes and patted John on the back. We clinked glasses and I wished them the best.

"I had to make it strong," said John, trying to hand me

the dish towel, which I refused. "There wasn't much ice and everybody except Penny wanted Coke."

When I went to check on Jimbo and Katie, I found them sitting quietly on the front steps. Katie, sitting on the upper step, staring at something across the street while Jimbo, seated one step lower, was sprawled out top to bottom, looking up at the stars. Neither of them said a word.

"You guys, OK?"

"Something moved," said Katie. "Over there behind that car."

"What is it?"

"Don't know."

"How big?"

"I just saw it out of the corner of my eye."

"Big Dipper," said Jimbo, pointing up. "Which one is the North Star?"

"The one in the north," said Katie, laughing. "Duh."

Jimbo was quiet for a minute and then he started laughing. "That's funny."

"What's funny?"

"What you just said."

"What'd I say?"

"I forgot. But it *was* funny."

"Then quit laughing."

"I can't get this grin off my face."

I could not imagine Jimbo with a grin. This whole conversation and their complete lack of intolerance for each other was, for me anyway, suspicious.

"Jimbo?"

"He's not home, right now."

"Look at me."

"Why?"

"I want so see your face."

"Why?"

"Because I can't imagine you with a grin. Let me see."

"No way, man."

"Just look at me."

"Which one's the North Star?"

"Don't change the subject. Look at me."

"I don't think so."

Suddenly, Katie stood. "My mouth feels like the desert. You've got something to drink?"

"Talk to Penny. She'll fix you up."

When she left, I sat down on the steps with Jimbo. He didn't make eye contact and he had this weird smile.

"Hey, you doin' OK?"

"I'm doin' just fine."

"Did you take a pill, or something?"

"Can't talk about it."

"You're acting weird."

"I'll tell you tomorrow."

"Promise?"

"Promise..., what?"

"That you'll tell me tomorrow."

"Right." Jimbo got up, steadied himself a bit and then headed back up the stairs. "I'm thirsty. My mouth feels like sandpaper."

Back inside, Belafonte had finished playing. John and Penny turned out the kitchen light and followed Katie, who was holding two drinks, one of which she handed to Jimbo, back into the main room.

I put Belafonte back in its' cover, picked out Stan Getz and João Gilberto, put it on the turntable, told everybody that after this album they were going to have to leave because I'm not supposed to have a party, and put the needle down before they could say anything. *Girl from Ipanema* filled the room.

I returned to the conga drum. Harold went back to work on the guitar. Jimbo found the marimba and, much to my surprise, tapped lightly with the mallets. His disposition, normally, is to treat things roughly. So, I added this to the growing list of things not normal about Jimbo tonight.

John and Penny found the stuffed pillow chair in the corner while Katie, standing in between the two speakers in our darkened room, lit on one side by the hallway light, closed her eyes and started dancing.

Swaying with the music, arms reaching upward and

then slinking down to her hips, going forward, fingers beckoning our attention, inviting us in, hands moving like two snakes in some sort of mating ceremony, her head tilting side to side, blonde hair falling over her shoulders, hips swaying, all of her essence casting long shadows across the wooden floor and onto the opposite wall.

I could not read her smile and became fixated on it. This was not the impetuous girl wrangling her way into everything. Her smile suggested that she was a young woman, enjoying the music, happy with who she was and where the music was taking her.

Standing in my dark corner and watching her exotic, sensual moves, letting my hands do what they will with the drum, I noticed that she had captivated everyone's attention.

The room was quiet when that side played out, everybody motionless, waiting. When I went over to flip the record, almost as if it was a wake-up call, they all remembered their drinks. No one said anything.

Side two was good, but the magic was not the same. When it was over, Penny drug John back into the kitchen to dry while she washed glasses. Jimbo and Katie left still looking as if they were in a daze. Harold left with them.

John and Penny finally gone, I checked on the girls and left the hallway light on in case they got up. Returning to the quiet of living room, leaving it dark, I sat on the pillow couch and reminisced about the evening.

When Katie wasn't being a pest, she could be quite charming indeed.

Jimbo had a friend, Buzz, who needed a place to keep his motorcycle until the driveway was fixed at his house. That didn't sound right, but I figured that it wouldn't harm anyone if he parked it in front of my Dodge out in the alley. Still...,

"Why doesn't he just park it on the street?"

"It's a brand-new bike. He's afraid it might get stolen."

"Oh. Doesn't he have a garage?"

"If he did, he'd put it in there."

"How long is he going to keep it here?"

"Until the driveway is fixed, I guess."

It didn't feel right. Surely, Buzz had other places where he could keep it. He had no other friends? I didn't know him. Jimbo had never talked about him before.

Also, the ordeal with the Dodge had not been resolved. If parking his bike here brought unwanted attention, how might this affect me? The last two things I wanted was thieves in the area wanting to steal his bike or, even worse, police investigating the theft and then noticing my car.

"Has he got a cover for it?"

"No idea."

"Because if the bike's bright red, it's gonna attract attention and...,"

"I don't know what color it is."

"How come he asked you?"

"Because we're friends."

"You've never talked about him before."

"You tell me all about your friends?"

"You know all of my friends."

"Well..., can he? Or, not?"

"He has to keep it outside the fence and if he's got a cover to hide it, that's even better. Two nights, no more."

"Thanks. I'll let him know."

Buzz came cruising in about three hours later. The bike was beautiful, a red and silver Triumph Tiger. I could see

88

why he would be worried about someone stealing it. But I didn't care much for Buzz. He wore Levi's, black, steel-toed boots, a white T-shirt with a pack of cigarettes rolled up into his sleeve, Lucky Strikes.

Buzz had a flat-top haircut, tobacco stained teeth, a chipped front tooth, bruised knuckles like he'd been in a fight recently and, holding his pants up above his lanky frame, a thick, black leather belt with a silver, turquoise inlaid buckle.

He didn't have a cover for the bike and wanted to put it inside the fenced yard. Nope. No deal.

"You got a tarp I can put over it?"

I did. But that wasn't part of the deal. Jimbo wasn't here and I was having to deal with him. I took him to the trunk of my Dodge, opened it and showed him a greasy piece of carpet that I use when I have to get beneath the car.

"That's it? That's all you got?"

"The deal was, I give you a place to park. Everything else is up to you."

He was sizing me up. I could feel it. My heart stepped up a bit. But that was the deal. I had to stand by that. And, I was hoping, that he realized it wasn't going to do him any good to have an altercation here. I hoped he was that smart.

"You're right, kid. I'll just put it between that car and the fence, if you don't mind. I won't need a tarp."

I didn't really like that either because if I wanted to leave, I only had a few inches between my car and the bike. But if it got me rid of him, I was for it. "No more than two days, right?"

"I'll be outta here tomorrow."

"OK." I turned to go. I was furious with Jimbo for not being here to deal with him, for getting me into this situation in the first place, and not checking it out to see if the need was real. It didn't feel right.

"Hey, kid."

"My name's Calvin."

"Calvin." He reached to shake my hand. "Thanks. I

appreciate it."

I shook his hand, headed back through the gate and for the first time in a long time, pushed the stick between the two U-bolts where the post and gate came together. Sure, anybody could get in just by removing the stick, but I didn't have a padlock. At the same time though, the insinuation was that this property was private and secured. If you remove the stick, wouldn't that be breaking and entering?

I went inside, got myself a glass of water and, thinking about it, decided to go back out and remove the stolen tags from the license plate. My car might be stolen, but I had already reported that. There was no way I could explain the up to date tags.

I didn't sleep well at all. I kept thinking that I heard voices out back and even got up once around midnight, grabbed a flashlight and scanned the back yard. Nothing. Shining my light over the fence, I didn't see anything unusual. Bike and car were just how we left them. That did not keep me from imagining, throughout the night, that I heard voices out there.

Everything looked normal on my way to school the next morning, but coming home, I spotted a police car blocking the entrance to the alley. The other end of the alley dead-ended, so to speak, into a canyon.

I walked past the alley and entered the house via the front door. Looking out back, I saw that the motorcycle was *in* my back yard, sitting between my dune buggy and the fence. There were two policemen standing next to it, one reading something from a piece of paper, the other inspecting the bike.

A knock on the front door. I was hesitant to answer. Looking out the front window, the police.

"Are you the owner of the motorcycle in your back yard?"

"No."

"Is the owner here in the house?"

"No. Some guy came by yesterday and asked if he could park it here."

"In your yard?"

90

"No. Out in the alley."

"Did he have permission to park it in your yard?"

"No. I told him he could not park it in my yard. The alley is public property. I've got no control over that."

"What time, yesterday?"

"Afternoon, about three."

"Did he give you a name?"

I was going to get caught between two opposing forces, thanks to Jimbo. If I identify Buzz, sooner or later, when he gets out of prison, he'll be back. Or, I get involved in some kind of crime thing like receiving stolen goods. "I'm not sure. Bud, or Buzz, something like that."

"Did he give a reason why he wanted to leave it?"

"Something about his driveway was being repaired and he was afraid that it might get stolen if he left it on the street."

"Well, it is stolen..., from a good friend of mine, another policeman. Did you know this person prior to yesterday?"

"No."

"Any idea why he chose here?"

I was very tempted to bring Jimbo into the mess. "I just figured that he thought it would be safe."

"You're *sure* that you did not give him permission to park the bike inside?"

"I'm very sure. Last I saw, it was in the alley."

"Any idea who owns that car?"

"Which one?"

"That old Dodge."

OK. He got me. I was hoping to slide out of this before my parents got home in another hour and a half. With a sigh, I invited him in, showed him the receipt and explained how I reported this situation to the DMV and showed him all of my paperwork.

"Have you driven the car on the street since you've owned it?"

"No. I'm too young to drive."

"You know it's going to have to have insurance and current registration before anybody drives it."

"Yes. I know that."

91

"And..., since it's not on your property. You might have to move it. Or..., we might have to tow it, if that turns out to be the case."

"I'll move it into the back yard."

Jimbo owed me one, I could claim to my parents that the car was his and I was going to help him work on it. I followed the policeman out to the back yard and listened to their conversation. It was taking place in my yard, so I figured that I had the right to watch. I kept my mouth shut.

It wasn't me that got Buzz busted. On the other side of the alley is a duplex that faces Winona Avenue. Across the street, living in the second-floor apartment, another policeman had seen the bulletin and watched the activity between Buzz and myself. He had already identified Buzz and, yes, the motorcycle was parked outside the fence. I was vindicated and I did not rat out Buzz. A sigh of relief.

They hauled the bike away and left my car alone. I was told that they would investigate ownership and if it turned out that the car was mine, and if that was public property, I'd have forty-eight hours to move it. They were nice about it.

My parents got home about ten minutes after the area cleared out. By then, I had the back gate closed, stick back in place and made myself busy watering plants. They were happy that I was taking an interest in the yard. Some days are diamonds, some days are stone. Not quite sure how to describe this one.

Turning sixteen, I was eligible to take the driving test for my license, once I got a car to drive. Our family car is not available all week long and one of my parents is usually using it on Saturday. The DMV is, obviously, closed on Sunday.

Jimbo and I went down to the DMV, me riding on the back of his bike, took the test and got our learner's permits. I drove the Dodge around long enough to decide that I could pass the test. Jimbo was usually there riding shotgun, telling me all the things that I was doing wrong, not that he was any expert.

I'd chance taking the driver's test in the Dodge, but I read that the vehicle has to have current registration and proof of insurance, bad news. The good news was that the DMV sent paperwork saying that I can register as the new owner after I fill out a certificate of non-operation, update the registration and pay the fees. One last thing, I could not be the legal owner of the car because I was not eighteen.

My parents were reasonably understanding. After I got off restriction for not telling them in the first place, they agreed to sign on as the legal owners provided I kept up with the insurance. Uncle Wally offered to pay for that up front, but I'd have to pay back with interest.

Working for him, moving jukeboxes and pinball machines around town, provided enough money for gas and maybe an occasional cruise through Oscar's Drive-in for a Coke and hamburger. Not much else. I quit the paper route.

But through a friend of the family, I got a job at a local donut shop working three to six in the afternoon. I would work behind the counter, clean up the cooking area and, after they got to know me, close up the shop.

A teenager in a donut shop? I could not think of a better way to spend the afternoon. The first week, I cannot even begin to count how many glazed donuts I ate before I

93

discovered that I liked the chocolate ones better. Getting tired of those, I moved on to maple bars. There's something about raised donuts (the ones that have yeast and have to proof before cooking), and maple frosting that goes beyond glaze or chocolate. Take your time eating these. They're kind of special.

Tiring of raised donuts, I moved into the cake donut realm. One of my jobs was to move all of the unsold donuts of the day into the day-old donuts case and wipe down the other cases, getting everything ready for the fresh batch in the morning.

What I noticed was that the cake donuts held up much better than the raised ones. The frosting on the raised donuts seemed to melt and fade away by the end of the day, whereas the caked donuts stayed moist, firm and the frosting stayed put. I went through all of the flavors and coatings and by the end of the first month, I pretty much knew every product that we had to offer. Also, I was sick of donuts.

Early one Saturday morning, my boss, Tony, asked if I could come to work. There were customers waiting when I walked in. Tony was waiting on customers and frying donuts at the same time, a work skill that I was soon to learn, something akin to bucketing out the water of a sinking boat while rowing toward shore.

In a rare lull, he showed me how to fill the hopper with cake dough, guide it over the top of the oil, turn the handle, get thirty at a time and don't land one donut on top of another because then they're both bad.

"Flip them when they're golden brown and don't stab them with the stick. Tap the donut at the edge to turn it over. When both sides are the same color, pull up the screen, bang it on the lid here to knock off the extra oil and then slide the donuts onto the cooling rack."

"Got it."

"Do thirty each of all of the icings."

I was busy frying when a customer, a clean-cut man in his thirties wearing a sports jacket and tie on a Saturday morning, walked through the front door.

I made eye contact. "I'll be right with you."

He nodded, smiled knowingly, and waited while I put the first six donuts in the icing.

"Thanks for waiting. What'll it be?"

"Coffee...,"

He was looking up at the price list on the wall...,

"Here? Or, to go?"

"Oh. Here."

I grabbed a tray, poured his coffee.

He looked at me, quizzically. "What's good?"

"It's all good."

"What's *your* favorite?"

What does that matter? "Depends on the day of the week and what I had last."

A short laugh. "Ha! I guess that's true. You must eat a lot of donuts, working here."

I gazed longingly at icing tray on the other side of the partition. "I did at first."

"How about a chocolate and a...,"

His eyes began wandering over the different trays of donuts in the display cases. Odd, I was thinking. He had several minutes to make up his mind.

"Your chocolate donut. Raised? Or, cake?"

"What's the difference?"

I pointed them out. "The raised donut is like bread, light and airy. And they're a little bigger. Cake donuts are more like cake and slightly smaller."

"How do they do that?"

"One has yeast and the other doesn't. I'll be right back while you decide."

I hurried back to the icing area and dipped as many donuts as I could before he looked over at me, suggesting that he had made his decision.

Another customer came through the door, an elderly lady, gray hair pulled back, wire rim glasses and black thick-heeled shoes. I noticed that she assessed the donuts in the case and already had her mind made up. She smiled and waited patiently for customer number one.

Having finished icing donuts, I hurried back to the counter. "Have you decided?"

"Yeah," he said, looking up at the menu again. "I guess I'll take a coconut."

There were no coconut donuts in the display case. How could he miss that? "We haven't had a chance to make them, yet. I can make that happen with the next batch out of the fryer."

"How long will that take?"

"That, my friend, depends on you. About ten minutes."

While he was back to studying the menu, the lady made eye contact and said quietly, "Two plain donuts, one cup of coffee for here, no cream. Here's the exact change."

Oh, how I love customers like that! I served her, put the money in the register and waited for customer number one.

The customer's always right. Isn't that what they say? In my mind, a good customer is always right. A bad customer I can do without. He seemed to have no clue as to what the situation was in the shop.

My boss was over at the cutting table trying to get an order ready for a ten o'clock delivery. Meanwhile, donuts are not being fried or iced and this guy thinks I have nothing to do except wait for him to make up his mind.

"Not yet?"

His response was slight shake of his head and something between a smile and a grimace.

"May I recommend a maple bar? They're really good."

"I don't know that I'd like a maple flavor on my donuts."

"Take your time. I'll be right back."

I headed for the icing tray, mumbling. The elderly lady, sitting at one of the tables along the wall, looked over at me with a knowing smile. I acknowledged her unspoken comment by smiling and rolling my eyes.

Back at the fryer, I glanced over at customer number one, saw that he was still occupied with some dilemma and started cranking donuts into the hot grease. By the time I'd plopped thirty of them, two more customers came through the front door.

"Tony? I'm kind of committed here."

He glanced over at my situation, dropped what he was doing, took the money that customer number one had tentatively placed on the counter, rang him up, put the change on the tray with his coffee and donut and slid it toward him.

"I'm going to buy another donut."

"Let me know when you're ready. Next!"

I just learned from the expert.

When I asked Jimbo about his and Katie's change of mood the other night, he didn't answer, choosing instead to kick at the dirt.

"Man, if you can't tell me, who can you tell? Explain Katie, changed like night and day. What's with that?"

We were sitting out on the back-door steps of my house. We'd been talking quietly, but looking up at the open window to my bedroom, Jimbo nodded that we move. We walked over to the other side of the dune buggy and sat in the shade of the fence.

Jimbo picked a leaf off of some nearby weed and began tearing the edges back toward the spine. He smiled.

"What's so funny?"

"It was just a good night, that's all."

"How was it good?"

"You know, the music and all."

"And all of what?"

"You know, the vibes."

"Jimbo, fess up. You promised."

"Katie and I...,"

"Come on!"

"Outside, we had a long talk."

"And...?"

"Promise you won't tell anybody."

"My God, Jimbo. Spill it."

"When Katie and I went outside..., remember?"

"Of course."

"I took her over to the side of the house, you know, so the neighbors wouldn't see. I wasn't going to hurt her. Just get her to settle down. But before anything like that happened, we spotted an abalone shell that had a few butts inside."

"Cigarette butts?"

"That's what we thought. Instead of arguing, we broke away the paper, put the tobacco in my pipe and smoked it."

98

"Why would you do that? You don't even know what it is."

"If someone else was smoking it, it must be OK."

"So..., it wasn't tobacco?"

"Did you ever see the show, Reefer Madness?"

"Yeah..., so?"

"It's not like that at all. We just started laughing."

"What if it was something really bad?"

"Look at me. Am I dying?"

"Is it addicting?"

"Don't know."

"Do you crave it?"

"It's not like that. It felt good. Instead of being mad, I was happy. Couldn't get the smile off of my face and you kept asking why..., ass hole. That just made it worse."

"If something's not normal, I'm always curious. And *you* were not normal."

"Did we look normal? I felt like I was glowing."

"Normal, except for that grin. You look stupid when you grin, evil almost."

"It sure felt good."

"Katie is a really good dancer."

"I'd never seen her do that before. Now she does it all the time. We hardly argue. I think we both realized how stupid it was."

"So..., you're saying that you both are better off having smoked marijuana? Or, whatever it was."

"You saw it with your own eyes."

"Did you have a headache the next morning?"

"Nothing like that."

"How long did it last?"

"Don't know. I went straight to my room and crashed. Didn't want to talk to my parents."

"That wasn't yours to smoke. They probably think I took it."

"Looked to us like they butted it out, like a cigarette. They were done with it. That's not stealing. We were cleaning up!"

If I hadn't seen the change with my own eyes, I'd think

Jimbo was full of it. "You didn't get sick, like when we drank the wine?"

"Nope. And sipping on that Pepsi was like a river going down a canyon."

"I think you're full of shit."

"I'm not kidding. You should try it."

"Riiight. It's illegal. You go to jail for that."

"No. We're juveniles. We won't be going to jail."

"Well, in any case, we don't have any and I have to go to work tonight."

"What time?"

"Midnight. That's what sucks about this job. Everybody else is out having fun on the week-ends and that's when I have to go to work."

"What time is it?"

"We had dinner at five, so I'd guess that it's about six."

"That's enough."

"For what?"

"Let's go sit in the Dodge."

"Why?"

"I kept one of those butts. It's in my billfold."

"I've got to work tonight."

"You'll be OK by then."

Midnight, driving into the parking lot next to the donut shop, I noticed that there were several people standing outside the bar across the street, rowdy and yelling.

The donut shop was the third storefront in this complex, about two hundred feet away. I walked quickly past the lighted signs in the windows and by the time I got to my door and was hunting for the right key, some guy started yelling.

"Bastards won't serve me! Sayin' I'm *drunk*? What the *fuck*? I've been coming here for thirty years! I'm their best customer! I'm not *drunk*!"

I thought he was, wobbly, aggressive and loud. I opened the door about the same time he stepped off of the curb, heading toward me, which got my heart racing.

My state of mind could be classified as, still stoned. Jimbo assured me that I wouldn't feel anything come midnight. Wrong.

My car felt like a spaceship on the way to work. I was in some sort of exploratory vehicle traveling through some kind of alternate world, a rat working my way through a maze. It all looked the same but felt so different. The night lights were beautiful and all songs played on the radio seemed like masterpieces. The single speaker mounted above the radio in the dash never sounded so good, even though the speaker rattled, torn cone.

Hours earlier, sitting in the Dodge with the windows rolled up, we each got one big puff off of the pipe and held it as long as we could. We turned on the radio and waited.

"I don't feel anything, Jimbo."

"You will."

"What am I supposed to feel?"

"It's not like drinking. Just the opposite, actually."

"I can't imagine what the opposite of drinking is."

"Oh! Here's, *Under the Boardwalk*. I'm gonna turn it up."

101

"Not too loud, I don't want to talk to anybody."

"That's why you turn it up, so you don't have to."

"Who?"

"Anybody."

"I don't see anybody."

"That's because it's working."

"What's working?"

Jimbo started laughing. "Nobody. Nobody's working."

"I don't feel anything."

"You sure? You're talking like you do."

"How does one talk if they...,"

"If they're..., what?"

"Did I already say that I don't feel anything?"

"About ten times."

"Really? Didn't they just play this song?"

"It's the same one."

"As before?"

"It just started. If you shut up we can hear it."

"Same song..., really?"

"Your mind is mush."

"I am very thirsty."

"Let's drive up to Dowd's Liquor and get a Coke."

"No way I'm driving."

We both got a drink from the hose, after which, Jimbo had to go. I went to bed around eight-thirty, hoping to get a couple hours of sleep before going to work.

Would I remember the formulas? Would I set the fryer to the right temperature? Did I know how much water to add per pound of flour? A mistake is hard to clean up and a complete waste of time. I got no sleep between eight-thirty and now.

Instead of crossing the street, the drunk stopped at a car parked along the curb, flung the driver's side door open, causing a passing car to honk and swerve, flipped that driver off, retrieved something from inside the car, headed back to the bar and threw whatever it was through their storefront window.

It came down like thunder, glass splintering across the blacktop, followed by a string of customers, drinks in hand, cigarettes glowing. They kept him from getting into his car, took his keys and within the next fifteen minutes, the cops were there.

I didn't have time to watch. I went inside, locked the door behind me and went to work. Tony had shown me how measure out the flour, add water at the right temperature, heat up the fryer and run the three-speed mixer with the big, steel bowl.

Once inside, I found a note saying that he would be in a little late and to make a large batch of the raised donut dough about an hour before I was done with making the cake donuts.

That seemed optimistic. Making up a large batch that early, and if Tony was late coming in, the dough would rise up out of the container, oozing up from beneath the cloth cover like a big ominous worm.

If he was late, it would fall upon me to scrape all of that out of the bowl, cut it up into workable piles and start rolling out and cutting filling up the screen with donuts until, at some point when the proof box was full, that I'd have to start frying and icing at the same time. I was not enthusiastic about that. I put on a pot of coffee, turned on the radio and went for flour.

A Hard Day's Night.

My mind is mush. I'm here to do..., *what?* I have to force myself to concentrate. Measure flour, got it. Water. Got it. Mix it up. It's a big mixer and the dough hook stops for nothing. Finish mixing. I can hear the radio again. One good thing, there are less commercials at night.

Glad All Over.

It seems like, for the first time, I see a clear order of things, how everything fits into its own little niche, taking up space and time, little compartments of stuff everywhere. Frying donuts, coffee in hand, I'm rolling along, getting into the rhythm, feeling smug. Someone's banging on the front door.

Suspicion.

Two policemen, standing on the other side of the glass, peering in. Coming to arrest me for smoking pot? How could they could know? Maybe they know I'm under eighteen, out after curfew. Shit. Be cool.

Maybe they just want donuts. I point to the fryer, which they can't see, and motion for them to wait. I feel like I'm glowing. Don't...,

Let It Be Me

They stood on the other side of the partition, eating donuts and watching me make them. Kit, the younger one, inhaled a warm Old Fashioned, still crispy around the edges.

"Man! They're really good right out of the fryer. Thanks."

Flipping the donuts in the hot oil, "Yeah. First time I tasted them like that, I couldn't stop."

An odd feeling, being stoned *and* on the right side of the law. I had a hard time keeping the smile off of my face.

Bill, the older of the two, put his coffee down and reached for his billfold. "Thanks for serving us. We appreciate it."

"Actually, I didn't serve you. I pointed to the coffee and donuts and told you to help yourselves."

"How much do we owe you?"

"No charge."

"No? Really. We want to pay."

"How about a hundred dollars?"

He laughed. "That seems a little high."

"Better if you take the first offer, free. I'm glad to have you here."

"It's a deal. Thanks."

"Were you the ones that handled that drunk across the street?"

"Yeah. He could hardly stand up. Lucky, he didn't get behind the wheel."

"What did he throw into the glass?"

"Paperweight. Who drives around with a paperweight in their car?"

I measured out the flour, took its temperature, retrieved the cake of yeast from the fridge and worked out the formula for water temperature, all with the intensity of being stoned.

All talking ceased. They both grabbed another donut,

refilled their coffee cups, sat down in a booth and filled out their paperwork.

This was a comfortable arrangement. I had protection! I laughed at the irony of it.

We'll Sing in the Sunshine.

After Uncle Wally and I removed all of the pistons in the old Dodge, re-seated the rings, put it all back together, gave it another tune-up and after I washed and waxed the car, Jimbo offered to buy it.

"I'll give you two hundred."

"I just did all of that work! It's worth more than two hundred now."

"That's what you originally wanted."

"Before all of that work. Besides, it's not for sale."

"OK. I'll give you two, twenty-five."

"If you wanted the car so much, why weren't you here helping us fix it? Or, at least help me wash and wax it."

"I've still got a paper route, remember?"

"It doesn't take that much time. You've got an easy route. And you've got a bike."

"But if I had a car, I could go get a real job."

"Which is why I'm not selling this one. I need it to get to work."

"If you got a deal on a newer one, you'd sell this one?"

"That depends."

"On what?"

"It's gotta be in better shape. It's got to be special."

"That won't be too hard. This is a pile of junk."

"Says the man with no car."

"What kind of car do you want?"

"Never thought about it. I like this one."

That wasn't quite true. I didn't like that the speaker rattled when I turned up the sound and this car only had an AM radio. I'd heard FM on Uncle Wally's new Chevy. The sound is much better, no static, and the station doesn't fade when you go under a bridge, a huge technology leap.

"Well? What kind of car?"

"Why don't you go buy something, leave me out of it?"

"I've got a paper route. I don't make that much. You're working at the donut shop. You can afford it."

106

Fifty-five Chevy Bel Air's were hot, especially the ones with the power pack, the two hundred and sixty-five cubic inch engine with the three-speed synchro-mesh transmission with optional overdrive. But they were out of my price range.

A nineteen fifty-six Ford Fairlane Victoria caught my eye, one that had dual exhaust, a two hundred and seventy-two cubic inch engine, a four-barrel carburetor and front and rear speakers. I fell in love.

Yes, I would have to make payments. And, if I was even going to consider the transaction, I'd have to sell the Dodge and use that money for a down payment, meaning that I'd be relying on Jimbo to pay promptly, right after he collected for his route and before he could go spend the money elsewhere. They did not want the Dodge as a trade-in.

Funny thing about this. I was happy with the Dodge until Jimbo pointed out that I could afford better. Did I really need this powerful vehicle with all of the new bells and whistles? No. But after I saw the Ford, I could think of nothing else. It wasn't going to get me to work any faster and it was going to set me back financially.

I think what happens is, working hard, trying to get ahead, the promise of a reward for all of the effort is too much to resist. I quit my three to six shift at the donut shop on the condition that I got it back when school resumed in the fall and took on the night shift as donut maker, which earned me a lot more money.

Hoping to ensure that Jimbo held up his end of the bargain, now that he had a car, I persuaded Tony to let him work my afternoon shift. Everything was working out OK, so far.

San Diego River meanders through Mission Valley on its way to the Pacific and it floods almost every time we have heavy rains, a night like tonight. So, what did they do? Put in a big shopping center and lots of apartments right next to the river. Made sense to someone. Or, as my economics instructor always said, "Follow the money."

I had just replaced the windshield wipers on my car and was pleased to see how well they worked on my way to work. Fifty-fourth and University was flooded. Fortunately, I was warned by the rippling reflection of the traffic lights before I got to the intersection.

Inside the donut shop, at four in the morning, there is no one else around to bother, so I turn up the sounds. To get my attention, you have to knock louder than the radio, or at least wait for a pause in between, which is what this girl just did.

Hello Dolly

She was standing out there, arms crossed, hunched slightly forward, her dishwater blonde hair dripping rain. I walked around the donut cooling rack, past the glass cases and opened the door. "Can I help you?"

"Can I buy a donut?"

I had explicit instructions, don't let anyone in. Talking to Tony, the police were the only exception. "We're closed. Sorry."

"Just one donut?"

"There's no money in the register. I can't make change."

"I'll give you a dollar. I don't need change. I just want a donut."

"Well...,"

She was getting wetter by the second, the top of her blouse now getting soaked. She was about my age, mouth teasingly ready to break into a smile. Too cute to resist. I stepped back to let her in.

"I'll get you a towel."

"It's OK. I'm waterproof."

108

She followed me to the other end of the shop, stopped at the counter and put a dollar down. I went around to the other side.

"What kind?"

"Glazed."

"All I've made so far are the cake ones." I pointed to the pile of dough on the table. "Glazed donuts come from that."

"How long will that take?"

"About an hour."

"For just one donut?"

"I can't make just one. I have to make them all at once."

"Why?"

"Well, for one, if I try to push one donut through ahead of all the others, it won't turn out right. The dough won't have risen enough and it'll taste like yeast. I don't want to make yeasty donuts."

She started to laugh. Looking around, she spotted the coffee. "Is that fresh?"

"Yes."

"Can I get a coffee and a donut for a dollar?"

"I suppose."

"OK. I'll wait. Can I serve myself?"

The Way You Do the Things You Do

I nodded, slightly uncomfortable with her assertive behavior. She put a dollar next to the cash register, poured herself a cup and found the cream in the fridge. I started cutting the dough into piles.

She sat on the counter facing me. I couldn't help but notice how short her skirt was. She wasn't concerned about it and instead blew the steam off of her coffee while I rolled out the dough.

"Do you like making donuts?"

"It's a job."

"Are you in here every night?"

"I get Tuesdays off."

"Why Tuesday?"

"It's the slowest day. We only have to make a few dozen donuts for the day."

"What's your busiest time?"

"Saturday night. All of the churches want donuts for Sunday morning."

I grabbed a cutter and began cutting up the dough, carefully putting each piece onto a screen, six rows of five, offset.

"Those don't have any holes in them."

"They're going to be jelly-filled." I rolled the remaining dough back into a ball and covered it.

"What do you do with that?"

"I'll roll it out again later and make chocolate and maple bars."

"Is there always some left over?"

"No. First cut is for donuts and jelly filled. Second cut is for maple and chocolate bars. Pretzels come last."

"Why?"

"If I roll them out too soon, the dough will have too much rise and the pretzels will come out like bread. My boss wants them to have a slightly harder crust. You writing a book?"

She was drying her hair with a handkerchief and it was already soaked. Was she out walking in the rain? I didn't see any cars parked out front.

"No. Just waiting for my donut."

"What're you doing out this time of night?"

"Couldn't sleep."

"I don't have that problem. Mine is to stay awake."

"Is that why you keep the music so loud?"

Come a Little Bit Closer

We *were* competing with the radio. I turned it down and returned to my cutting table. "I don't normally have anyone to talk to."

"How's it feel, working Saturday night while all of your friends are out having fun?"

"Depressing." I shrugged. "Pay's not bad. And if I were out with my friends, I'd probably be getting into trouble. Did you *walk* here?"

Big smile. "No. I parked down in the lot, on the other side of that Ford. It started pouring as soon as I got out of the car."

I put the cutter down, went into the back room, grabbed a clean towel, came back and tossed it to her. The handkerchief wasn't going to make it.

"Thanks."

Her skirt rode up a bit as she let herself off of the counter. She went back out to the customer area, bent over and dried her hair. My God, she had nice legs. Tony would understand, should he walk in right now. I lost count of the donuts on the screen and had to do a recount.

Baby, I Need Your Loving.

The proof box was getting full and the top rack donuts were going to be over-proofed soon. Start frying whatever's on top and fill in with new racks full of whatever, keeping a space in between.

Once frying is started, it's a hectic circle going from cutting, to frying, to icing. Although I needed help, I didn't want Tony to arrive. If he did, she would leave and I would never even know her name. She was combing her hair now, length just past her shoulders. She looked good with wet hair.

"Hey! What's your name?"

"Do I need to give you my name just to get a donut?"

"I like to know my customers."

"You know all of your customer's names?"

"All the one's I want to know."

"What's yours?"

"Vinny."

"You don't look like a Vinny."

I laughed. "What does a Vinny look like?"

"You know, black hair combed back, a day's growth, T-shirt...,"

"What's your name?"

"You're not a Vinny."

I opened the proof box, took out the top wire screen that held the future jelly-filled donuts, placed the screen between the two wire handles and carefully dropped it down into the hot oil. They all disappear for a second and then pop back up, sizzling. "If I agree that I'm not Vinny,

111

you'll tell me your name?"

She smiles, liking the challenge. "OK."

"You're right. I'm not a Vinny. So..., what's yours?"

"Bambi."

"You're not a Bambi. You don't look like a Bambi."

She laughs. "Now it's your turn to stereotype."

"You don't have floppy ears."

"That's it?"

"I don't think you have a wet nose." I peered over the partition. God, she was pretty. "Nope. You're not a Bambi."

I had to get back to frying. It was going to be very busy for the next hour.

Dancing in the Street

"Cassi," she said, at last. "My name is Cassi."

She looked like a Cassi, although I had no idea what a Cassi might look like. I didn't know any, so why I would even have an opinion? Do people really resemble their names? Do they grow into them?

"Cassi? OK. Even if you aren't one, I'll call you that."

"So..., what's yours?"

"Calvin."

Her glazed donut was finally ready. I tried to give her two, but she only wanted one. She left before Tony arrived. The first place Tony goes to, entering the shop in the early morning hours, is to the coffee pot next to the cash register.

"What's this dollar doing here?"

"Oh. I sold somebody a coffee and donut to go. They didn't want the change."

"What's with this towel? It's all wet."

I took it from him and headed for the dirty clothes basket in the back of the shop. "I got soaked coming in, got busy and forgot about it." The towel smelled of her perfume, compelling.

Tony took over cutting while I settled into frying and icing, a repetitive motion that allows plenty of time to think of other things.

I didn't get her number and I'm not sure that's her name. We seemed to hit it off pretty well. I liked her interest in making donuts, her disregard for being soaked, how pretty she was dripping wet, her smile, her perfume and her willingness to tease and be teased.

Was I thinking about her? Of course. In the wee morning hours, after a stranger has come and gone and left such a powerful impression, there is no space for anything else.

Wishin' and Hopin'

The thing is, you don't really know anything about anyone, even when they tell you. I didn't see a ring on her finger and there was no conversation about spouses, boyfriends, girlfriends or significant others. It's a mystery and that makes it all the more compelling.

Was she just passing through and was I never going to see her again? Does she live somewhere nearby? Out driving around because she had an argument with her boyfriend? All I know is that there's something special about someone coming in out of the rain. Your heart goes out.

You Don't Know Me

Coming back from Potrero County Park, located in the back country of San Diego County, there is a long, straight stretch of two-lane blacktop road that is a relief to drive after passing over all of the curved sections.

I had been following a Chrysler through the winding curves and he was dogging it. I tried, at first, to nudge him along at a faster pace by following a little too closely. When that didn't work, I dropped back and hoped that he would get the message and pull over into one of the available sections of road that would allow that. Nope.

So when the solid yellow, no-passing line changed into a broken yellow, I had a long stretch where I could see what was coming and figured I had a pretty good chance to go around. I punched it and all four barrels of that two hundred and seventy-two cubic inch engine kicked into passing mode. I swung out into the oncoming lane and surged ahead, engine roaring.

To my surprise, he did the same and it became a race to see who was going to get ahead of whom before the passing lane ended. We had plenty of time to accelerate, a couple of hundred yards and we were both going way too fast into the curve. When I knew I was a car's length ahead, I pulled back into our lane.

I had never been on this road before and was utterly surprised by the sharpness of the curve. I hit the brakes hard, hoping that the idiot behind me wasn't going to shove me over the side.

To his credit, if any is due, his braking skills were equal to mine, not that either of us was any good, but his car stayed back and let me negotiate the curve. My passenger side tires hit gravel, I could hear it kicking up into the wheel wells, and the car started to skid. The drop-off was steep. I don't remember how far.

I knew I was going over. I could feel it. My heart was in my throat. This car was going to roll and I was going to be in it. Seat belts? Never heard of them. My only hope was to let off of the brakes and hit the gas. Tires spinning, spewing gravel, they finally caught a bit of blacktop and, surging forward, I came out of the curve still on the road.

I had never faced death before. You know, *instantly*, what's important in your life. Was this road race necessary? No. Did it prove anything? No. Was winning worth my life? No.

I braked heavily and slowed down to a safer speed with this other driver right on my tail, no more than a foot or two off of my rear bumper. I kept expecting his car to ram into mine. When there was a chance to pull over, I did and waved him by. I was shaking from head to toe.

Passing, he honked his horn and, laughing, gave me a thumbs-up before gunning it down the road. I pulled back onto the blacktop and continued on at a much safer, relaxed speed. I hardly even reached the speed limit all the way home.

My mind kept coming back to those few seconds when I was sure I was going over the side. There was no guard rail to prevent it from happening and, had I not gunned the engine, I would be at the bottom of that curve right now, either in or out of my car, hurt and bleeding, dead or alive. It was a moment of utter disbelief, my actions causing my own demise.

Was it a desire to teach the other driver a lesson, to prove what an idiot he was? Was it a show of power between two egos? A challenge between two fast cars? Stupidity? All of the above.

Starting school again, with the new schedule, the only chance I would have to see Cassi was on a Friday night when I'd be working alone until Tony came in sometime around four. I didn't think she'd knock if he was there, and even if she did, he would frown on her presence. She *would* be a distraction.

Several times over the last few weeks, working the night shift, someone honked passing by, but I couldn't see the car through the store's reflected light off of the front window. I liked to think that it was her.

Now, other than Friday and Saturday nights, my only other shifts would be from three to closing at six on Tuesday, Wednesday and Thursday. Jimbo works that same shift Friday, Saturday, Sunday and Monday, a schedule he doesn't approve of.

"This messes up my entire weekend."

"So? I've got to work nights."

"How about you take Friday afternoon?"

"I have to work Friday nights. I'm not going to take two shifts in the same day."

"They're different days, Friday afternoon, Saturday morning."

"No."

"I know you won't take Sunday. How about Monday?"

"No That's my only day off."

"All of my weekends are fucked up."

"Preachin' to the choir, man."

"This sucks."

"What? You want to go back to a paper route?"

Jimbo shook his head. "No. But I would like to get my hands on some more dope. You ever go back and check out those abalone shells?"

"No."

"You should."

"What if I'm caught? They know who I am."

"They're already smoking it. They won't care."

"No."

"Tony said you were going to transfer over to Crawford?"

"Yeah. It's in the same direction as the shop. I can't get there in time if I stay at Hoover."

"That sucks."

"I wonder what the teachers are like."

One of my new teachers was Ida Brinks, my English instructor who preferred to teach through creative writing. After a couple of weeks of basic stuff, our assignment was to tell a story between one hundred and two hundred and fifty words in length.

"Make it good," she said, adjusting her pink, rhinestone-rimmed glasses to the tip of her nose, looking over the top with a thin, fleeting smile. "Each of you is going to read it in front of the class."

She seemed to enjoy the collective groan as she walked back to her desk, sat on the edge and began fielding questions from the ten, or so, raised hands.

"Yes. Every word over two hundred and fifty will drop your grade by one. Anything under one hundred words will be an automatic F. Think carefully about handing in a paper with one hundred and one words. What kind of message will that send?"

"Yes. It is harsh. Count carefully."

"I don't care if it's handwritten or typed."

"You can't type? Oh. Well..., now's a good time to learn."

"Yes. You heard right. Over two-fifty and under a hundred is a recipe for disaster."

"You don't know any stories that short? You must have a very interesting life. Pick one. And keep your eraser handy."

"How many pages is two hundred and fifty words? About one typed page, double spaced."

"You are right. It's very hard to tell a story in one page. Glad you brought it up. So, let's change it to two pages and up the number of words. The story has to be between two hundred-fifty and five hundred words...,"

A collective groan from the class.

"One typed, double-spaced page is about two hundred

and fifty words. If you go past two pages, you're probably rambling. Thanks for the suggestion, Pat."

From somewhere in the back of the class. "Nice going, Pat."

"Yeah, Pat. Really?"

"Slightly different rules," said Ms. Brinks. "Under two-fifty, an F. Over five hundred, an F."

"Yes. It can be fiction, science fiction, romance. I don't care if it's a trip to the grocery store to buy toilet paper. Write it well and watch your punctuation. Apply what we've learned these last two weeks."

I liked how she was throwing it right back at us. No excuses. This is the framework. Live with it and within it. Period. Nice and clean.

I was tempted to write about my bomb dismantling experience, but decided that, in everyone's eyes, I'd look pretty stupid. I was no longer proud of that moment.

I considered writing about the stolen motorcycle, thinking that might be more interesting, but I didn't want that story to get back to my parents any more than I wanted to talk about the road race out near Portrero.

So, what to write about? Making donuts while stoned? Nope. Putting an engine back together? Yawn. Getting drunk and throwing up? Nope. Talk about Cassi coming in out of the rain? Nope. That would kill my chances with any of the girls in this class. But I liked the idea of meeting a stranger in dark times...,

After the rain, a thick fog crept through the trees, smothering the lingering sunlight and changing the soft, hazy yellow glow of the forest into a darkening, dusk-colored gray.

I was having trouble focusing and my balance was shaky since the fall. Hearing water roaring down the gully above, it was all I could do to scramble up the bank. Grabbing that branch, I started to pull myself up when the water ripped us both away from the side and pummeled us downstream.

My head throbbed and my ankle felt like it was on fire. I couldn't put any weight on it. I lost my gear and with that,

118

my compass, but I still had a pretty good sense of direction until the fog arrived.

I knew that if I headed west, I would run into the road sooner or later, but the fog put a stop to that. Wandering without knowing where you're going is futile, so I stopped at a clearing to rest.

I was exhausted, in pain and without food or water. Funny. Fog all around, recent rain, and not a drop to drink. I laughed at the irony of it. At some point, leaning up against the trunk of a tree, I passed out...,

She was standing over me, full moon backlighting her head and torso in a soft, silver light. She retrieved a leather pouch, hung diagonally from hip to shoulder by a thin leather strap, untied the top, knelt beside me and touched a few drops of water to my lips. I couldn't get enough of that sweet-tasting drink. She examined the side of my head, cleaned the wound with water from the pouch and then placed some kind of compress over the whole area, wet, soothing leaves.

Examining my ankle, turning it this way or that until I gasped with pain, she finally placed one of her feet between my legs and used her other leg to hold mine in place. She massaged the swollen area for some time, I don't know for how long, and when I was least expecting it, suddenly twisted my ankle back into place with a loud Pop! I think I screamed.

I remember looking up at her face, smooth and tanned, her long, black hair pulled into some kind of loosely-tied pony tail, her eyes darker than night. I tried to ask her name, but she placed her finger on my lips, shook her head with the slightest of motion and offered a gentle smile.

With a bit more water, her massaging my forehead and with some kind of liquid she made me drink, sour and biting, the pain began to subside. I started to relax and must've drifted off.

When I awoke, she was gone. Sitting up, my head exploded with pain, but settled back into tolerable when I slowed my actions down. I didn't detect any blood on the side of my face. It felt like the wound was clean. And, to my surprise, I could move my ankle. It hurt, but I could walk on it.

I found no sign that she had ever been there. The ground was full of leaves and footprints were impossible to find. I did see a broken branch to my left and another some distance beyond. Following them, I was led to a small concave rock filled with rain water. Drinking what I could, I felt refreshed and began my trek back to camp.

I'll never know if she was really there. I can't imagine that she wasn't. Sometimes, I see her in my dreams.

Several of the students had really good stories and we all had a lot of laughs. Ida Brinks, beaming with enthusiasm, decided that we would do this again.

"Next time," she said. "We'll do the same thing with dialogue."

A collective groan from the class.

I was at home alone, sitting in the over-stuffed chair in the living room watching TV when the old, wooden rocking chair next to the television began to rock. Not a lot of motion, but there shouldn't have been any. I thought maybe a breeze could have come through, but I didn't feel anything.

I had been told by both my mother and sister that they had seen it move. Both claimed that the chair was haunted, that my great, grandmother had died sitting in it.

Haunted? I never really thought about it until now. I closed the front door and the door leading to the back of the house off of the kitchen, wanting to eliminate any possibility of wind.

It would take a substantial breeze to make it move. The chair was solid, heavy, made in Norway some hundred years before, complete with a carved, growling-hound's head at the end of each arm rest, a design that, when sitting in the chair, the heads of the beasts fit neatly into the palms of your hands.

It rocks farther backward than what's comfortable for the sitter, but always stops at the moment of panic and reverses direction. Whoever made it, I was thinking, was well aware of the balance and tipping point and that they probably had a mischievous smile on their face when they fashioned and cut the arc.

If not wind, perhaps an earthquake? A small tremor might make it rock. I was sitting in the over-stuffed chair at the time and it was quite possible I wouldn't have noticed.

I had worked a night at the donut shop the night before, was tired and dozed off. I woke up to, *Amos and Andy*. The rocking chair was moving ever so slightly, yet the glass of water on the table next to my chair was absolutely still. No one else was in the house. I will be keeping my eye on this thing.

121

After the rocking chair episode, ghosts were on my mind. In our English class, we persuaded Ida Brinks to let us do the a hundred and fifty to five-hundred-word story instead of three-hundred words of dialogue. I wanted to write about ghosts...,

Sometime around midnight, I was trying to stay awake while studying for a test when I heard a light tapping sound coming from the window across the room.

Tap..., tap, tap.

I assumed that it was caused by the wind, but the timing between taps seemed suspicious. Going over to the window, I noticed that the branches of the shrubs that I'd been told to trim last week were close to the window and, yes, if the wind were to blow hard, they could touch, don't know about tap. It was raining, but there wasn't much wind.

Thinking that I solved the riddle, I returned to my studies. But in the back of my mind, I was listening for wind. In past times I've heard gusts come through that rattle the glass, but there is nothing like that tonight.

Tap, tap..., tap.

Crossing the room, I opened the window, broke off the suspect branch and threw it down to the ground. There was now a good six inches between branch and glass. Good riddance.

Back to my studies. It seems like the storm is building. I can hear bursts of rain against the glass from time to time. I can't concentrate, fold up my notes and get everything ready for class tomorrow...,

Tap..., tap, tap, tap.

It's not a clanging sound, as if someone used a metal object. If wood was used, the stick would have to be..., hardwood? No. That would make too sharp of a sound, something a little softer like a..., a fingernail or claw. I shiver at the thought of it.

Do I want to go look? Not really. Do I want to know what

it is? Yes. Am I willing to risk my health to find out? Maybe.

I turned out the light, grabbed the flashlight from the drawer, walked quietly to the window and waited. Minutes passed. Standing in the dark, I was beginning to wonder if all of this was just my imagination. But as I was leaving...,

Tap..., tap, tap.

I pulled back the curtain and shined the light outside. What I saw was my rain splattered face looking back at me.

Opening the window, I cautiously leaned forward and scanned the area with my light. I saw no footprints, humans, animals, nothing. Maybe a bird..., at night in this rain? I doubt it. Yet, there was no other explanation.

I've read, usually with a large dose of doubt, about people internally combusting, levitating, disappearing without a trace, so many things.

Tonight, I have no tracks to follow, no recording to prove what I know I heard, no image to convey. I, too, am left with doubts.

If there is such a world that can interact with ours, how would we communicate? Tea leaves? Crystal balls? Dreams? Haunting images? Or, maybe just a simple tapping on the glass.

And if that's what it was, what does it mean? Was it a warning of some kind, a message? That's the problem. I just don't know.

Feeling something like a large spider crawling across the back of my neck, I threw my books into the locker, slapped my hand on top of whatever it was and attempted to fling it off. Spinning around, I was face to face with Letti, laughing. "Don't like spiders?"

"Jesus!"

She held out her hand. "Don't know if you remember me. I'm...,"

"Letti. I didn't forget.

She had a firm handshake. "And you're Calvin. You're at Crawford now?"

"Yeah. It's closer to my work."

"Where's that?

"Over on University. How about you? Did you ever work at the zoo?"

"For a month."

"Doing what?"

"A sweeper. I had to walk around sweeping up trash.

"Was the pay good?"

"No. But I've got friends there, now. Next summer, I'll have a real job."

"Are you still in track?"

She smiled. "That's one of the reasons I stopped by, to see if you're going to keep your promise."

"What promise?"

"If you enrolled at Crawford, you'd try out for the track team."

"Did I say that?"

"You did."

"But I work after school during the week and nights on weekends."

"Oh." She sounded disappointed.

"What are the others?"

"What?"

"You said that's one of the reasons. What are the others?"

A slight blush from Letti. "I wanted to say, Hi. What classes are you taking?"

We went through all of her classes and mine and determined that we were on opposite ends of the campus most of the time, but that we did have the same lunch hour.

"Maybe I'll see you at lunch?"

She smiled. "Maybe."

The bell was about to ring and it seemed like there was nothing more to say. She turned to go.

"Hey..., Letti."

"Yeah?"

"Thanks for stopping. I was hoping to see you again."

That brought a smile, refreshing. I liked very much how she wore her feelings on her sleeve.

"Maybe you can watch us work out one day and get inspired. I probably can't beat you in the one hundred, but I bet I can take you in the two."

"I might take you up on that. What do you want to bet?"

"Ten bucks?"

"I don't want to take your money."

"That won't happen. What do you suggest?"

"A kiss."

This time she did blush. "Ten dollars is safer."

"You've got to make it worth my while. "If I lose, you get ten bucks. If I win, a kiss."

"Are we talking a peck on the cheek?"

"On the lips."

"For how long?"

"Until you push me away."

"Let's just stick with ten dollars."

The corridors were empty now. The bell was going to ring any second and I didn't want to lose this chance. I shrugged. "Well, I tried. Ten bucks, it is. When?"

"At the track. Friday, after school?"

"OK."

The bell rang as both of us hurried off in different directions. I was happy with the date, but wondering what I'd gotten myself into.

What if a bunch of her friends hung around to watch and Letti won? That would be embarrassing. What if she beat me by a lot? I'd been eating many donuts over the summer and knew I'd put on some weight. I finally reasoned that on any Friday after school, probably no one else would be out on the track. That turned out to be the case.

I changed clothes in the men's room after classes and wandered over to the track. Letti was already there, stretching. She had beautiful, tan legs. Facing her, I did some of the same stretches and then a couple of short runs, ten or twenty yards, starting slowly and then breaking into a sprint.

At the starting line, Letti patted me on the back. "I'll give you one last chance to back out."

"No way. I'm going to take the money and run."

She laughed. "I'll just run and take the money."

There was no starting gun or anything like that. We just made eye contact, agreed that it was time and started. I took the lead and immediately regretted it. It would have been better to let her set the pace and then outrun her in the last ten yards.

As it was, I had no idea if she was struggling, getting ready for a surge or just hanging back, doing what I should have done.

Halfway around the track, my breathing was becoming strained. I had set the pace too fast. I could hear her behind me, her breathing smooth, steady. Three quarters of the way around the track, she was on my heels. Knowing that she was going to turn it on when we hit the straight away, I gave it ninety percent, keeping a little for that last surge.

When you don't have enough air, you don't have enough air and all the rest of the parts, legs and lungs mostly, give out. We ran neck and neck down the stretch and in those last few feet, she pulled ahead.

There were no words for the first minute or so, both of us gasping for air. But when I looked over at her, she was grinning. She was also getting her wind back faster than

I. "You did better than I thought you would."

"Same, for you."

Another long pause for breathing. Letti was holding her arms up, breathing deeply. Seeing me watching her, she smiled, slightly embarrassed. ""It's how you breathe."

"I heard you, behind me."

"I also jogged the track twice before you got here."

"What does that do?"

"Gets my muscles loosened up and puts more oxygen in my blood. I'll have an advantage right from the start."

I handed her the money. "Ten bucks for the lesson. I'll remember that for next time. Thanks."

"Next time?"

"I deserve a rematch, don't I?"

"Let's race the four hundred, twice around."

"What am I, nuts? If I run out of air at two, the four will kill me."

"You have to pace yourself."

"I'll stick with the two. And…, I'm sorry, but I have to get to work."

"Sorry for what?"

"Ending this conversation."

She smiled. "Oh."

"And I'm sorry I didn't get that kiss."

To my surprise, she reached up, placed her hands on the back of my neck and kissed me on the lips, lingering for a second, before turning and grabbing her towel.

"That's for runner-up."

"I'll be that every time, if that's the prize."

Blushing again, I loved that about her, she waved and headed back to school, towel around her neck.

I didn't have time to change back into street clothes and entered the donut shop wearing gray shorts and top. Ruth, the girl working the day shift, looking over the glass counters, took note.

"You coming to work like that?"

My head was in the clouds. Letti's smile, her easy laugh, those soft lips touching mine, her hands holding me. Was I smitten? Dumb question.

Realizing that I'd left my street clothes in the car, I turned and headed for the front door, high on presumed romance as only a teenager can be. "I'll be right back."

Did I hope we'd have lunch together at school on Monday? Another dumb question. Was I willing to join the track team just to be near her? Maybe. Was she all I was going to be thinking about for the rest of the week? Of course.

Parents in Mexico for the week-end, rest of the family gone for one reason or another, Jimbo was staying at my house for a couple of days, just so he could be away from his parents and, more likely, they could be rid of him. He went to the stove, turned the burner onto low, leaned down and lit a joint.

"Shit! Burned my eyebrow!"

"Just hold it over the flame. It'll light itself."

"Last time I did that, the paper burned all the way back to my fingers and all the pot fell into the flame. That sucked."

"You must've rolled it too loose."

"Like you're an expert. You've never rolled a joint."

Jimbo took three short puffs and when the tip was glowing bright orange, took another, much longer drag. He handed it to me and, coughing to hold the smoke, pointed to the section that was burning too fast and motioned for me to wet it with my spit.

Completing that, I took a long drag and handed it back to him. "Where did you get this?"

"Outside Menlo Market. I was going to my car. This guy asked if I wanted to buy some."

"What's his name?"

"Like he's gonna tell me. I bought a lid for ten bucks."

He took another drag and handed it back to me.

"How much is in a lid?"

""It was supposed to be three fingers. Mine was more like two. If I squeezed it thin and spread it out in the baggie, like he did, it was three, but just sitting on the bottom, it was hardly more than two."

"You got gypped."

"I got dope. That was the point."

There comes a time, handing this thing back and forth, when it becomes too short to hold. Any sane person would simply let it go out and save it for harder times. Beginners don't think like that. Burning our fingers, passing it back and forth was a badge of honor, stick with it no matter how tough the going gets, seeing who gives up, the triumphant winner smoking it all the way down. Jimbo got the last hit and a blister on his thumb.

I headed for the stereo out in the living room. "We need music."

Money. (That's What I Want)

"And food," Jimbo yelled, from the kitchen. What's to eat?"

Eight eggs, scrambled, four pieces of toast and six pieces of bacon later, we decided that the dishes could wait. Eating is so much easier if you don't do dishes, especially with the problem of bacon grease in the pan. We were just lighting another joint when the phone rang.

"Calvin. Tony here. Ruth went home sick. Is Jimbo around? His mom said he was there."

I handed the phone to Jimbo. "It's Tony."

He exhaled, cringing, and took the phone. "Oh. That's too bad."

He's gritting his teeth and shaking his head side to side, rolling his eyes.

"Yeah. I guess. Yeah. I'll be there. Sure. No, that's OK."

Hanging up the phone, Jimbo glared up at the ceiling.

"Fuck!"

"What's the matter?"

"I've got to go to work."

"When? Now?"

"Ruth's sick."

"You're going to *drive*?"

"How else am I going to get there?"

"Take the bus."

"Right. I've got to be there in fifteen minutes. Besides, the bus won't bring me back. It doesn't run that late."

"Man. You should've just said, no."

"Too late for that."

"Maybe, throw some cold water on your face."

"Why would I do that?"

"Sober up."

"Let me take your car."

"Fuck you."

"I'm less likely to get stopped in your car."

"Don't even think about it, Jimbo."

"Well..., guess I'll clean up." He started for the bathroom. "Oh, forgot to tell you. Some girl stopped by, asking about you. She said, Hi."

"Did you get a name?"

"Bambi. She didn't look like a Bambi."

"What's a Bambi look like?"

"Hell, if I know."

"Let me guess. She bought a glazed?"

"Yeah. I think she did."

"Did you tell her I was madly in love with her and thinking about her night and day?"

"Fuck you. I gotta go sober up."

I was trying to think of what I was going to do while Jimbo was gone, when the doorbell rang. Looking through the glass in the front door, I shuddered.

Dawn (Go away.)

Answering, Katie was standing there, hands on hips, trouble on two feet looking for a place to land. The joint was sitting in an ashtray. Not smoking, but visible.

"Jimbo's got dope. I know it. Can I come in?"

"Um, sure." I turned to give fair warning. "Jimbo! Your sister's here!"

Jimbo came into the room bare chested, wiping his face with a towel. "What're you doing here?"

"You've got dope, bro. And I need some."

"Who said I have dope?"

"You left Zigzags on the kitchen table. I grabbed them before Mom woke up."

"*That's* where I left them. Thanks."

"So..., you owe me."

"You're not old enough to smoke."

"What does that even mean? You're only seventeen. What makes you so special?"

"One. It's my dope."

"And it won't be if I tell Mom."

I was going to say, "Sounds like blackmail," but decided

131

to stay out of it.

"OK. When I get off work, I'll roll you a couple of joints."

"You don't work today."

"He just called." Jimbo glanced at his watch. "Jesus. I've got to be there in five minutes."

"You're just saying that."

I held up my hand. "It's true. I just talked to him. The day girl went home sick."

"Why don't you go?"

"Because I'm working tonight."

"Oh." She seemed out of avenues to race down.

Jimbo hurried back into the bathroom and returned wearing a shirt and combing his hair as he headed for the door. "Wish me luck."

When he was gone, Katie strolled around the room, studying the knickknacks, glancing at the magazines on the coffee table.

"Smells like dope in here. I wonder if I can get a contact high. Jimbo didn't leave any with you, did he?"

How to answer that? Am I contributing to the delinquency of a minor if I'm under eighteen?

"Oh. I see there's something right there. Probably enough for both of us, don't you think?"

There was no way that I could get out of it. I already knew that Katie wasn't going to let up. I handed her the roach, still quite long since Jimbo was the only one to hit it, lit a match and held it up. We passed it back and forth in silence. I wondered when she would give it a pass.

She motioned for me to keep the roach and then, searching through her pockets, grabbed it with a roach clip. I had never seen such a thing.

"That's clever."

"Only a fool would smoke it all the way down with their fingers." She pointed to the brown marks between my thumb and forefinger and smiled. "I see you've done it a few times."

"That's not my only talent."

She laughed, losing her hit. "Not fair."

She took another hit and handed me the clip. I was amazed at how efficient this thing was. Smoking it all the way down, seeing who was the bravest was just dumb. Think through the problem. Don't dwell on it.

Katie looked at me with her mischievous eyes and I found myself being a bit afraid of what was going to happen next. Sex with a fifteen-year-old? I'm under eighteen, so I guess it's legal.

What if she goes crazy? What if she runs outside screaming that I tried to rape her? What would Jimbo say to that? What will Jimbo say when he finds out that we smoked that roach together? I think I'm in trouble no matter which way it goes. I am one guilty mother...,

Pointing at me, Katie burst into laughter. "You look...," more laughter, "You look like I'm going to hurt you! Are you *afraid* of me?"

"No. Just trying to figure you out."

She stood, put her hands on my shoulders and kissed me on the forehead. "Don't worry. I'm not dangerous. What have you got to drink?"

We didn't have much of anything and I wasn't going to mention the bottle of cheap rum hidden away. I made a pot of strong coffee while she made herself a bologna sandwich.

"Calvin, right?"

"Right."

"Nickname?"

"I don't have one."

"Why not?"

"Don't want one."

"Anybody call you Cal?"

"Nope. Calvin, is just fine. Is your name, Kathryn?"

"How about, Calie?"

"No."

"I like it, because it suits you."

"I'm not a Calie."

"You're too uptight. Loosen up, laugh!"

"Nobody can laugh, just for the hell of it."

Katie had this gleam in her eye that convinced me that something, I couldn't fathom what, was going to happen as soon as she finished swallowing her last bite. I'm not comfortable with how her mind works.

She laughs. "What goes *on* in that head of yours? I think you're going to crack!"

"I'm not sure what to do with you."

She took on an innocent look, slightly tilted head, sad eyes. "What would you like to do with me?"

OK. If I did anything with Katie, it would get back to Jimbo in spades. Both Katie and I knew this. She could be as bold and teasing as she wanted, knowing that I would do nothing.

"Calie?" Puckered, pouting lips. "You didn't answer."

I laughed at the trap. "That's good, Kathryn. But I think I have a headache."

"At least I got you to laugh. What would you do if I wasn't here? Wander around the house and do nothing?"

"I was going to do my homework."

"You're kidding, right?"

"It's due next week."

"What's the assignment?"

"Three hundred words or less, but more than a hundred, all dialogue."

"What've you done, so far?"

"Nothing."

Katie got a big mug out of the cupboard, filled it halfway with coffee, the other with milk and stirred in several spoons of sugar. "Let's go do it."

"I'm thinking you're nuts. Waste a good high on homework?"

"You were going to."

"Because I have to."

"I'll be Jed. You be an old friend. We haven't seen each other for a long time. How hard can this be?" She pulled three sheets out of my notebook, set herself at the dining room table and started writing. "Who are you?"

"Ben."

She wrote, *"Hey, Ben!"* Grinning, she handed me the pen.

"Jed! Long time, no see. What've you been up to?"

Katie laughed. "Long time, no see? That's the best you can do?"

"You picked, Jed. It doesn't leave me much to work with."

"What do you want, Samantha? Bridget? What kind of conversation are we having?"

I was finding Katie more interesting than dangerous. "Let's keep going with this."

She took a long gulp of her coffee and stared at the first two entries. I noticed a big smile come across her face.

"Been plantin'. Bought this new dirt. Amazing!"

OK. She's got me smiling. This could go any which way. "*What's so good about it?*"

"*Powerful stuff. Cherry tomatoes came out big as oranges. Should a seen 'em.*"

"*That's just..., really?* We were both giggling now. "*As big as oranges?*"

"*I dug around the roots to see what was goin' on and the dirt was full a worms.*"

"*I wonder what's in that dirt.*"

"*One cherry tomato was all each of us could eat at one time.*"

"*I'll bet.*"

Katie is laughing now. I know that she has some kind of devious plan. I can see it in her eyes.

"*And you know they come in bunches on the vine. We got, oh..., six, eight, maybe ten per bunch.*"

"*That must've been a heavy plant.*"

"*Fifteen or twenty bunches.*"

"*Incredible.*"

"*And they all came ripe at the same time.*"

"*Drowning in tomatoes, huh?*"

Katie started laughing, started to write and then burst into laughter again. She tried to explain, but couldn't get the words out, holding her stomach and banging her feet on the floor.

"*Just the...,*" She had to stop and wipe her eyes. "*Just the opposite.*"

OK. Both of us are in hysterics. I got the Kleenex out of the bathroom and put it in front of us, a pause while we dried our eyes.

"*How so?*

"*Did you know tomatoes give you the runs?*"

"*Hadn't thought about it.*"

"*And we've only got one toilet.*"

"*Man...,*"

"*We had to form a line outside the door.*"

"*Every house should have two toilets.*"

"*At least.*"

"*What happened to all those tomatoes?*"

136

"We've got enough stewed tomatoes for ten years. I just happened to have a case here. Would you like one?"

"Um, no. I think I'm allergic."

"And then came the oranges. I had to get the wheelbarrow just to carry five of em back to the house."

"That is hard to believe."

"Would I lie?"

This was an interesting question. Smiling slyly, Katie handed me the pen. More was going to be read into this answer than what was on the paper.

"I..., don't know."

"Each orange makes a quart of orange juice."

"Incredible."

"Hard to believe, huh?"

"I've known you for some time, Jed. And I've never known you to lie. So, if you say it's true. I'll believe you until it's proved otherwise."

I saw a satisfied look come across her face. I think, in that moment, I caught a glimpse of a girl wanting to be accepted, if not as a woman, certainly as one of the crowd, not just Jimbo's impetuous, little sister.

And then she picked up the pen and wrote, *"You won't believe what the pumpkins turned out like."*

Laughing, we shook hands. Neither of us felt compelled to add anything more.

I got to know Katie pretty well that day, at least the parts that she wanted to show. She loves acting, is interested in history, loves the Beatles, dances in front of the mirror and knows all of the words to all of their songs. She liked the weird music that was played the night I was baby-sitting, but admitted that could've been the dope.

She looked puzzled, head tilted. "Maybe that's what happened today. I actually *liked* writing."

"It's not so bad. You get to say things and nobody can interrupt."

"Wow, Calie. Maybe you'll be a philosopher."

"I don't think they make any money."

"Donut makers do?"

"Probably more than if I was a philosopher."

Katie finished her coffee, cold by now, gave me a hug and headed for the door.

"I'll give you a ride."

"No. You're stoned. And I need to clear my head before I get home."

"Hey, Katie!"

"Yeah?"

"Thanks for the help. I had fun."

"Good to see you laugh, Calie. I had fun, too."

Saturday morning, after finishing the night shift, I got back to the house around eight, made myself some breakfast and crashed. Sometime around ten, Jimbo called.

"Man! You knew I'd be sleeping!"

"Let's go surfing."

"I don't know how to surf."

"Body surfing. I've got an extra set of fins."

Coming from the mid-west and never having seen anything like the ocean before the age of fifteen, I am slightly intimidated by the waves. "That doesn't sound as good as me going back to bed."

"What a party pooper!"

"You got a good night's sleep."

"Just for a couple of hours. I've got to be to work at three anyway."

"Isn't the ocean still cold? It's March."

"March twenty-eighth. So, what? If it's too cold, we'll just leave and I'll buy you lunch on the way back."

On our way down to Mission Beach, we heard on the radio that there had been a nine-point-two earthquake in Alaska the night before.

I pulled into the parking lot and began the search for a spot. "Nine-point-two. Isn't that pretty huge?"

"I think it only goes up to ten, right?"

"I think so. Could we get a tidal wave here?"

"Look at all those people out there. If it was dangerous they'd get everyone out of the water."

"It's still cloudy. Water looks cold to me."

"It's not bad, once you get used to it."

We laid out our towels and raced into the water. I can't go in slowly if the water's cold. I put on the fins and dove headfirst into the next wave. The ocean seemed a little rough to me, waves certainly bigger than the last time I was here, and colder. I caught a few waves, lost track of Jimbo, surfed a few more and then headed for shore.

The sun was starting to break through and, lying on my towel shivering, I settled in on my stomach, concentrated on the heat and fell asleep. I was awakened sometime later when several drops of cold water splashed onto my back.

"Jimbo! What the hell?"

"Man!" He straightened out his towel and plopped down next to me. "I'm lucky to be alive!"

"You keep splashing water on me!"

"Didn't you see it?"

"See what?"

"The waves, man! You missed that?"

"What waves?"

"A *huge* set came in, biggest I've ever seen!"

"I was sleeping."

"You didn't hear them? It was like thunder."

"If I did, it was in my dreams."

"Only a couple of us were that far out. The wave started to break and I thought I was going to catch it. But then the bottom fell out and it just slammed me down into the sand! I didn't know which way was up."

"Did you smoke anything while I was sleeping?"

"I'm not shittin' you. I thought I was gonna die. When I did come up, the waves were so big I could hardly get any air. I didn't even know which way the beach was. Shit. My ears are full of sand."

"So..., you going back out?"

"Hell, no."

"Must've been from that earthquake. How fast do waves move?"

"No idea."

"A hundred miles an hour?"

"Jesus, man! I almost died and you're doing math?"

"What do you want me to do? Hold your hand? I'm trying to figure out if the earthquake caused it."

"Of course, it did."

"You don't know how fast waves move."

"I know how big they normally are. Those were huge."

"Huge, yes. But you can't say they came from Alaska."

140

"What the fuck else happened in the last day that would cause that? It doesn't matter! Let's go eat. I'm starving."

After lunch, I dropped Jimbo off at his house, went home and checked out a map for the distance between Anchorage, Alaska and San Diego. I didn't have much of a map, but calculated the distance to be about eighteen hundred miles. I also discovered that, depending on depth and type of wave, speeds can vary considerably.

Normally, I would just let it go and take Jimbo's word for it, but later that day the news reported that the earthquake occurred at five-thirty-six in the evening, Alaska time. The crummy map I had did not show time zones.

According to the news, it took the waves about seven hours to reach our shores, sometime around midnight, twelve hours before we were in the water. I called Jimbo up at work to let him know.

"Those waves hit San Diego about midnight the night before."

"I don't care what the news says. I was there, dying while you were sleeping."

"They travelled at about two hundred and fifty miles an hour."

"So..., what?"

"Just thought you'd like to know. Pretty fast, huh?"

"Don't you have more important things to do?"

"I like to know things."

"How is that ever going to help you? As for me, I'd like to know the color of Bambi's panties."

"Man! I'm working on her."

"You've only seen her once. I've seen her twice. She stopped in today. I had a minute, so I sat down and had a cup of coffee with her. Sweet!"

"Not cool, Jimbo."

"You gotta love those short skirts."

"Fuck you."

"Just so you know, I asked her out."

"You're an ass hole."

"She said, yes. I'm a happy ass hole."

141

"Did you get her number?"

"No. She wouldn't give it."

"When are you going out?"

"Friday night."

"I *hate* working nights."

"Oh! Got a customer. See, ya later, loser."

There were several aftershocks following the main event, some occurring hours later. Any one of them could've caused the set that Jimbo talked about.

But I didn't feel like talking to him.

John spotted me crossing the courtyard at lunchtime and waved me over. Penny arrived at the table at the same time and sat next to John. I took a seat opposite them. We'd been out of touch over summer vacation.

"You two still going steady?"

John put his arm around her and pulled her in. "Why wouldn't we be?"

Penny held the chain up and let the ring swing. "I guess I'm stuck with him."

"When's the big day?"

"What? Getting *married?*"

"You both look so happy."

John, talking between bites of his sandwich, "We've gotta finish school first."

Penny, stealing a few of his potato chips, "And college."

"San Diego State. I'm going to play for the Aztecs."

"He says that," said Penny. "But I don't want him getting hurt. What if he blows out a knee?"

John looked a little irritated. Apparently, they'd had this conversation before. He finished half of his sandwich in three bites. "That's part of the game."

"I don't want to spend my life taking care of a cripple."

"I'm not going to get hurt. I know what I'm doing out there."

"They're called accidents, John. You don't see it coming. Everybody's bigger and faster in college."

I unwrapped my sandwich and bit into the meager bologna, mayonnaise and wilted lettuce. "I didn't mean to start an argument."

"You didn't," said John. "Are you going to try out here at Crawford?"

"Can't. I work after school during the week and nights on the week-ends."

"You're too young to be working nights."

"Trying to get ahead."

"Ahead of what? Are you going to college?"

"Maybe."

"Is that what you're saving for?"

I laughed. "Who said I was saving anything?"

"Which college would you go to?"

"SDSU."

Penny had brought to the table a chocolate milkshake and a bag of Planter's Peanuts, both of which looked far better than my measly sandwich. "I'm going to San Jose."

The second half of John's sandwich stopped halfway to his mouth. "What? We're both going to San Diego State."

"That was your conclusion. I didn't agree to that."

"We talked about this."

"We did. And I said that I hadn't made up my mind yet."

"And now it's San Jose?"

"I don't want to see you get hurt. If you're going to play football, I'll go to San Jose."

Clearly, John was irritated. I was trying to think of how to change the subject when I felt someone's hand on my shoulder.

Penny looked up with a smile. "Hi, Letti."

"Mind if I join you?"

She seated herself next to me and opened up her lunch, apple slices, orange wedges, nuts, celery and some other green stuff I could not identify. "How can you live on that?"

"I see you're still eating the same old bologna sandwiches. How can you live on that?"

"It fills me up."

"So, does this. And I'm not eating pork guts, or whatever that is."

"Bologna is not pork guts."

"Have you read the label?"

I had to admit that I had not. Penny was watching us with interest. "Do you two have a class together?"

We both answered at the same time. "No."

"How do you know each other?"

"I'm trying to get him to join the track team," said Letti, peeling an orange wedge away from the skin.

John, happy with the change in conversation. "You just

144

said that you didn't have time for football."

"Same thing for track. No time."

"He's really fast," said Letti, crunching on some almonds. "For the first hundred yards. But he runs out of gas before he gets to two."

John pulled an apple out of his lunch bag, polished it on his sleeve and bit into it. "How do you know that?"

"I raced him."

"Oh? On the track?"

"Right."

"And?"

"I'll let Calvin tell you."

"Not much to say. I was ahead for one hundred and ninety-nine yards."

Everybody laughed. I didn't see quite as much humor in it.

Letti patted me on the back. "He set a fast pace. I was thinking, oh boy. This is gonna be tough."

"And I was thinking, damn. I'm a fool for taking the lead. I should have let her have it and just stay close. I figured I could beat her in the last twenty yards."

"So...," John leaned back on the bench, smiling. "There must've been a bet. What did you lose?"

"Ten bucks. But it was worth it to see her run." I patted Letti on the shoulder. "You're gonna go all the way, kid."

"You didn't see me run, except for that last yard."

"*That* was worth ten bucks."

Neither of us mentioned the kiss, something that was on my mind much of the time when it was out wandering.

I wondered if she felt the same.

Inserting the key into the lock, I'm hating Friday nights. While all of my friends are out having fun, I have to be at work by midnight.

Walking past the empty glass cases to the other end of the room under the low intensity lights, I found Tony's note on the cloth-covered, cutting table telling me how much of everything to make.

My choices, before coming to work are; stay at home, get some sleep so that tomorrow morning after work, I'll feel like doing something or, stay up, party with friends and leave when the liquor is flowing and everyone's having a good time. And if I do that, go to work feeling like crap, crash when I got home and lose half of the next day.

Or, I can quit. I'd get my Friday and Saturday nights back. But if I quit, Jimbo would jump at the chance for the job, probably get it, and then he would be making the money. Nope. Not quitting until something better comes along.

I flipped on the switch for the overhead lights above the preparation area, turned on the radio and hurried into the back room for flour.

It's a tube radio and takes a minute to warm up. Therefore, a ritual, of sorts. Can I get the flour into the prep area before the sounds come on? Not much else to do at midnight. Coming back into the room, I set the bag down...,

I Get Around

Two good things about working alone at night, less commercials between songs and I get to choose the station. When Tony comes in? Easy listening. Yawn.

Ninety dollars a week in nineteen sixty-four for a teenager is good money. I'm saving it, not because I want to, but because I'm too busy or too tired to spend it. Basically, my social life is a wreck.

Jimbo wouldn't talk about his date with Cassi...,

"Where are you going?"

146

"Don't know. We'll decide that when she gets in the car."

"What are you going to do?"

"Try to get laid. If that works out, you want me to talk about it?"

He was right. None of my business, so I quit asking.

It Hurts to be in Love

At least Jimbo, always complaining about having to work weekdays and weekends, still has every night to go out and do things. And because one of us is off when the other is working, we hardly see each other.

After his Cassi (Bambi) comment, neither of us brought that subject up again. I had first contact. It seems like I should have first try. There's no written rule for that. But she asked Jimbo about me, so doesn't that indicate that she is interested in me? Unless she used that as a ploy to get to know him. There are no rules. That's the conclusion I'm coming to.

Did John and Penny getting together bother me? At first. But their relationship developed over time and we all got a chance to get used to it. Cassi and Jimbo is like..., *what?*

I measured out the flour and water, rolled the bowl over to the mixer, raised it up to the dough hook and eased the mixer into first.

Actually, there's probably nothing going on between the two and Jimbo is probably pulling my chain. Just like him. Thinking about it, if the situation was reversed, would I do the same thing just to irritate him?

Jimbo is also my connection for pot and I'm not about to jeopardize that over a girl that I'd only met once. Working nights, I get a lot of time to think about things. Did I fantasize about Penny before John and her hooked up? Of course. Even now? Not answering that. Letti? Of course. Cassi? Certainly.

I'm young, trying to figure out what works and what doesn't. How to make money? How to move away from home? How to get laid?

Turning off the mixer, I hear somebody knocking on the front door, Cassi, smiling, wearing a miniskirt. Her date with Jimbo must've been cut short. Hmm. Should I let her in? Dumb question.

Everybody Loves Somebody

Cassi walked behind the counter, put a dollar next to the cash register...,

"You don't have to pay."

grabbed a cup and stared blankly at the empty coffee pots.

"I thought that was the first thing you did."

"I wasn't expecting company."

She smiled. "Or, you'd have baked a cake?"

I put one of the Farmer Brothers pre-measured bags of coffee into the holder and poured a pot of water into the top. I love how that works, pour cold water in the top, get fresh brewed, hot coffee out the bottom in seconds. She watched, slightly amused at my hurried demeanor.

"I could've done that for you."

"It's faster if I just do it myself."

"I can follow instructions."

"I'm sure you can. I can't think about what I have to do over there and give you instructions at the same time."

"Well, then, you should get back to work. I'll bring your coffee to you. You take it black?"

"Right. When I'm here, it's all about getting done on time. I'm not normally like this."

"What are you normally like?"

"Not like this. More easy going. How about you?"

"What you see is what you get."

"Really? Cause I'd like to have what I'm seeing."

Cassi laughs. "Not in *that* way."

"Oh, well. I tried."

I hurried back over to the fryer and plopped the first batch of donuts into the oil. There's a rhythm to it, one revolution of the handle makes one donut. If the revolutions are matched up to the correct speed, it's just one smooth motion. Practice, practice, practice.

Cassi brought my coffee over to the frying area and put it on the shelf next to the radio. "Here, OK?"

"Perfect. Thanks."

148

Dancing in the Street

She returned to the customer area, poured herself a cup and sat on the counter, the only place to sit that had a view of the work area. With that short skirt, I wasn't going to complain.

I started to flip the donuts with one long, wooden stick, done by pushing down the top right edge and in the same motion, the top left edge of the adjacent donut. It's easy to flip the whole batch in seconds.

I've seen other donut makers use two sticks, but I also see them make mistakes and poke holes or disfigure what should be a perfectly round donut. I've tried two sticks, but I'm not good at it. The only person I've ever seen that is really good with two sticks is Tony.

Cassi laughed. "You're pretty good at that."

"First time I tried it, I spent as much time cleaning up as I did frying. Can I ask you a question?"

"Sure."

"Why are you out running around all alone at midnight?"

"That's two questions."

"What?"

"Are you asking why I'm running around at midnight? Or, why am I all alone?"

"I was trying to sneak an extra one in."

"So...," sipping her coffee, watching me over the rim of her cup. "Which one?"

I pulled the screen of hot dripping donuts out of the oil, banged it down on the fryer lid on the side and then slid the donuts onto another rack where they could cool while I cranked out the next batch. I can't talk when I'm doing all of that.

Coming back over to the icing tray, "They're both good questions. I think they should both be answered."

Baby Love

She smiles. I think she likes this little cat and mouse game.

"What I have to go through just to get one donut."

"Not just *a* donut. The best donut in town."

"I didn't know there was a contest."

149

"You're right. There is no contest, compared to these."

"OK. Still…, pick one."

I had to think about that. If I ask why she is alone, she could give me any reason, something like, I was just on my way home. On the other hand, if I ask why she is out running around at midnight, she would have to be more specific. "Why are you out running around at midnight?"

"I'm on my way home."

"Oh? Where's that?"

"That's another question."

"You're pretty stingy for information."

A slight, pouting smile. "I answered your question. What more do you want?"

"How about your phone number?"

This caused a belly laugh and a slight spill of her coffee onto her skirt. "That would not be good for either of us."

"How so?"

Do Wah Diddy Diddy

"I've already answered your one question."

"You're a mystery. I love mysteries."

"Then, don't ask so many questions."

"But there are so many. At two in the morning, you can't sleep and crave a glazed donut?"

"I didn't say glazed. And I didn't say I couldn't sleep."

"So, you're here to learn how to make donuts."

"No way."

"Because you want to make passionate love with me?"

OK. That brought a belly laugh. "Never!"

"So sure?"

"That's another question."

"Will you go out with me?"

As soon as I asked her, I realized that I had stepped over some kind of red line. Was she Jimbo's girl now since they had already gone on a date? He didn't hesitate to ask her out when I thought I had first chance. Do best friends do this to each other? Suddenly, I regretted asking.

A World Without Love

The thing about Cassi was that she was hard to read. Amused with my question, she sipped her coffee and

150

watched me make donuts, silent for a long while. "Maybe," she said at last. "Tuesday is your night off, right?"

"Right."

"What would we do?"

"Dinner and a walk the beach?"

"Nothing more?"

"I'm open to suggestions."

"No. I meant, you wouldn't expect anything more?"

"That's depressing. But I can live with it."

"Then..., OK."

"Phone number? Address?"

She laughed. "Where do you want to meet?"

I've got a date! Do I tell Jimbo? Neither of us are talking about her, so I guess this is a secret? She did not mention her date with him tonight, so..., what?

I was standing at my locker and searching for my English book when somebody bumped into me from behind. Turning, I saw that it was two of Carlo's friends, Dante and Angel, both of them laughing. They kept going, but after a few steps Dante, the one that had bumped into me, looked back apologetically.

"He pushed me."

It could've been an accident. I didn't think it was on purpose and he did look apologetic, although he never said he was sorry.

I didn't think any more about it. I was still thinking that, because I was John's friend, I was safe from Carlo and friends. Maybe they had forgotten?

But that would be hard to forget. I'd seen them walking around at lunch hour and I was always sitting with John, Penny and Letti. So, they must know. I decided that it was just an accident and to leave it at that.

Friday, during lunch with John and Penny, Letti asked if I'd like to join her up on the track after school and run a few laps...,

"Don't worry. We won't race."

"I'm not worried."

She smiled. "I don't want to take your money anyway."

"You won't."

John laughed. "Man, I detect some serious competition between you two."

"I give him a hard time," said Letti. "Because he should be on the track team."

"Would if I could."

"You don't have to come to all of the practices. Coach will understand if you have to work."

"I'd miss too many. It wouldn't sit right with anybody else that comes to all of the practices."

Penny, scooping one of the peanuts out of her chocolate shake with a spoon, nodded. "I agree. You can't just be half there. You have to be committed and let others know

152

that you are. Otherwise, it affects team moral."

"Like you know," said John. "You aren't a member of anything."

"Because I'm busy with my studies. I want to get through college in three years and get on with my life."

I couldn't resist. "So, you can support John while he plays for the Aztecs?"

John winced. "Low blow, Calvin."

"Sorry. I couldn't help it."

"Are you going to college?"

"I don't know what I want to do, yet."

"Did you get a notice to report for the draft?"

"Yeah."

"You wait too long, you're going to be drafted."

"If it comes to that, I'll probably take the test to get into the Air Force. They'll give me some kind of training. Better than the Army for two years, anyway."

Letti bit into one of her apple slices. "Back to the original question. Do you want to run a few laps with me after school?"

"Sure. Just don't take advantage of me."

We were running together, side by side. Letti set the pace.

"I start out slow, just to get my muscles warmed up."

Running slow, for me, was about the same thing as lazy. I fought an urge to break into a run. You put me on a track and if I know that there's a finish line somewhere, I'm going to race toward it.

"I know how you feel, Calvin. Trust me. Just do what I do."

After the first lap, Letti picked up her pace to what I estimated to be about half speed and I was happy with that.

"You're bouncing a lot." She reached over and put her hand on my arm and pushed gently downward. "It's wasted energy. You don't need to go up and down. Lean forward a bit and let that bounce push you forward."

I had never thought about it, but it made sense. When I sprint, that bouncing is actually propelling me forward because I'm going fast enough and am airborne long enough that it works. With the slower pace, it's wasted energy.

By the end of the second lap, I was glad that the first had been a warm-up. The third lap, now approaching six hundred yards, was testing my endurance.

"Breathe in deeply," said Letti. "Hold it in a little longer and let it out slowly."

I tried that, found that it worked at first, but soon I was back to what I would describe as gasping.

""Last lap," said Letti. "Fourth time around."

In between breaths. "I wish..., you would have told me..., that we were going to..., run the eight, freaking hundred."

She laughed and picked up the pace even more. I was just keeping up. About halfway around...,

"OK, Calvin. You can turn it on now, if you want to. I know how fast you are."

If I want to? Of course! That's the whole point! My brain and my ego want to put this last hundred yards behind me, finish with a flair! But I just didn't have the air.

I thought of all those times Jimbo and I had fired up that pipe and held the smoke in our lungs until we could hold it no more. How does that affect me now?

And I was glad that I had not taken up smoking cigarettes, like Jimbo, who smoked whatever he could whenever he could. I had been noticing lately, that he was developing a cough.

Letti was pushing the pace now. I was staying with her, but struggling. I was amazed at how much stamina she had. Going into the final stretch, she could've pushed it. She could've embarrassed me, but she didn't. We crossed over the line together.

"You're a great runner, Letti," I gasped. "I *am* impressed!"

She smiled. "You're not so bad yourself."

"I ran out of air."

"You don't know how to breathe. With practice, you could break records."

"Too many donuts in my life."

154

"You don't have to eat them."

"How often do you run this?"

"I only do the eight hundred on Friday. My three races are the two hundred, the four hundred and the four hundred relay. This is just to test my endurance."

God, I wanted to hug her. "You're amazing."

That brought a slight blush. She grabbed her towel, threw it over her shoulder and waited for me to gather my stuff. We started back toward the gym.

"Thanks for running with me."

"Thanks for the lesson. I can't see me doing eight hundred in a race."

"You don't have to. Use that to train for the two."

"Don't know that I can do that."

"You can do two." She patted me on the back. "But you can't do four, yet."

"I don't have time to train."

"You can do whatever you want to do."

If she only knew. I laughed. "*Whatever* I want to do?"

"You know what I mean."

Leaving the field, I noticed that Carlo was there with a friend, not close enough to hear us, but close enough to watch.

Tuesday night, a little after ten, Cassi turned on the radio as soon as she got into the car, her miniskirt, as always, drawing my attention. We didn't kiss, but she gave me a quick hug.

I was hoping to have a quiet conversation with her on our way out to La Jolla, but with the sounds turned up, I decided that she didn't want to talk.

Game of Love

When I took the Ardath turn and headed up toward La Jolla, I turned the volume down.

"Where do you want to go?"

"Let's drive through the residential area."

"Where all the expensive homes are?"

"The ones that have a view of the ocean."

It occurred to me that, in my neighborhood, she never got out of the car. Drive-in's, like Oscar's, were OK as long as we parked away from everybody else. At first, I thought it was because she wanted to be alone with me. I'm now thinking it's because she doesn't want to be recognized.

Driving slowly through the winding roads we found a dead-end street with a view of the ocean. I parked the car, rolled down the window and listened to the waves crashing onto shore. I was content to stay there, but she opened the door.

"Let's go."

"What? Down there?"

"It's a dead end. There's got to be a path somewhere."

"At night?"

Slamming the door closed, "Let's go!"

Seeing what the wave might do with her miniskirt was a compelling thought. I quickly followed her down a path. We took off our shoes, played hide and seek with the waves for half an hour and then settled in on top of a rock far enough away that we wouldn't get swamped.

On this night, Cassi was more aroused than usual. She

156

let my hands roam farther than ever before and I was thinking that this was the night.

How cool! Right out here on the beach in the moonlight with the waves rolling in. It doesn't get more romantic than that.

About the time I thought it was going to happen, she pulled away, took a deep breath and readjusted her clothes.

"What's wrong?"

"I'm sorry, Calvin. I can't do it."

I felt like I'd just been hit with a hammer. "You're kidding, right?"

She abruptly stood, brushed off the sand and extended her hand to pull me up. "I wish I was."

We walked back up the trail, got in the car and drove home in silence. I was at a loss for words. She didn't want to answer any of my questions and I couldn't think of any other conversation that I wanted to have.

When I reached her car, she leaned over, squeezed my hand, kissed me on the cheek and got out. I could see that she had been crying.

Neither of us had seen her for a month. I did not want to admit that even after several dates I hadn't gotten much farther than making out. Jimbo didn't want to talk about it either, so I assumed that he had fared no better. One night, while playing a game of chess and drinking beer...,

"She must like you, Jimbo. I can't get past first base."

Jimbo, contemplating his next move, looked up, surprised. "I was thinking the same thing about you."

"She's always ready to go out and we always have fun, so I'm always thinking tonight's the night. But it never happens."

"Same here."

"What the hell is going on?"

"I think she's got another boyfriend."

"I can see why she would reject you, but...,"

"Screw you."

"It's your move, by the way."

"I'm thinking."

"I'm sick of working nights."

"I'm sick of donuts. I can't believe that I used to like them. What are you going to do after you graduate?"

"Not make donuts."

"Go to college?"

"Don't know. How about you?"

"I'm sick of school. I want to go get a real job."

"With your talents? Like, what? Insurance salesman? Door to door?"

Jimbo advanced one of his pawns. "Maybe, I'll just sell dope. I can make a lot of money off of slime balls like you."

"Screw you."

"Maybe we should just confront her. Ask her which one of us she likes best and the other one bows out."

"Who would you date, then?"

"Screw you."

"Besides, she's not around to ask."

"You got a point."

"You got any more weed?"

Jimbo pulled a joint out of his pocket, lit it, took a hit and passed it over. "Where the hell has she been for the last month?"

"You're right, another boyfriend."

"Your move, man. Keep up."

"I take your white bishop with my knight."

"Shit. I didn't even see that. I hate losing a bishop. The other one's useless after that. Hey! Let me have some of that."

I took another hit and passed it back. "We need to date more girls, give her some competition."

"Right."

"We don't have too many eggs in one basket. We have one egg in two baskets."

"That sucks. I take your rook with my pawn."

"I was hoping that you wouldn't see that."

"I got a thing in the mail yesterday. It said. "The friends and neighbors in my community have chosen me to serve our country...,"

"I got one of those."

"Some friends."

"I'd like to know *which* neighbors chose me."

"I have to go up to L. A. for a physical."

"Me, too. And unless we sign up for college, we're going to be classified, 1A."

Jimbo chugged about half of his beer, burped. "After we're classified, how long before we're drafted?"

"I heard that when you get a second notice for another physical, they're getting ready to draft you."

"That sucks. What's with this war, anyway? Why are we even in Viet Nam?"

Jimbo tried to hand the joint back to me, but I waved it away. "No idea. I don't even know where it is."

"If we're drafted, do we go into the Army or Marines?"

"What's the difference? You gotta go through boot camp and in the end, they've got you for two years."

"Maybe I'll go to Canada."

"I'll go visit the Air Force recruiter and take a test. They don't see combat, do they?"

"I think helicopters get shot down all the time. Is that Air Force? Or, Marines?"

"How would I know?"

"I thought politicians were supposed to keep us out of wars."

"Well, we had Kennedy, but they killed him."

Jimbo took one last hit and put it out. "If you enlist, that's for four years, right?"

"Right."

"So, if I go in for two and you're in for four, I'll have Cassi all to myself for two years."

"She's gone, Jimbo. She just played us along."

"I hear Thailand's got pretty good dope. If I'm sent to Viet Nam, maybe I could get over there on leave."

"What are you, nuts? Jimbo, those are real bullets they're shooting."

"I'll volunteer to be a cook, dishwasher, anything that doesn't involve bullets."

"Asian women are beautiful. At least we'll get laid."

"No telling what else you're gonna get."

"I take your pawn with my queen. Check."

"You, ass hole."

We didn't talk about it, but we both knew that we were coming to an end of an era. The war was going to suck us up into its gigantic web. We were probably going to the other side of the world and do things we've never done before. Our decision for the future came down to whether we wanted to do a high risk two-year stint, or a safer, four-year stint, or Canada.

Coming soon was a time when I would never make another donut. I would sell my car, get my head shaved, wear a uniform, salute people I'd never seen, stand at attention, obey commands even if I thought them wrong.

It seemed so sudden, graduating from high school and going to war. Hardly a break in-between.

Jimbo bought a new carburetor for the old Dodge, drove the car into my back yard and parked it so when he opened the hood, he'd be in shade. I had him stop on top of a piece of carpet that I'd scrounged from one of my customers during my paper delivering days. Jimbo popped the hood, got out and put the bar in place to hold it up.

"What's the carpet for?"

"In case you drop something."

"It's only four bolts and the fuel line. I'm not going to drop anything."

"If you do, you're not crawling around looking for it in the dirt."

"Oh. Right. Thanks."

"And the air cleaner."

"What?"

"You've got to remove the air cleaner."

"Well..., yeah, that."

"And the linkage. Make sure you mark it, so you know how it goes back together."

"I'm not a dweeb, like you. I got this."

"You got a new gasket?"

"Right. Go do whatever else it is you have to do. Where do you want me to leave your tools?"

"Beneath the steps at the back door. Close the gate on your way out."

"Right. Thanks."

Coming back to the house two hours later, Jimbo was still there, now standing in the sun, shirt off, hunched over the carburetor.

I laughed. "It's only four bolts and a fuel line. How hard can it be?"

"Fuck you."

I know that tone of voice. Nothing helps invent new strings of curse words better than mechanics.

"What's up, Jimbo? Can I help?"

161

"It's this frickin' fuel line! It doesn't line up."

"Wait. Stop. I remember that problem from when I put it together. Stop, Jimbo. Really."

Reluctantly, he backed away, glaring at the defiant tubing. I leaned over the engine and saw that he had bent the fuel line too far away from where it was supposed to reattach.

"If you bend it that far, it gets out of whack. You should move it as little as possible."

"Too late for that. It kept getting in the way when I was putting the new carburetor on."

That would be like Jimbo, not the most patient person in the world. "I remember..., you have to loosen the other end, not all the way, just enough so that you can get another quarter inch at this end. Hand me, what is this? Seven-sixteenths?"

"Fuck if I know."

We fixed the trouble, tightened all of the fittings and started it up. It sounded like crap, coughing, sputtering.

Jimbo killed the engine. "What the hell! It's brand new!"

I grabbed a screwdriver. "I just remembered. You have to adjust the air-fuel mixture."

"Where's that?"

I pointed to a screw on the side of the carburetor. "I think this is it. Did it come with instructions?"

"No. Is it supposed to?"

"No idea."

The screw was tightened all the way down. Checking the old carburetor, we found that the screw was backed out two and one-quarter turns. We matched that setting on the new. Jimbo turned the key. It started right up, sounded good and then he was all smiles.

"Let's take it for a spin."

I motioned for him to go and started putting my tools back. Five minutes later, pulling back into the yard, Jimbo killed the engine and joined me on the back porch.

"Man! It's running really good. You sold me a car that had a bad carburetor. I think you should pay half."

"Fuck you."

162

"No, really...,"

"Then I'm going to charge you a hundred bucks for carburetor installation and tune-up."

Jimbo pulled a joint out of his pocket. "Well, in that case, you're not getting any of this."

"You'd still be out there messin' with that thing, if not for me and all of my talent. Hand me that joint, will you?"

"Go to hell."

"Well..., at least your car's fixed."

Jimbo took a puff and handed it over.

"I have an idea. "Let's go out to Borrego Springs, give the car a good run. I'll borrow my old man's telescope, grab a couple of sleeping bags and we'll sleep out under the stars."

"You're kidding, right?"

"You ever see the night sky from the dessert? There's so much starlight that it's like daylight. My dad's scope is pretty good and...,"

"What kinds of things are out there?"

"Bugs, spiders, snakes, coyotes. Everything."

"And I want to go..., why?"

"Jesus, Calvin. You finally get a night off and you don't want to go anywhere?"

"What would we do for food?"

"We've got a Coleman stove and some pans. We'll just buy a dozen eggs on the way out, some bacon, stop by the shop and get some donuts."

"You really think that carburetor's OK? I don't want to get out there and have us break down."

"Bring your tools. Hey! Hand that over."

"And the old carburetor. Why do I have a bad feeling about this?"

"Cause you're a dweeb."

Ten-thirty at night, Jimbo driving, we're heading north on Highway Sixty-seven, wanting to connect into Highway Seventy-eight. It's a two-lane road and there's not much traffic.

"Are your headlights adjusted?"

"Listen to that engine, Calvin. It's purring!"

"Seems like the passenger headlight drifts too far to the right."

"Why would I care about that?"

"It kind of gives you a blind spot in the middle."

"I kind of like it. One for the road. One for the scenery."

"Kind of dangerous."

"Why don't you adjust it when you get a chance, if it bothers you so much."

"It's not my car."

"It was probably like that when you sold it to me. Actually, it's on you to fix it."

"All of the stations are turning into static."

"Yeah. AM sucks. No range. It sounded good when we were in town, though. Right?"

"Yeah. How did you fix the speaker?"

"I just put a piece of tape on the cone where it was ripped."

"Did you get both sides?"

"Why would I do both sides if taping one side fixes the problem?"

"I guess it'll work until the tape falls off. What you really need is a new speaker."

"I figure I've got a year before the tape comes loose and I've got a whole roll of that. I can go twenty..., that car coming at us. Are they in my lane?"

It was hard to tell. We were doing about fifty going into a section of the road that curved left, coming up in about a hundred yards. The oncoming car, already in that curve, seemed to be drifting into our lane.

"Jesus! I think so...,"

164

"Fuck!"

Jimbo flashed his high beams, swerved hard to the right, honking his horn and braking heavily. That car hit us just behind the driver's side mirror, shoving us into the gravel where we skidded toward a telephone pole. Our car came to a stop about ten feet from it.

Jimbo still had his hands on the wheel. *"Holy fuck!"*

I took a deep breath. "That would've been head-on! Thank - you - Jimbo!"

Jimbo forced his way out of the car, shoving the mangled mess of his door outward with a string of curses. He was going to kill somebody. My door worked fine.

After glancing off of Jimbo's car, the other car came to rest in a ditch on the other side of the road about a hundred yards away, a little less. Their horn was blasting non-stop.

Neither of us were hurt, but going to the other car, we found the driver, a middle-aged woman who reeked of alcohol, draped over the steering wheel, unconscious.

We did not smell gasoline, didn't think there was any chance of a fire, so decided not to move her. We did pull her away from the steering wheel, which stopped the horn and returned some measure of calm to the evening, silence at first and then crickets.

I was struck by the oddity of the situation, two cars going in opposite directions through a quiet night, smashing together in some sort of metallic BANG, with lots of sparks and possibilities of explosion, both skidding off in different directions, us across gravel, the other into a ditch, horn blasting and the crickets just waiting patiently until it was OK to chirp again.

Jimbo pointed to the open passenger-side door. "You think that just popped open? Or, was there somebody sitting there?"

The passenger side seat was folded forward. "Maybe they were in the back." Going around the car, I spotted two kids, maybe four or five years old, running across the field. "I'll get them. You see a house where we can make a call?"

165

Jimbo took off running. "There's some kind of store up there. Maybe they've got a pay phone."

I climbed between the wires of the fence running parallel to the road and went after the kids. They started screaming and were running from me. I could easily catch them, but what kind of trauma might that bring? I stopped, knelt down so I wouldn't seem so big and ominous, and yelled.

"Hey, you two! This was an accident. Your mom is hurt. She needs you. I'm not going to hurt you. Come on. Let's go back."

They stopped running, whimpered a bit, but they were not about to return to me. I stood and pointed to their car back in the ditch.

"Your mom is in the car. She's hurt. I'm going to go try and help her. Don't you want to help her?"

They followed me back to the car, but stayed on the other side of the fence when they saw Jimbo running toward us, gasping.

"Police..., are on the way, tow truck and..., ambulance."

I ran back to Jimbo's car and grabbed a couple of donuts to take back to the kids. They were wary at first, but who can resist a donut? They took them and after a bite, or two, climbed through the fence and joined us while we waited for help to arrive. She was breathing, becoming aware.

The police were the first on the scene, setting out flares and warning the few passing cars to slow down, sweeping up the glass and other miscellaneous scattered parts.

The ambulance whisked away the woman and her two kids. A tow truck hauled away her car and after the police hailed Jimbo as the hero of the evening for his exemplary driving skills, the tow truck arrived to haul away Jimbo's car. Before they did, we took everything out of the trunk.

Three in the morning, sitting at the side of the road with all of our stuff, waiting for his dad to come pick us up, Jimbo was getting impatient.

"I think he went back to sleep."

"How come the police didn't take us home?"

"I told them my dad was on his way."

"Well..., this sucks."

"My car's a wreck. I hope she has insurance."

"They're not going to offer much. Car's too old."

"Hey! It was running good."

"Police smelled alcohol on her. Good. Drunk-driving charge."

"With two kids in the car."

"Never heard so many crickets. Listen to that."

"Fuck the crickets. I'm hungry."

"Let's fire up the stove and have some eggs."

Jimbo unfolded the Coleman and began pumping air into the tank. "Bacon?"

"Might as well. Did we bring coffee?"

"Instant."

"Good enough."

"How about you cook and I'll set up the scope?"

"What? You're going to star gaze?"

"We're not going to make it to Borrego Springs. We're doing what we came to do, sleep out under the stars...,"

"We're not sleeping."

"Yeah. But we're outdoors having breakfast. Stars won't look much different whether we're here or in Borrego Springs."

I got bacon sizzling in the pan, water boiling for coffee.

"You got a point. How many eggs?"

"Four."

"I'll do eight. Man, this fresh air makes me hungry."

"Yeah, camping out always does that."

"You got a joint?"

"You bet. Fuck this night."

The other driver, Lynn, did not have insurance and Jimbo was carrying only the minimum. His insurance company was glad that he reported it, apologized for not being able to help more, but shouldn't he have purchased a better policy? They made a few phone calls, no results.

She was living in a trailer out in the back country with her boyfriend, Buck who, when we went out to talk with them, was combative and unwilling to deal with the problem. Lynn claimed she didn't have any money and for a while it looked like Jimbo was going to suffer a total loss.

It was the letter from the DMV stating that she would lose her driver's license for two years if Jimbo did not sign a form releasing her from her financial responsibility.

We were sitting at a dilapidated picnic table alongside her trailer. Lynn was wearing a neck brace and had a cast on her arm. She offered us some lemonade, but both of us refused.

"How about I give you twenty dollars a month from my disability check until we're even?"

Jimbo, I could tell, was clearly irritated. "That's not going to get me a car. I need one for work."

"That old car can't have been worth much. Would you settle for a hundred dollars?"

"I paid twice that for the car, rebuilt the engine and had just put a new carburetor on it. It's worth five."

Buck was standing in the doorway of the trailer. "You're full of shit. That car's not worth five."

"It's worth more than a hundred. Quit trying to screw me and let's get down to business."

One thing I'll say for Jimbo. He naturally has a face that says, "I'm already pissed off. Don't fuck with me." When he really gets mad, his eyes narrow and, with jaw set hard, furrowed brow, pursed lips and red face, he looks like a madman getting ready to explode. It's very impressive.

"How about," Lynn paused while she lit a cigarette. "How about I give you two hundred. I'll borrow it from somewhere."

"No deal. I put a lot of work into that car. Two hundred is the starting point. It wasn't me that caused the accident."

"I guess I'll just have to lose my license." She blew the smoke in our direction. Really?

"I'll notify the DMV about my neck problems since the accident. I'll make sure that they understand the full extent of your problem."

"You don't have a neck problem."

"I've got a pain in the neck, right now."

I held up my hand. "Who owns that old Buick out back?"

"I do," said Buck, now glaring at me.

"Does it run?"

"No."

"Engine blew up?"

"Why you asking?"

"It might be part of a deal."

"I'm plannin' on fixin' it."

Lynn laughed. "He's been sayin' that for five years."

"Gotta get the money first."

Lynn turned on the bench, took a long drag on her cigarette and blew it out slowly. "For that, Honey, you've got to get your ass out of the house."

"Can Jimbo and I go look at it?"

Lynn got up and waved for us to follow. "It was a fine-running car when it ran. Might be just what you boys want. Clean it up and it'll look like new."

It was a nineteen fifty-one Buick Special, two-door, two-tone, white top, blue bottom, covered in mud, dust and surrounded by weeds, a sweet looking car that, if it had a good engine, would get up and go. Jimbo was doubtful.

"I don't think so."

Turning, I noticed that Buck had followed. "Did the engine stop? Or did the transmission go out?"

"Engine over-heated, blew up."

Fortunately, the windows were left up so the interior wasn't too bad. Popping the hood, we discovered a rat's nest, which we quickly broke up, several black widows and whatever else had made the compartment home for the last five years. We dragged a hose out from the trailer and sprayed it down. The radiator had no water in it.

"Yeah," Buck admitted. "Had a leaky freeze plug. Must've blown when I was driving."

"Probably sucked a valve, huh?"

"Don't know."

Lynn peeked inside, rubbed her hand over the dust on the dash. "Leather seats. Won't take much to clean that up."

Jimbo, shaking his head. "Too much work. I need a car that runs."

I pulled him aside. "That car, when it's running, is worth about five hundred. We can probably fix it for a hundred."

"How long will that take? I've got to go to work every day. And if we can't fix it, I'm stuck with a piece of shit."

"Let's make a deal. We take the car and they pay for half of a rebuilt engine. We do the work."

"How are we going to get it out of here?"

"Uncle Wally moves vending machines around town. He's got access to trucks and trailers."

"How do we get the old engine out?"

"We'll need a pulley and some kind of A-frame."

"Jesus, Calvin."

"That's a hot little car once we get it running, Jimbo. Can't you see yourself in that when it's all waxed up? Did you see that it's already got front and rear speakers?"

"It does have nice lines."

"Picture yourself with Cassi in there."

"Fuck her."

"Whomever."

"You're going to help me with this, right?"

"Right."

"How am I going to get to and from work?"

"I'll take you."

"Can I borrow your car while you're at work?"

"No way."

170

"Even if I have a hot date?"

"Not even. If I'm not getting laid in my car, you aren't either. I want to be the one to break it in."

"It's gonna rust out before that happens."

"Fuck you."

Jimbo looked the car over one more time, checking the tires, chrome and looking for dents. The body was in good shape. "OK. Let's go do this."

Overriding Buck's objections, we got the car, pink slip, registration and her promise to pay up to one hundred dollars toward a replacement engine, to be paid at twenty dollars a month in exchange for Jimbo's signature on the release form, which he was withholding for the moment.

To get uncle Wally's assistance, Jimbo and I had to agree to help move several vending machines around town and clean up the warehouse.

His friend, Benny, loaned Wally a truck and trailer to haul the Buick back to Benny's place where we washed the car, vacuumed it out and wiped everything down. The car was looking pretty good.

Jimbo was curious to know if the radio worked. We jumpered the battery from my car over to his and turned it on.

Hang on Sloopy

Front and rear speakers worked and sounded good. Jimbo, sitting behind the steering wheel, was smiling. I could see him falling in love with this vehicle.

Just hearing that little bit of sound brought the car back from the dead, letting us feel that, yes, there are so many possibilities.

Benny cut a round figure. I cannot say that he looked like a beach ball in coveralls with four protrusions, short neck and a mostly bald head, but he comes closer to that than anyone I've ever seen. He has a pencil moustache and a space between his two front teeth that looks like it should whistle. Benny builds race cars.

He went to the garage on the far right of a three-car garage located behind his house, fired up a modified, number thirty-two, backed it out and parked it alongside the building.

"Let's push your car in there, open the hood and see what you got."

Peering inside, he moved the spark plug wires around a bit, popped the distributor cap and checked out the points and rotor, pulled out the dipstick, noted the level, low, and then rubbed some of the oil between his fingertips.

"You see the metal shavings? We can do a compression check to see where the trouble is, but you should pull the head off and take a look. You want to rebuild the engine? Or, replace it?"

Jimbo cleared his throat. "Which is faster?"

Benny laughed. "Here's how it works. You've got fast, good and cheap. Pick any two."

"Fast and good."

"Fast and good means a new engine and it won't be cheap. You still have to take this one out and put that one in."

"Good and cheap."

"We pull the head off of this and see what kind of mess you've got and rebuild it. That can get complicated, depending on what you have to do. It takes a little longer."

"Fast and cheap?"

"You call junk yards and find out if there's an engine out there that has your name on it. Sometimes you get lucky."

Jimbo looked at me. "What do you think, Calvin?"

172

"I'd say we check this engine out before we think about replacing it. Like Benny said, let's see what kind of mess we've got."

Benny went through the door leading into the middle garage and rolled his tool cabinet back into our room.

"There's some tags and a pen in the top drawer. You might want to mark where the hoses and wires go before you disconnect. It goes back together a lot faster later on. These are all the tools you're gonna need. What I ask is that after you've used one, wipe it off and put it back where you found it. There's some rags in that box over in the corner. Don't leave tools lying around and at the end of the day and you clean up the day's mess. Fair enough?"

Both of us nodded. Jimbo shook his hand. "Thanks, Benny. We really appreciate it."

What a joy it is to use good tools. And we had a smooth concrete floor beneath our feet. No crawling around in the dirt. Truly a luxury. Jimbo and I removed the head and discovered that the exhaust valve in the number seven cylinder disintegrated, taking out the piston as well. Benny came out to inspect it.

"For sure, a valve job, replace that piston. You might have to put a sleeve in this cylinder. And if you're gonna do that, you might as well do rings and bearings at the same time."

Jimbo sounded disappointed. "That sounds like a lot of work."

"Well, now you know where the trouble is. Once you remove the oil pan...," He paused, sizing us up. "It's gonna take some work. Tell you what. I've got a friend who's pretty good at locating parts. He owes me a favor. Let's see what he comes up with."

"Another engine?"

"If he can find one, how much you willing to pay?"

Jimbo looked over at me. "One hundred?"

"If it's a good engine that we won't have to mess with, three hundred."

"I'll give him a call. Let's see. This is the Fireball Straight

Eight, isn't it?"

I nodded. "How many cubic inches is that?"

"I think, two hundred and sixty-three."

No more progress, Jimbo needed to get to work. I dropped him off at his house and waited outside while he got cleaned up.

During that time, Katie came out to wait in the car with me. Since our day of writing together, our conversations continue along that line. She sat in the passenger seat, closed the door and leaned against it, studying me with a seductive smile. She has an uncanny ability to unnerve me.

"Calie. Been a while."

"Katie." I reached over to shake her hand. "Long time, no see."

She's laughing already. I think she's stoned. Her eyes are red and her smile does not go away.

"Long time, no see? That's the best that you can do?"

"I've been searching everywhere for the love of my life. But now I see she's sitting right here in front of me."

She laughs. "Now, I know you're full of shit."

"That's not my only asset. I'm also boring."

"That, I can believe. I hear you helped Jimbo find a car?"

"A fifty-one Buick Special."

"And it is..., where?"

"At this guy's house out in Lakeside. We're going to rebuild the engine."

"He bought a car that doesn't run?"

"We'll get it running."

"So sure?"

"Nothing is *for* sure."

"You're right. You are boring."

"I warned you. What kind of trouble are you getting into these days?"

"I'm taking an art class."

"I didn't know you liked art."

"It's better than basket weaving."

"What are you doing in class?"

She smiles. I can see her mind working, concocting

a devious plan. "We're supposed to draw a portrait of someone."

"Really? In a beginner's class?"

"Yeah. So?"

"I'd think you start off with shapes. You know, cubes, pyramids, easy stuff."

"A portrait's a shape."

"It's about ten thousand shapes inside one. Whose portrait are you going to do?"

She framed me inside a makeshift square formed by her hands. "I want to do you."

"No way."

"Naked."

I laughed. "I don't think so."

"Why not?"

"Because I'm the one that would get in trouble."

"Is that all you can think about? I thought you'd be excited about it."

"I'm excited *thinking* about it. But I won't do it."

"Because I'm Jimbo's sister?"

"Partly. Besides, a portrait is a face and torso. What you're suggesting is a nude."

"I didn't really want to do you anyway. I just wanted to see what you'd say."

"Ask me again when you're eighteen."

"You'd do it then?"

"Depends."

"Nothing is for sure?"

"Right. If I take up art and want to do a nude, would you do it for me?"

"Sure."

"After you're eighteen."

"There you go again, Mr. Boring."

She giggles while her hands unbutton the top button of her blouse, giving me an innocent, little girl smile. "And," leaning forward, "when I say sure, I mean *for* sure. I'll do it right now." She's unbuttoned her second button. "I'll just take this off...,"

"No, no, no! Here comes Jimbo. *Jesus!*"

Katie laughs, opens the door, gets out and blows me a kiss before she waves goodbye. This girl baffles me. Is she so free and easy because she knows I won't do anything? Or, is she really interested? And, if she is, how will that go over with her brother?

Jimbo got in, slammed the door too hard, as usual, and rolled down the window. "What was that all about?"

"What?"

"She blew you a kiss?"

"Your sister's a tease."

"No shit. Let's get this over with. Onward, James."

Benny's friend, after calling his cousin who worked at a junk yard in Otay Mesa, found the same engine in a Buick that had been rear-ended. They sold us the engine and transmission for a hundred and seventy-five, delivered it to Benny's house for another fifty and hauled the old stuff away. Such a deal.

The engine was clean and, inspecting it, Benny said it was in excellent condition. Two days later, after we got everything bolted into place and hooked up, we started it up.

There's always the initial tinkering, getting gas to the carburetor, adjusting the linkage, setting the timing, checking for leaks.

But when Benny finished tuning it up and told Jimbo, who was sitting and fidgeting behind the wheel, to start it up, you should've seen the smile on his face when he turned the key and heard it purr.

Letti and I were becoming a thing around school and there was no reason for it. Yes, we ate lunch together every day. But a big reason for that was because Letti and Penny were friends, same as John and I, and that they could do their homework together. The only other time that we were together was on Friday afternoons when we worked out at the track.

I wanted more time with her, but working afternoons during the week and nights on week-ends, I didn't have much of an opportunity. Also, she was not allowed out on a date with anyone unsupervised. In other words, we were not to be left alone.

Heading out to my car after classes, I found Carlo leaning against the driver's side door and Angel sitting on the front fender.

Carlo made no attempt to move, ignoring my approach while he cleaned his fingernails with the tip of his knife. When I tried to reach around him to unlock the door, he moved in the way. Angel slid off of the fender and moved behind me.

Instinct tells me to run, but Carlo had no reason to assault me. I had done nothing to him or any of his friends and I still thought I had protection because I was John's friend.

"What's up, Carlo?"

"You're becoming a problem to me."

"How?"

"You don't *know?*"

"I don't know..., what? What have I done?"

"Letti is my sister."

OK. That is bad news and it explains their presence up on the field when Letti and I worked out. And it puts a new perspective onto the incident where Angel bumped into me. I saw my fantasies of dating Letti come to an end. Carlo was watching me closely.

"I had no idea."

"So…, you understand my problem. Comprende?"

"I do."

He moved away from the door and, standing next to Angel, folded his knife. "She is not for you."

They left without another word. Getting into my car, my mind was whirling and my palms felt sweaty. Adrenalin does that? My hands were shaking as I put the key into the ignition.

A knife is such a dangerous thing. It doesn't have to make any noise to serve the owner's purpose. A small slice on someone's fingertip can be a powerful reminder to behave, a silent, behind-the-scenes persuader. Comprende?

Got it. The problem is, Letti and I are friends. We like being together, are comfortable teasing each other and I love to make her blush.

How is this going to affect our relationship? Should I change where I sit at lunch? No. There would be questions. Stop the work-outs at the track? No. I enjoy those as much as Letti.

If I stopped doing either of these, she would demand some kind of explanation. I take that back. She would quietly inquire and listen carefully, weighing my words. I cannot lie to her. No. I cannot change what already exists.

But this sure blows a hole in any kind of designs I had for her. In a way, it was doomed from the beginning, restrictions on her, work hours for me.

And, while I respect Carlo's desire to protect his sister, much like what Jimbo did with Kenny that day, I resent being threatened. What business is it of his if Letti and I have a thing for each other? Does she tell him who he can and cannot date? I doubt it. There seems to be a double standard here.

On the other hand, he did not say to stop seeing her or to stop doing what we are already doing. He was just letting me know to not take advantage.

Right?

I was out front washing my car when Harold crossed the street and joined me, sitting on the rail of our fence. I turned the nozzle off, grabbed a towel and started drying the top.

"Harold. What's up? I haven't seen you since Hoover."

"Not much. How's Crawford?"

"About the same as Hoover. Are you trying to grow a beard?"

"I'm growing one." He laughed. "Doesn't it look like it?"

"How many day's growth is that?"

"About four weeks."

Harold gets a, wait until you hear this kind of look when he launches into an explanation, a slightly crooked smile, his laughing eyes amplified through his extra-thick glasses, that implies that it's going to be extra-good, so listen up. "Can't you tell? I'm going to Berkley in the fall and I want to fit in."

"I see your hair's getting longer."

"That, too."

"Has anyone at Hoover told you to cut it?"

"They can try. But I'm already done with all of my classes. Aced the finals."

"And you're still going to school?"

"Yeah. The teachers want me there. We get good talks going and I help other kids."

"What are you doing in this neck of the woods?"

"I've got a student over on Chamoune."

"You're still walking?"

"Yeah. I like to walk."

"How much is Berkley costing you?"

"I'm on a scholarship."

"You won't be classified 1A, then."

"I wouldn't be anyway. I've got terrible vision and flat feet."

"Lucky you."

"I'll probably be 4F. I don't mind. That's better than a

179

bullet."

"I hear you."

"What are you going to do?"

"Try and get in the Air Force, I guess."

"No college?"

"I don't know what I want to do."

"Don't wait too long. You don't want to be drafted and have them assign you."

"I hear you."

"You want to smoke a joint?"

"*What?* What did you say?"

He laughed. "You never knew?"

"No. You aren't kidding..., right?"

"One of my students always gives me a joint as a tip. I can't take it home, so I have to smoke it before I get there."

"The whole thing?"

"Sometimes I walk a couple of miles. I take different routes and when I get to a place where nobody can see, take a couple of hits, put it out and wait until I get to the next place."

"You're amazing."

"Just before I get home, I chew two sticks of Double good, double good, Double Mint gum. Sometimes I do Juicy Fruit, but it doesn't work as well."

I laughed. "I *never* suspected."

"So, do you want to?"

"What makes you think I smoke?"

"Jimbo told me. He gave me a ride in his Buick a couple of days ago. He calls it, Blue Beauty."

"He named his car? Boy, he's gonna hear about that."

Harold helped me wipe down my car. We drove up to Dowd's Liquor, bought a couple of sodas and, on the way back, he lit the joint, took a puff and offered it to me.

"Not while I'm driving. Did you want for me to drop you off someplace? I don't want to drive stoned."

"Back to your house is OK. This won't hit you before you get there, anyway."

I took a hit and passed it back. "Jesus. I can't believe

180

this. Do you do math when you're loaded?"

"That's when it's the best. I'll work equations all weekend long if I can."

"Do you go to school loaded?"

"Naw. There's enough going on already."

We parked in front of my house and, sitting in the car and listening to the radio, talked for another hour. In the end, I realized that just about everyone I knew was going to college or getting married after we graduated.

What kind of crap is that? Get married or go to college or pick up a gun and fight. And..., why?

If I knew what I wanted to be, I'd go to college and study for it. At Harold's insistence, I went up to the Air Force recruiter on El Cajon Blvd. and took a battery of tests.

I was hoping they would let me in and give me some kind of training that would get me through life. When I asked Uncle Wally what field I should go into...,

"Communications. Electronics."

"I was thinking jet mechanics."

"The pay'll be good when you get out. But you're going to be around loud noises and cancer causing chemicals for how many years after that? You might want something a little cleaner and quieter."

"Got it. Thanks."

Senior prom. There should be another name for it. I can agree with the first part, senior; on top, at the end of this stage of our lives, end of the rope, time to move on.

But between the end of the rope and moving on is the second part, prom. I wondered about that. Did prom mean promenade, parading, strutting? Or did it come from prominence, pinnacle, popularity? Maybe, prominent, as in obvious, unavoidable.

Looking it up, prom comes from promontory, a body or mass projecting into a low land. I don't really care what it goes down into. It's the obstacle in front of me that gets my attention. So…, in my mind, senior prom should be renamed to senior obstacle.

Why would I want to get dressed up in clothes that I don't have, go to a place where socializing and dancing are the main events, when I can't dance and am not very good at socializing?

John and Penny are going, same with Kenny and Gwen. They already know who they're going with and any other option is out of the question. As for me, I will be one of those people that stays away. I will work on my car, maybe give it a wax job. Or, head down to the beach with Jimbo, go to Belmont Park and check out the action. Anything except go to the prom.

When the subject came up at our lunch table, Letti said that she'd been asked twice, but hadn't made a decision. Because the discussion was taking place next to me, loud enough for me to hear, it felt like pressure was being applied for me to pop the question to Letti.

This doesn't work on so many different levels. First and foremost, Carlo. If I went with her, I have this sinking feeling that, if not on that night, then sometime in the near future, something bad is going to happen to me or my car.

Second, the prom is on a Friday night and I have to be at work early, sometime around ten. Some convention in Mission Valley ordered a hundred dozen donuts to be delivered by seven in the morning, that in addition to the normal extra orders for Saturday. It was already going to be a long, hard night and I needed the sleep.

Third, I am a lame dancer, terrible, in fact. While Jimbo can fly across the floor, do several fancy pieces of foot work and swing with his partner, I look like I'm rowing a boat and basically, sinking. Many hours in front of the mirror did not help. My mind does wonderful things, but my body misinterprets the masterful moves that I envision.

"Calvin, would you like to go to the prom with me?"

Letti said it with a proud smile and, glancing over at Penny and John, both of whom were watching, I had this feeling that they had this planned all along.

I hadn't talked with anybody about my encounter with Carlo and the last thing I wanted to do was hurt Letti's feelings. Had Carlo not threatened me, would I say, yes? I cannot answer that question. This is so sudden.

"Letti, I would love to go with you, but I have to be at work Friday night by ten. We have an extra big order due Saturday morning."

She looked disappointed. "I see. Oh, well."

"Besides, I'm a terrible dancer, probably the worst in the world."

"I've seen him," said John, coming to my defense. "He's worse than that. He can run, but he can't dance."

The conversation around the table dwindled after that and I felt like crap for declining her offer. Am I a coward? I ask myself why I said, no. And I'm confused about the answer.

Did Carlo intimidate me that much? What would've happened if I told him that Letti and I have a thing for each other? Would he have stabbed me? Would I have been his and Angel's punching bag?

Or, was my concern about having to be at work early a legitimate reason? No doubt that it was going to be a hard night, but I'm young. Surely I can go to work one night and work the whole night without sleep. The more that

I realized this, the more I came to the conclusion that intimidation from Carlo was the deciding factor.

Letti and Penny went back to their homework, but it sounded half-hearted. I noticed several glances between them and I suspected that there was a lot more to this prom thing than what I knew. John was looking at me like I was nuts. I ran into him between fifth and sixth period.

"Calvin, what is wrong with you? That was your chance."

"I had a run-in with Carlo."

"How?"

"He told me to stay away from Letti."

"Why?"

"She's his sister."

"I didn't know that. He threatened you?"

"He was leaning against my car door cleaning his nails with his knife. Angel was with him."

"What did he say?"

"He told me to stay away from Letti."

"I'll talk with him."

"I really do have a big night, Friday night."

"Yeah. That, too. She likes you, Calvin. How do you feel about her going with somebody else?"

"It's not like we have a track record."

"Actually, you do. Just not in the sense that you'd like. Would you go if Carlo backs off?"

"I'm still a terrible dancer. God, I hate senior proms."

"You can't sit on the fence. Make a choice."

In between classes, when I had stopped to get a drink from the fountain next to the bathrooms, Carlo and Dante pulled me aside.

"You're still seeing her, Calvin. Tell her to go away."

"She's my friend. I can't do that."

I had to stand my ground. What was already happening between Letti and me was because we both wanted it and he had no right to step in-between. I wondered what would happen if Letti knew about this. Would she tell him to back off, tell her father? What would he do?

"If you don't want us together, you tell her."

"Sit somewhere else for lunch."

"John and Penny are my friends. Letti joined us. Nobody forced her. Letti and Penny are friends. They do their homework together."

Not that I wanted to, but getting into a fight with Carlo at school would get us both expelled. I thought I could hold my own against him, but he was always with friends and I had little doubt that they would jump in. With knives?

It was then that I decided that I would go to the prom with Letti. This cannot be the reason that I do not go. I was not going to go through life being a coward.

A few students took note of our conversation as they passed by. No crowds gathered, but this thing was now breaking into the open. It would get back to Letti.

Carlo did not hit me or threaten me further. His look was a warning that things were not going to go well for me later on. He studied me with a cool disregard and without another word, turned and headed for class, Dante alongside.

Suddenly, I had the same kind of sick feeling in my stomach that I had when I was on my way to fight Harvey back at Hoover.

When the final bell rang, I went to my locker, gathered what I needed for homework and headed for my car. I was hoping beyond hope that it was untouched and that there wasn't an unfriendly crowd surrounding it.

Approaching, my heart sank. Carlo was there, with friends. His power came from surrounding himself with his little personal army. Without that, I was thinking that he was nothing more than a punk with a knife.

I had parked on Orange Avenue, about a block from school. Approaching, I noticed a few words being spoken between them, but could not hear what was said. I was not about to turn around. I had to make a stand.

When I was about fifty feet from the car, I heard footsteps coming up behind me and had a sudden fear that I was going to be jumped from behind. Was I going to make the news again? If I got my whole fifteen minutes of fame this time, would I be alive to view it? Dumb questions come to mind when you think you're going to die.

Turning, John had fallen in behind me and, behind him, several others, among them Brad, Aaron, Sonny, a couple of guys from the wrestling team.

I have the same kind of feeling that I had when Jimbo and I got into that accident, several seconds or minutes of disbelief, walking not quite on the ground, in shock. The same feeling now, elongated, happening in slow-motion, still engaging. Crap!

My heart is beyond my throat. How is it that I've come to be the focus of this? Twice! How did I get to be in the middle?

"John?"

"Not going to let you down, buddy."

"How did you know?"

"Half the school knows, except for Letti. No one's told her, far as I know."

Slowing as I approach my car, I'm searching for some kind of solution. I figured that I could use my books as a shield if someone pulled a knife. Maybe I'll just walk to work. Would they understand if I was a half hour late?

Hoping to avoid a confrontation, I walked around the car and inspected it for damage. None. Coming back to the driver's side, keys in hand, I hoped that Carlo would step aside and let me in.

186

They say that sometimes tension feels so thick that it can be cut with a knife. It's true. My ears are ringing and I feel like I'm walking underwater, that slow. I'm not sure how I appear.

We're blocking west-bound traffic, cars taking turns passing in both directions, everything seemingly happening in slow-motion. Jesus.

Looking at Carlo's face, I could see that things were not going as he planned, winced eyes, stone-faced, hand in pocket holding his knife. He and his friends were out-numbered, out-sized, and on the wrong side of the conversation. Was he going to move out of the way?

Two police cars arrived, one on either side of our crowd, two policemen per car, radios turned up, crackling through the thick air, red lights flashing. They stepped out of their cars and, pushing through the crowd, made their way to Carlo and me.

If ever a fox was trapped, this was it. On a sudden impulse, and I don't know why I did this, maybe because of my fight with Harvey and how that turned out, I reached out to shake Carlo's hand.

"Thanks for protecting my car..., my friend."

I couldn't think of anything else. Carlo studied me for a long moment before letting go of his knife. I saw it fall back into his pocket.

A strained smile at first, but as we shook hands, it felt like the tension surrounding us began to dissolve. We both breathed a sigh of relief.

"No problemo..., amigo."

I put my key into the lock, opened the door and then turned and waved to the crowd. "Thank you. Sorry to leave, but I have to get to work. Ruth doesn't like it when I'm late."

Driving away, looking in my rearview mirror, they were still standing there, looking like they'd lost the script.

As I've said before, it's a good day when an enemy turns into a friend. I don't really believe that I'm suddenly Carlo's friend, but I suspect that when our paths cross, we can each give the other a nod.

John offered me some whiskey from a flask that he kept inside his suit. I was tempted, but the idea of a long night at the donut shop held me at bay like an invisible leash. I'd had no sleep since I got up early Friday morning and I wasn't going to get any until sometime Saturday, probably late morning. "No..., thanks."

"It's the one thing that makes this slightly tolerable."

Penny slapped his shoulder. "Hey!"

"It's true. I go through this to get what comes later."

"It's going to be a cold night for you."

John poured whiskey into his and Penny's drinks, offered some to Letti, who refused, and then came back to me.

"No, thanks."

A little pot wouldn't hurt later on, once I got the dough mixed and could step out back for a minute or two. Jimbo had given me a pin roll in anticipation of my four AM need-to-be-awake mode. I didn't mention that to anyone at this table. I didn't think that the conversation would go over very well.

Letti, looking absolutely stunning in her red gown, grabbed my hand and led me out onto the dance floor.

"Since you're leaving so soon, we have to dance."

I'm uncomfortable wearing a suit, feeling like I'm a phony and wondering if all of the other males here are feeling the same way. This was a slow song, much to my relief.

When a Man Loves a Woman

I do like being close to Letti. Her perfume draws me in and I can feel the heat from her body next to mine. Could I dance like this all night? I could think of only one other thing that would be better, not allowed. She squeezed my hand.

"That was very brave."

"What was?"

"What you did."

"I didn't do anything."

"Penny told me."

"Oh?"

"You could've talked to me about Carlo."

"I didn't want to get you involved."

"I can handle him."

"Why doesn't he want me to see you?"

"His two best friends, Dante and Angel, have been hitting on me for years. It's a competition."

"And then I came along?"

"Right."

"So..., how do you feel about that?"

"It's very tiring."

"Am I tiring?"

Letti laughed and pulled me in a little closer. I pushed out of my mind the idea of dancing nude, but it kept creeping back in.

"No, you're refreshing."

"How so?"

"For one, you're not drooling."

"Oh..., I am. You just can't see it."

"Drooling will get you nowhere."

"I have to beat you at the two-hundred?"

"Worse."

"The four hundred?"

"Worse. Papa has to like you."

"Ouch."

"He's not that bad. I'm his little girl and he wants to make sure I don't get hurt."

"You're the one beating up on me. He's got nothing to worry about." I tickled her in the ribs. God, that would be fun, wrestling, tickling, touching. I'm a pervert. No. I'm a teenager in love.

"You know what I mean."

"I wish I didn't have to work tonight."

"If you didn't, what would we do?"

"We'd go walk along the beach."

"That would be fun."

"Your dad could join us, if that would help."

189

Letti laughed. God, I love how she laughs, so clear, genuine.

"I don't think he'd be interested."

There wasn't much more to say after that. I tried to pull her in even closer. I wanted no space between us, but she resisted, signaling with her eyes, a smile and a slight tilt of her head, to respect that.

I had no desire to go to work. The idea of leaving this girl at the prom with John and Penny and a multitude of other males who would ask her to dance after I departed was depressing.

This is what happens when you work nights. Everyone else gets to follow the evening's pleasures all the way through, while I have to leave just when it's getting good. Conclusion? Working nights are the reason that I'm not getting laid. Not that I would with Letti tonight. She would never allow that.

I stayed past my planned departing time and said my good-byes. Letti followed me to a quieter place and, making sure that no one else could see, kissed me, not passionate like I wanted, rather, long and gentle. When it was time...,

"John's taking you home, right?"

"Yes. That's the third time you've asked."

"I just want to be sure."

She gave me a hug and another quick kiss. "Thank you for a lovely evening. Now..., go to work. I can take care of myself."

On my way out to my car, I got jumped from behind. I don't remember much, a couple of hits to the back of my head, a kidney punch or two and, as I was going down, a few kicks to my ribs. I was not hit in the face and I never saw my attackers.

Hurrying past the glass cases, I'm trying to remember the names of the two policemen waiting at the front door. I've got donuts in the fryer.

I can't take a deep breath, bruised ribs. I've taken two extra-strength aspirin to help ease the pain. I don't think I'm limping. I've got a swollen middle finger on my left hand when it got caught on the car door handle as I went down. I don't look like I've been in a fight.

I unlocked the door, stepped back to let them in and locked it after them.

"Kit and Bill, right?"

"Right. You don't mind?"

"Not at all."

They followed me back to the other end of the store and waited in the customer serving area. I didn't have time for that.

"Help yourselves. I've got to get back to frying. Cream's in the fridge."

"Thanks."

Watching them devour the first donut, I was thinking I could make a million dollars selling donuts fresh out of the fryer if I had a good location. If I didn't sell to the churches I wouldn't have to get up early. Come in at five, open at six, close by noon, a seven-hour workday and I would have all of my nights to do whatever I wanted.

Wait. Tony's paying me to take his place for the night shift and he pays my wages by garnering special orders from the churches.

Hmm. The more I work, the more he makes and the less time off I have. He has all of his nights off except Tuesday when he comes in at five and is out of here by ten. I'm on the wrong end of this deal.

"I said it before and I'll say it again," said Kit, devouring half of a chocolate donut. "Just out of the fryer, these are better than anything. Man!"

I nodded. "Yeah. You get spoiled. Nothing else compares."

My kidneys hurt the worst. Bruised ribs, I can handle. That's just a dull, lingering pain until I try to breathe too deeply. Sneezes brings involuntary tears. I can live with all of that.

Pulling screens of donuts out of the hot oil brings pain from the area around my kidneys, any action that forces me to use my lower back muscles. Banging the screen of donuts onto the drip tray when they come out of the oil isn't too bad, but the quick motion required to slide the donuts off of the screen and into the icing area is very painful. It's going to be a long, hard night.

Bill noticed my wincing. Blowing the steam off of his coffee, he watched me crank another batch of donuts into the fryer.

"Calvin, right?"

"Right."

"You doing OK?"

"Yeah. Why?"

"You look like you're in pain."

This conversation was going to get me nowhere. If I say that I was attacked leaving the senior prom, I'm basically admitting that I'm not eighteen and am out after curfew, or at least put my age into question. I probably wouldn't get into too much trouble, but Tony would. And if I mention that I was jumped, I would have no information about my attackers. This conversation will only lead into a bad place.

"I was playing football with some friends and got hit in my kidney, somebody's knee."

Bill nodded. "I took a hit like that in a martial arts class. Drink lots of cranberry juice. That's what they told me."

"Thanks. I'll try that. Any action out there tonight?"

Kit poured himself another cup and, crossing over to the partition, refilled Bill's cup. "Drag racing on El Cajon Boulevard."

"Oh?"

"We got three of them," said Bill. "Exhibition of speed. That's going to cost each of them a couple of hundred. One of the cars got away."

"Oh?"

"Yeah, an old Buick."

"Really?"

"Blue body, white top. That's about all we know. Didn't catch the license number and if we went after him, the other three would've gotten away."

Jimbo drag racing? Can that be? Hard to imagine. He's normally a careful, conservative driver. Still...,

"There was some kind of altercation over at Crawford tonight," said Bill, reaching for a maple cake donut.

"How so?"

"They had their senior prom tonight. Somebody dancing with someone else's girl. There was a big fight."

"Anybody hurt?"

"Couple of kids with bloody noses, couple of black eyes. Everybody's going to live."

I would love to see their report on that, get names and hear the official version, but didn't think they'd show it. I'll have to call John.

They seated themselves in a booth and filled out paperwork while I cranked out donuts. Twice over a fifteen-minute period some car passing by out front honked their horn. Cassi?

I have to admit that I'm confused. Letti acts like she wants our relationship to go further, but look at all of the obstacles.

Cassi wants to keep what we have, but won't let it go any further and Katie acts like she'd do it in a heartbeat. I can't tell if she's teasing or serious. I wouldn't do it anyway. Not that I hadn't thought about it.

None of these relationships are going to mean much within the next few months because, one way or another, I'll be dealing with the military.

All of this seems unfair.

As soon as we set our towels near the fire pit and brought in a bunch of stuff, John picked up Penny who, screaming and kicking all the way, was carried out into the waves.

Ken was following Gwen around like a little puppy, moving their towels from here to there, massaging oil into her shoulders, placing their sandals side by side, switching sides when she didn't like the one she was on.

Annette, Jimbo's new girlfriend, struck me as an odd choice for him. Where he always looked rather stern, she had a perpetual smile. Jimbo lumbered along. She was light on her feet. Annette wore a gold cross on a chain around her neck. Jimbo wondered how anyone could believe that kind of crap. I wondered how that was going to work out. Jimbo sour. Annette happy. Jesus.

She had brought a couple of pails, some garden tools, plastic glasses and some carving things for Jimbo and anyone else who wanted to help build a sand castle. Glancing over at Jimbo, I laughed. Frowning, he gave me a mouthed, silent, "Fuck you."

While everyone was getting settled, Harold tapped me on the shoulder. "I forgot something in your car. Did you lock it?"

"Yeah. You want the keys?"

"Naw. Just walk up there with me."

Halfway to the car, Katie was by my side. "Where you two going?"

"Just to the car."

"Oh?"

"Yeah. No big deal."

Katie went over to Harold's side and put her arm through his. "You have a joint, don't you?"

"What makes you think that?"

"Because both of you smoke dope and you're walking up here to smoke one."

I'm more naive. "No. Harold just forgot something.

Right, Harold?"

"Right."

Katie squirmed in between the two of us, her arms through ours. "What did you forget, Harold. Lighter?"

"How'd you guess?"

"Really, Harold? I thought it was something important."

"This is important."

"I can't get stoned right now. John and Penny don't know that I do. Neither do Kenny and Gwen."

Katie elbowed me in the ribs. "Or, Annette. She doesn't know about Jimbo either."

Harold handed me a stick of Double Mint gum. "They don't have to know. Katie?"

"Sure. Thanks, Harold."

Getting into the car, Harold took a back seat, Katie took shotgun and, somehow, Jimbo was there with us, standing outside my door.

"Hurry up. Give me a hit. I told Annette I was going to get a Coke. If I'm going to build fucking sand castles, I have to be stoned."

"How'd you know we were coming up here for this?"

"Jesus, Calvin. I see three dopers walking away from everyone else, headed for your car. What else am I going to think?" He took another hit, handed it to me and hurried back across the parking lot, not exhaling until he reached the sand.

Katie tapped me on the shoulder. "Hey! Pass that thing over here."

Five minutes later, we got out of the car and headed back to our fire ring. I felt like I was on a different beach, visiting Rio de Janeiro, entering a new stage of my life, feeling like our time in my car happened hours ago. Did it really happen?

Unfolding her towel, Katie grabbed a frisbee and threw it at me. "Heads up!"

It bounced off of my chest and my several attempts to grab it, popping it up a couple of times, probably looked fantastic, but it landed in the fire pit. "Jesus, Katie."

"John said you had fast hands. Just checking."

I took it to the water, rinsed it off and launched it back at her. Harold joined us, each standing about twenty feet from the other. A few throws later and we're thirty feet apart. Within another five minutes, and this is how it always turns out, we're too far apart to make good throws and spend more time chasing than throwing.

After that, the exercise devolves into long throws veering off course, wind gusts, throws into the water, waiting, more chasing than catching and the ultimate crowning to the end of the game, "I'm going to get a drink."

Coming back from the water, Penny wrapped herself up in a blanket while John, Jimbo and I brought wood down from our cars. Benny had a bunch of oak pallets behind his garage that he wanted get rid of and was happy to see us bust them up and hall them away.

Tuna fish sandwiches, potato chips and sodas tided us over through building sand castles, an occasional swim and several trips up to the car for recreational purposes.

When it was dark, we were ready for the good stuff, charred hot dogs, potato chips and sodas, this time with vodka that John provided. With the fire crackling away, Katie used the hot dog at the end of her clothes hanger to try and knock mine into the ashes.

"Hey! Knock it off!"

"I'm trying."

"That's not what I meant. I don't want to eat ash."

"It's good for you, Calie."

"How?"

"It makes you want sex."

"I already have that. Ash isn't going to make it any better."

"Where's your girlfriend, Calie?"

"I don't have one."

"Even Jimbo's got one. Look at him over there. He's got one thing on his mind."

"Yeah, well...,"

Katie moved next to me and placed her hot dog over the fire next to mine. "I'll be your girlfriend for tonight. How's that?"

Actually, I liked the idea. Katie was turning into a very beautiful girl and I loved her teasing ways. But I could feel Jimbo's protective feelings for his little sister. "What all does that include?"

"You can put your arm around me if it gets too cold."

"That's it?"

"Don't get your hopes up. This is our first date."

"It's not a date, really. We're just at the beach together."

"There you go, Mr. Boring. I'm giving you an opportunity and you do your best to blow it."

"What will Jimbo think about this?"

"Jimbo is only thinking about one thing right now. He doesn't care what I do."

"I saw what he did to Kenny."

"That was Kenny. You're his best friend. He's not going to hit you."

"Not until I mess around with his little sister."

"Look at you! No wonder you haven't got a girlfriend. You *try* to get out of relationships."

"I have to work nights and...,"

"As soon as I get my license, I'll drive over to your donut shop and fuck you."

There was a cot in the back room of the donut shop. I'd never used it. But on occasion, if Tony had too much to drink, he'd crash back there and leave me instructions about when to wake him. If I had a chance to have sex back there, would I? Of course. Screw the donuts.

"Jesus, Katie. I think I believe you."

"Well..., don't. If I'm going to do it for the first time, it's not going to be in a donut shop."

"Where would it be?"

"That's for me to know and you to find out."

I wondered what Cassi would think if she stopped by and found Katie inside with me. Would she suddenly decide to go all the way the next time we went out? Hmm. These are pleasant thoughts.

Katie slipped her hot dog into a bun, poured ketchup over it and headed for the cooler. The ice was mostly melted by now, but she found a few cubes, poured in more than a shot of vodka and topped it off with Seven-Up. Watching her move around the fire pit area in her bathing suit, and after hearing what she just said, well...,

"Calie, you're burning the shit out of your dog."

The thing was on fire, streaks of pink splitting open lengthwise through the charred, black skin, spitting flames. John and Penny, sitting across the fire from us, were staring at me and laughing. Busted. Katie handed me a bun.

"Thanks. I like them well done."

John held up his cup. "To Calvin, who is full of shit!"

To my surprise, everyone had a cup of something, which they all raised and said, "Here, here."

It's good to be among friends.

Going home, Katie and Harold rode with me. I dropped him off first. Katie rode shotgun on the way to her house. When we were a couple of blocks away...,

"Pull over."

"What?"

"Pull over."

She scooted across the seat and put her hand on my leg. "Just wanted to thank you for today."

"I had fun too and...,"

She pulled me in for a kiss. Jimbo's little sister? No, no, no! But I didn't stop. Both of us were hungry. My hands found her breasts while she explored me, touching and kissing. Way too soon, she backed away, both of us gasping for air.

"We have to go, Calie. I have to get home before Jimbo."

I hated that she was right. We all left the beach at the same time.

After a quick, goodbye kiss, Katie got out two houses away from hers, waved and went inside. Jimbo had not come home yet.

Driving home, my mind was whirling. Jimbo's little sister? What just happened, was that mind-blowing? Dumb question.

After I received my second notice to report to LA for a physical, I went to the Air Force Recruiter and signed up for four years. Jimbo waited too long and was drafted into the Army for two.

It seemed like a short summer, a few more trips to the beach, washing and waxing our cars, driving up to Julian for apple pie, a trip to Disneyland and two trips to the zoo.

Katie seemed to be my default partner on most of these trips. We demonstrated friendship, teasing and the like in front of Jimbo, but were careful to keep our sexual desires out of his vision. When we thought we had a minute or two, sometimes even a second or two, we teased each other with light, seductive touches. My God, it was enticing. Do I feel guilty? Yes.

But how can you stop doing something when it feels so natural? Her touches to me and mine to her carried so much more weight than that kiss from Letti and all of those times with Cassi.

Letti's kiss held promise and she was a woman that I could love. But time and opportunity were not on our side. There were too many obstacles.

My time with Cassi, although driving me to the extremes of desire, seemed not so important anymore. She was using me. I was using her.

But Katie, so available, yet unavailable, was the girl who was always on my mind. She's driving me crazy.

Jimbo was busy with Annette. As much time as they spent together, much of it in private, I was half expecting to hear her say, "Surprise, Jimbo. I'm pregnant."

"If that happens, Jimbo. Will they reclassify you to something other than 1A?"

"Fuck, if I know."

"I'd check into it. It's gotta be better than Viet Nam."

"Maybe. Do you know that she's got a prayer for everything? When I take her out for dinner, she thanks

199

God for the meal. I tell her that I'm the one paying for it."

"What's she say to that?"

"That God brought me to her and helped me find a job so I could make money. It's driving me fucking nuts. Two years of not hearing prayers will be a relief."

"A bullet's better than a prayer?"

"Not when you put it like that. I can't imagine living with someone like that for the rest of my life. Besides, she thinks marijuana comes from the devil."

"Uh, oh."

"If she only knew how good sex is with it."

"Maybe you could explain to her that marijuana is one of God's creations."

"Riiight. Her dad's a cop."

"Ouch. Sounds like you got yourself into a fix. How are you going to get out of it?"

"Drafted, my friend. Nobody can argue with that."

"When are you going?"

"Two weeks."

"You gave Tony notice?"

"Yeah. I'm done after this next week."

"What are you going to do with your car?"

"Katie's going to watch it for me."

"She hasn't got her license."

"She's taking her driving test next week."

I feel like time is somehow leapfrogging over us. After high school, we're supposed to be testing the waters, getting better jobs, going to college, learning a trade, letting our relationships develop. Instead, we're off to..., *what?*

It's not just the breaking up of a small family of friends. It destroys the culture that has been built between them. Six months from now, one of us might come back for a week or two before leaving again, others will straggle in and out from time to time. Some may not come back at all. These friendships will never be the same. I understand that time and change go hand in hand, but this feels unnatural, out of whack.

Jimbo won't come back to Annette. I can just about

guarantee that. Letti will not wait for me. Her culture is too strong and, except for her, I don't feel welcome. I'll be gone for four years. She'll be married by the time I come home.

And, Katie. What about her? Just when we're hitting it off, we come to an end? Missing her is going to hurt the most. She will have lots of suitors while I am gone. And she'll have Jimbo's car to get around.

If she's getting her license, I wonder if she's going to keep her promise and come fuck me in the donut shop sometime in my last couple of weeks.

Oh. Wait. She said she wouldn't do that. I have to find the right time and place. I'll have a month to look after Jimbo's gone. Is that fair to him? Am I a traitor to our friendship? Is it fair to Katie? What is fair about any of this?

In six weeks, I'll be in Texas for basic training. After that, it's anybody's guess where I'll be and for how long.

Will Katie wait? I'm doubtful. She'll have too many opportunities to go have fun. Someone will steal her heart. This makes me very sad.

I will remember the agony of working nights for the rest of my life. All day long, every day, I feel like I'm walking around in a daze, yawning, eyes watering, not quite getting the full gist of any conversation.

My body wants to sleep between midnight and six and it peaks sometime around four. If I am going to die, it will be around four in the morning. Everything shuts down. My eyes cannot stay open. And when they are, they're watery.

Standing over the smoky fryer, I have to keep myself from nodding out. I have too much coffee in my growling stomach and I'm too sick of donuts to eat any of them to settle it. I waver and have to force myself to stay awake. My boss wants to hear easy listening. Bobby Vinton. Yawn. It would not be good to fall into the fryer.

The idea of being done with this job in two weeks is exhilarating. I'll be able to go to bed when it's dark and sleep in as long as I like. There are many creatures that can thrive being awake at night. I am not one of them.

But even this short reprieve is only going to last for two weeks. After that, basic training, and I'm pretty sure it's going to be on their schedule. If it's nights, I'm used to it. I can get by. If it's days, that's a present that keeps on giving.

I won't mind the athletic part of it. I'm looking forward to running some kind of obstacle course and would love it if they made us run the mile. I'd do well, thanks to Letti's lessons.

I think we both knew that it wasn't going to work. Last time we talked, when I called...,

"I got a job at the zoo."

"Congratulations. Doing what?"

"I'll find out on Monday, my first day. I'll work through the summer and go to State in the fall."

"Let me guess, women's track?"

"Go to college, Calvin. Get on the track team."

"I already signed up, four years."

"Can't get out of it?"

"Too late. What are you doing later on?"

"Helping my parents in the store. I do that four nights a week. I'm sorry I'm so busy. Anyway, we had fun, didn't we?"

That said it all, right there. Past tense. The relationship is now becoming a part of history. "Yeah, Letti. We did. Thanks for all of the lessons."

"Thanks for going to the prom with me. I know you hated it."

"You made it worth my while. I'll always remember your kiss."

"I'm blushing."

"I hope so."

"If things were different, this might have worked out."

"You made me dream about you, Letti. You still do."

Laughter. *"And did you win the race in your dreams?"*

"No. I won the girl."

"Now I'm really blushing. Can you see it?"

"I wish I could."

"Keep in touch, Calvin. Let's write."

That was a disappointing conversation. Enrolling for college might have bought me another year or two and I might've been able to move this relationship forward.

As it stands, this is just one more bridge that's collapsing, starting now. There will be a few letters in support of our friendship and I will appreciate them. But what won't be in those letters is information about all of her new friends, practice partners and relationships. Absence might make the heart grow fonder for a while, but it won't last.

Three in the morning, I've finished frying, icing and displaying the cake donuts and have cut the raised dough into workable piles on the cutting table. Tomorrow's a slow day as far as special orders are concerned and I'm slightly ahead of schedule.

Headlights from some car reflect off of the storefront window and, as often happens around this time of the morning, I'm expecting Kit and Bill to arrive for their morning coffee, donuts and a booth to fill out their paperwork. I never charge them. But sometimes I find a ten on the counter when they've gone. It all works out.

Instead, it's a lowered, nineteen fifty-nine blue, Chevy Impala that stops in front of the store. To my extreme surprise, Letti and Carlo get out and knock on the front door. I hurry past the glass cases to let them in.

Letti gives me a quick hug. "We're on our way home and I saw you in here."

"And you stopped by for..., donuts?"

"No, silly. To say good-bye."

"Oh. That's nice."

"It didn't feel right, saying good-bye over the phone."

I nodded to Carlo and motioned toward the other end of the room. "Donuts, anyone? You can't get them fresher than this."

Letti was reticent, but I could see Carlo eyeing the fresh trays of donuts in the cases. Following his gaze...,

"Chocolate? They're still warm."

It's really hard to resist a donut fresh out of the fryer, unless you're a donut maker. When the donut is still warm and the icing is just starting to set, the flavors engulf every taste bud so completely that it's like the sun breaking through on a cloudy, dismal day. Once you've had one, nothing else compares, for donuts anyway.

I went around to the other side of the counter, pulled two chocolate cake donuts off the tray and handed them to him. "Letti?"

"I shouldn't. I'm in training."

"Have you ever tasted an old-fashioned, fresh out of the fryer, crispy edges and freshly dipped into simple syrup?"

"No."

"One in your life won't hurt you. This will be the last time you'll ever get a chance to eat a donut that I've made."

She laughs. God, I love how she laughs. Her whole being lights up. "OK. Just this once."

Carlo is already finishing one. His eyes are glazed and red. I suspect that he's stoned and I'm guessing that he has dry mouth. I wonder if Letti knows. Can you hide that from your siblings? If she doesn't know the tell-tale signs, he might get away with it. It's easy to plead hay fever, a recent sneeze, or some such thing. Getting out of the car, he was the one driving.

"Carlo, you want something to wash that down? Coffee?"

Still trying to swallow, he nods toward the coffee pot. I pour him a cup and take it over to the nearest booth. Letti grabs two napkins and follows. I sit next to her, opposite Carlo. This is an odd situation. I'm not quite sure what to make of it.

"What are you two doing out this time of night?"

Letti swallows her first bite, wipes her hands on a napkin. "We're coming back from visiting relatives in LA. This is delicious."

"I hear that eating a donut before a race, will take five seconds off of your time."

"You mean, add, don't you?"

"Maybe. I always was bad at math."

Carlo finished his second donut. I would not be exaggerating to say that he wolfed it down. A couple more gulps of his coffee and he was anxious to go. I don't think that this was a stop that he wanted to make. Letti finished a couple more bites of the old fashioned, wiped her hands and nudged me out of the booth.

"It's been a long day. We have to get home."

I followed them out to the car and opened the door for Letti. Carlo shook my hand before going around to the driver's side, getting in, starting the engine and gunning it, dual exhaust, glass packs.

Before getting in, Letti turned, pulled me in for a hug and, surprise, surprise, gave me another long, gentle kiss.

"Write me. You have my address."

It was during that kiss that another car pulled in behind us, headlights on high beams. My back was turned to them and I was not about to break away until she decided that it was over. I could've stood there all night. To hell with the donuts.

I figured that the lights were from Bill's police car. The timing was about right. Turning to confirm, I was surprised to see Dante jump out of the car and come at me like a mad bull.

Letti stepped between us, hands outstretched. "Dante. *Don't!*"

"Out of my way. I'm going to kill him!"

"I was saying good-bye."

"I saw how he kissed you!"

"I kissed him. And it's none of your business who I kiss."

"Letti...,"

"No. I am not anybody's property."

Carlo killed the engine, got out. "Dante! What the hell!"

"And *you* let it happen!"

"They're saying good-bye. What the fuck! He's gonna be gone for four years. Jesus!"

"That was more than a good-bye kiss."

"It's her fuckin' choice, man! She's not married to anybody."

Letti reached up and put her hand on Dante's cheek and then pulled him in for a hug. "You're one of my best friends and I want to keep it that way. But you have to let me be me until I'm ready to settle down. Comprende?"

I thought she had him settled down. She gave him a kiss on the cheek and pulled away.

Turning to me, she took my hands into hers. "Good luck, Calvin. Maybe you can get on the track team in the Air Force."

"I didn't know they had one."

A big smile. God, how I love her spirit. "Silly, boy. You know you can run. Give it a try."

She squeezed my hands and turned for the car. As soon as she is seated, I hear the unmistakable sound of a blade snapping into place.

The door to the donut shop is behind Dante and to his right. No escape back into the shop. Before I can react, Letti is out of the car, getting between Dante and me.

He didn't lunge at me like he was going to kill, more like a warning swipe, but Letti got in the way. Blood spurted out of the gash across her left wrist, pouring off of her fingertips down onto the blacktop.

Letti stared at her wound in disbelief. "Dante! What the...?"

Wide-eyed, Dante turned and ran back to his car. Engine roaring, burning rubber, he drove off of the curb, raced down University to College Avenue and ran a red light turning left.

I grabbed Letti's elbow, applied pressure, held her arm above her head and dragged her into the front passenger seat of Carlo's car, her sitting in my lap. "Jesus, Letti. Keep your arm up, high as you can above your heart. Carlo! Let's go!"

"Where?"

"Hospital! Holy crap!"

"Where?"

"There's one on University and Sixth."

"Way over there?"

"Go, go, go! Use your horn!"

Carlo slammed his door shut, started the engine, but before we could go, a police car pulled in front of us, blocking our way, red lights flashing. Both Bill and Kit got out of their car, guns drawn. Carlo, hands frozen to the wheel, stiffened in his seat.

"Holy shit!"

Bill went to Carlo's side, motioned for him to roll down the window. "Nice and easy. Get out of the car. Hands high, in plain view."

Kit opened my door and motioned for us to get out. I held Letti's wound into the light of his flashlight.

"Kit. We have to get to a hospital!"

"Calvin? That you?"

"Yes! She's losing blood! Please!"

"Who...?"

"I'll explain later. Just..., *help!*"

Bill pushed Carlo back into the car. "Follow me, not too close. Don't lag behind."

At four in the morning there's not too much traffic on University Avenue. Still, it's quicker and safer going down El Cajon Boulevard. It's a wider street with wider sidewalks, easier to spot potential hazards. Siren blaring, flashing lights, we're hitting fifty, sixty miles an hour heading west, running red lights the entire way.

Even with my best efforts, Letti's blood was spilling all over. "How are you doing?"

"I..., light-headed."

"Stay calm. Try to relax. Do you know what blood type you have?"

"O positive, I think."

"Carlo?"

Carlo, intent on driving, did not even blink, much less take his eyes off of the road. He was hunched over the wheel and sweating. "Fuck, if I know."

Kit must've called ahead. They were waiting for us when we got there. Letti was strapped onto a gurney and rushed inside. Carlo left to park his car, Bill followed.

I found a rest room, took off my shirt and bent over one of the sinks, an odd feeling, washing Letti's blood down the drain. I rinsed out my shirt and put it back on wet.

Carlo, Kit and Bill were sitting in the waiting room when I arrived. "Any news?"

Carlo, staring at the floor, just shook his head. Bill, noting my wet shirt and bloody pants, gave me a smile that was more akin to a grimace. "Nothing, yet. Can you tell us what happened?"

He had his note pad out, one page already folded back and a bunch of scribbling on the next. He'd already talked to Carlo. I wonder what his version is.

"It was an accident."

"Why do you say that?"

"Dante was mad. But if he wanted to hurt me, he would have come closer. There was a lot of space between us. I think this was more of a warning."

"Dante?

I looked over at Carlo for confirmation. He did not make eye contact. "Yeah, Carlo's friend."

"Had he threatened you before?"

How to answer that one? He was with Carlo and Angel

when John warned that they were going to take my donuts up by Heavenly's Donut shop back when we were all going to Horace Man, with Carlo and Angel when saving my butt from Aaron and friends at Crawford, standing by Carlo when he was threatening me by my car, getting beat up by unknown attackers after the prom, one of whom I suspect is Dante.

"No. He's in love with Letti and I guess he thinks I'm in the way."

"Wouldn't you consider that threatening?"

"This one time, yes."

"Would you like to file assault charges?"

"No. I'm not hurt. That's up to Letti."

A Doctor Kittler entered the room. "Carlo?"

"Yes?"

"Your sister is going to be OK. We've stopped the bleeding, stitched her up and stabilized her condition. She's resting now. Have you notified your parents?"

"Yes. They're on their way."

Bill's radio crackled into the room, something about a burglary over on Thirtieth and University. They stood to go. Carlo and I went over to shake their hands. "Thank you. You saved her life."

Bill shook my hand. "No. You two did. We'll talk later."

"Donuts on the house next time you come by."

And then it occurred to me that I'd left the donut shop wide open. The door was closed, but not locked, fryer still turned on, probably smoking like hell, and the raised dough was probably spilling over onto the floor, unless Tony came in.

"Carlo. Give me a ride back to the shop?"

Relieved with the news, Carlo pulled the keys out of his pocket. "Let's go."

We were going east on University Avenue, driving into the sunrise. Carlo pulled down his visor and, stopped at a red light, reached over to the glove box and found his sunglasses.

"Can hardly see the light, man. Fuckin' bright lookin' into the sun."

"No shit. I hope Tony made it in."

"Who's Tony?"

"My boss. Cause if he didn't, that dough is going to be spilling off of the table."

"You sure make good donuts."

"They always taste good right out of the fryer."

"Is that a pretty cool job?"

"I hate working nights."

"Yeah, but look at all those donuts."

"That gets old."

Carlo pushed a tape into the player...,

"Light's green, Carlo."

"Yeah, I see it."

Come On, Let's Go

"Man. He's pretty good. Who is that?"

"You don't know who that is? Man!"

"Am I supposed to?"

"You know, *La Bamba*?"

"Everybody knows that."

"You know who sang it?"

"Same guy?"

"Hell, yeah. And you don't know who that is?"

"No."

"How about, *That's My Little Suzie*?"

"Oh, yeah. So..., who is it?"

"Do you know the song, *Donna*?"

"Damn it, Carlo. Who is it?"

"Ritchie Valens, man. You probably like Elvis Presley or some shit like that, huh?"

"I like The Rolling Stones."

"They're OK. Beatles?"

"Stones are better."

"Right."

"You've got AM, FM *and* tape?"

"Yeah. Only the best, man."

"This is stereo, isn't it?"

"Yeah. Hey...,"

"What?"

"Thanks for taking care of my sister."

"No problem."

"I watch over her."

"Don't I know it."

Carlo laughed. "If you two, you know..., make it. I'm OK with that."

"I'm not going to be around, Carlo. Somebody's going to snatch her up and it's going to break my heart."

"Probably not Dante. Not after what he pulled. He's a dumb shit, sometimes."

"It *was* an accident."

"And you didn't throw his shit in the street. You could've fucked him, man."

"Not my style."

"Hey...,"

"What?"

"You smoke dope?"

"Been known to. Not notorious."

Carlo laughed. "You're all right."

He pulled a joint from some handy place under his seat and handed it to me. "Light that up, will you?"

"Jesus, Carlo. I've got to go to work."

"This is good shit, man. It's smooth, like silk."

Pulling in front of the donut shop, Tony was not there. The door was closed, but not locked. The dough is on the edge of the table, just beginning the long fall to the floor. I'm coming on to the pot and feel like everything's under control. How can that be?

"Carlo, grab one of those coffee pots, fill it with water and wash the blood away from the front door, will you?"

"Sure."

I emptied the hours-old coffee from the burner, turned on the proof box and started to roll out the dough.

"Blood's washed away."

"Carlo, you contagious with anything?"

"Fuck, no. Why?"

"I need for you to fry."

"I know nothing about frying, man."

"How about make a pot of coffee?"

"Just pour water in the top, right? I can do that."

"Don't forget to put in the packet."

"No shit, man. I'm no dummy. Where is that?"

"And don't forget to put the pot at the bottom."

"Oh." Carlo laughed. "Riiight. I *was* going to forget that."

"I'm going to need help."

"Man, I want to go to bed."

"Coffee, donuts and ten bucks an hour?"

"Shit, man. For how long?"

"Couple of hours."

"What have I gotta do?"

"I need for you to fry and ice."

"You got music in this place?"

"There's a radio over there on the shelf next to the fryer."

Carlo set out two clean cups and then wandered over to the radio. "Jesus! This thing's ancient."

"It's better than nothing."

"It's got tubes! Man, if I worked here, we'd have stereo."

"Yeah, well. Welcome to Donut World."

"I'd change the colors in here, too. It's depressing."

"Customers don't seem to mind."

"Maybe change the seating around, make it more interesting."

"Let me tell you, Carlo. You work all night long, you're too tired to care and then the customers flock in anyway. Why change what's working?"

"Yeah. I hear you."

The raised donuts were still on the cooling racks when customers started coming through the door, not yet in the display trays. Seeing that they were extra-fresh, they bought more. Ruth came in and took over the counter

212

while Carlo and I made another, smaller batch.

Later, taking a break in the alleyway out back, Carlo lit a cigarette. "This place makes money, doesn't it?"

"It's a good business."

"What's the worst thing you have to do?"

"Work nights."

"Hell. I'm up half the night anyway. What else?"

"Clean the fryer."

"Who's taking your place?"

"Nobody, far as I know. Tony's going to have to hire somebody. One person can't do it."

"Except, I don't know how to make donuts."

"I'm here for two more weeks. I can teach you, but you'll have to get your health card."

"You gonna pay me?"

"I'll talk to Tony. He'll probably go for it. He doesn't like working nights either."

Bill and Kit stopped by sometime around seven. We got all of the latest news concerning the burglary near Thirtieth and University, an update on other things happening around town and served them for free.

It's good to know that you've got the law on your side. The way I see it, trust comes from giving. They've had a lot of free donuts over my time here, but they overpaid half of the time. It all works out.

They know they have a comfortable place where they can do their paperwork and I get to hear all about the comings and goings of the night and a little bit about them.

Bill has two kids, seven and nine, Lori and Seth. Lori plays the piano and guitar, loves percussion, that part drives them crazy, and Seth loves baseball, plays second base and is a good hitter. Kit's getting married next month. I'm invited even though I can't make it. We're a community of sorts.

That's part of what got Letti to the hospital so fast. They answered our call for help, no questions asked.

John supplied a bottle of whiskey, one of vodka and a six-pack of beer. If anybody asks, we found the booze in a paper bag sitting on a bus stop bench. Somebody must've boarded their ride without their booty. That's the official line. We've got to keep John out of trouble.

We, Jimbo and I, bought hot dogs, hamburger, snacks, sodas and ice. My parents are spending the weekend out at Lake Portrero in a friend's trailer. My sister is in Mexico with her boyfriend and the house is mine.

This would be our last party. I put on *Little Richard* and then went to the kitchen to pop popcorn. John handed me a drink, a whiskey and Coke mixed on the strong side, mixed drinks for everyone else and then joined Gwen, Kenny and Penny for a game of Hearts at the dining room table.

Harold, Katie and I went out back to look at the sunset. A few seconds later, Jimbo busted into our little circle and intercepted the joint being passed around.

"She's in the bathroom. I've gotta make this quick."

Harold laughed. "Pussy whipped already."

"No, dope starved. I won't be getting any after tonight."

I had to throw it in. "You won't be getting any of the other either."

"Like you even know what it is," said Jimbo, taking another hit.

"But you will be getting fucked," said Harold, with one of his grins that implies that the joke is funnier than it really is.

Jimbo took one last hit and hurried back inside. "See you suckers later."

Sitting at the small table in the kitchen, Katie watched me slice up some cheese. She'd taken a few hits over the evening and, due to the booze, her cheeks were rosy. If she didn't look so innocent, she'd be downright seductive. Does that make sense? How can she do both at the same time?

214

"Is it true, Calie?"

"Is what true?"

"You don't know what pussy is?"

"Jesus, Katie. I can't have that conversation with you."

"You've already had your hands on my breasts. I think you can answer that question."

I glanced around to see if there were any witnesses to our words. "Where's Jimbo?"

"In your bedroom with Annette."

"Really? He didn't even ask."

"It's his last night. Give him a break."

"Harold?"

"Passed out in the overstuffed chair."

John and Penny?"

"Making out on the couch, doing shooters. Kenny and Gwen went out to his car and it's rocking like they're having sex. This is your nightly news report."

"You're all right, Katie."

"You didn't answer my question."

"What was that?"

"Have you ever seen a naked girl up close?"

"I'm not going to answer that."

"You haven't, have you?"

"Just..., not saying."

That innocent, little girl look again. "Calie? Talk to me."

I don't know what's holding me back. Is it that I'm over eighteen and she's under? That she's Jimbo's little sister? Does she want sex? I think she does. Otherwise...,

"Why? Do you want to show me?"

"I want to know *if*, first."

"No."

There is a small add-on off of the kitchen that serves as a washing room and as a getaway if anyone ever wants to crash on the old couch along one of the walls. Katie grabbed my hand and led me over to the couch, closing the door behind us. She unbuttoned her top, removed her bra and left the front of her shirt open. Not sure how she did that.

"Kiss me, Calie. Kiss me all over."

You cannot resist once you begin. We're kissing each other wherever we find skin, removing clothes, touching, exploring on an old, dusty couch in the dim light coming in from beneath the kitchen door. I hear Jimbo's voice.

"Where is everybody?"

We're scrambling. I'm freaking out and Katie is stifling a laugh. How can she be so nonchalant? I still don't know how her mind works. I've got my pants on, but I feel like there is something else, another piece of clothing suspended in the crotch of my jeans. No time to take them off and check.

"Calie," she whispers. "You seen my bra?"

"I think it's inside my pants."

She's laughing.

"Shh. This is serious."

Mimicking a terrified look, she takes my hands and holds them against her breasts. "Oh, Calie! What are we going to do?"

I pull away and, buttoning my shirt, tip-toe over to the door leading outside. "Let's make it look like we're smoking a joint."

She's buttoning her shirt. "Except, we don't have one."

"Doesn't matter. He'll think we just finished, if he sees us standing out there."

"I'm impressed, Calie. I didn't think you had a devious bone in your body."

"Shh."

She giggles, softly. "I did feel the other one, though."

"I don't know how to respond to that."

Standing outside in the smoker's area at the back of the house...,

"It's stuck in the crotch."

"Unzip your pants."

"No."

"I need my bra."

"Well, you can't have it right now."

"Calie?"

"You can't just pull it out."

"Why not?"

216

"There are parts down there that could get caught up in..., well, they're vulnerable."

She's giggling. "I'll be gentle."

"Somebody might see."

"What are you, a priest? Jesus, Calie."

"I'll do it in the bathroom."

She shifts easily to the innocent, little girl look. "Calie? Don't you want to show me what you've got?"

"You're a tease."

"And you love it. Admit it."

"Here comes Jimbo."

"What are you two up to?"

"Checking out the stars."

"Riiight. Got any dope left?"

"We were hoping you had some."

Katie looked over at me with a big grin, happy with that save. We're learning how to read each other. I like that.

"No? Just as well. I've got to get Annette home. Katie, why don't you ride with us? That way Calvin won't have to drive."

Katie shrugged, glancing at me, apologetically. "OK."

Walking back into the house, I held the door open. "I'm picking you up at eight, right?"

"Yeah. I'll be ready. Thanks for taking me down there."

"I'm going, too," said Katie. "If my brother's leaving, I want to be there to say good-bye."

On their way inside, Jimbo led the way. Following, Katie rubbed her hand across the back of my neck and down my front. I wanted to squeeze her butt, but refrained and was wondering how it was going to go tomorrow when I returned her bra.

Do I feel guilty about this? Yes. Am I going to let whatever happens run a natural course? I don't know how to answer that.

Jimbo grabbed his suitcase out of the back, slammed the trunk back down too hard, as usual, and then met Katie and me on the curb. "Now, I'm wishing I'd gone to Canada."

There were several cars unloading future soldiers, lots of hugging, promises to write and nervous-looking young men heading inside the bus terminal. Jimbo reached out to shake my hand. "Wish me luck."

"Good luck, Jimbo. I'm going to miss you, buddy."

"When are you going in?"

"Three more weeks."

"You'll be gone when I get back."

"Well, then you might have a chance with Cassi."

He laughs. "Screw you."

Katie looked at me quizzically. "Who's Cassi?"

"A girl we met."

"Nobody, really," said Jimbo, turning to give Katie a hug. "We used to date her."

"We?"

"Calvin's first love."

"Jimbo's first failure."

"What happened to her?"

Jimbo turned, picked up his suitcase. "Nobody knows."

"She just..., disappeared?"

"Right."

"How long ago?"

"Months."

"Doesn't matter," said Jimbo, shaking my hand one last time. "Take care of Katie for me. I'll send my address. Write!"

Jimbo waved and disappeared inside. I opened the door for Katie, went around to the driver's side, got in and pulled away from the curb.

"Did you love her, Calie?"

"What?"

"Did you love Cassi?"

"I couldn't love her. I don't know anything about her."

"But you dated."

"She came into the shop one rainy night and we got to talking."

"Did you do it with her?"

"No."

"Why not?"

"She was a tease. It never went that far."

"But you would've?"

"Yeah."

"And Jimbo was dating her, too?"

"Yeah. Actually, he was dating her first. It was kind of a competition."

"To see who could do her first?"

"I guess. Anyway, she's gone and I don't care. Jimbo doesn't either."

"Why'd she go away?"

"No idea. She just stopped coming around."

"If she stopped by your work tonight, would you do it with her?"

"No."

"Why not?"

"Because, for her, it's just a game."

"What is it with us?"

"I don't know what it is with us."

"Calie? Be honest."

"I am."

"You find me sexy?"

"Of course, I do."

"Am I a tease, like her?"

"No."

"What's the difference?"

"She's doing it for whatever reason. You're the real thing."

"I'm a real tease?"

"No. You're trying to figure out what works and what doesn't. And I'm very glad that I'm a part of that."

"I was really drunk last night."

"You're a happy drunk."

"Was I sexy?"

I looked over at her with a big smile. "Katie..., you're always sexy. You drive me crazy."

"Jimbo asked you to take care of me. You going to do that?"

"As best I can."

"How?"

"How about a walk around La Jolla Cove and then we discuss it over a hamburger and fries at Oscar's?"

"Is this a date?"

"No. We're just on our way home from dropping off Jimbo."

"Too bad. I was going to fuck you, if it was a date."

"OK. It's a date."

She laughs. "Too late."

"It's never too late."

"It is, this time."

"Harsh, is the word I have for that."

"Did you bring my bra?"

"Better than that. I slept with it."

"Add weird to the list, along with boring."

"That was as close as I could get to you."

"Did you kiss it?"

"Of course."

She laughs. "You didn't fuck it, or anything like that, did you?"

"What? No. I put it under my pillow."

"So, how is this taking care of me, you sleeping with my bra?"

"I was protecting it, looking out for you."

We didn't say much while out walking the cove, climbing across the rocks, feeling the spray off of the waves, both of us lost in our thoughts, this new life without Jimbo, us with each other.

There is another side to Katie. She is quiet, insecure and sensitive. She wants to be held. We can be honest with each other and, if we make love, or not, before I go, I am really going to miss this girl.

220

At eighteen, I'm trying to figure out all of the moving pieces and it seems like the closer I get to my departure date, the faster everything moves.

Katie? I will do everything I can to keep her in my life. We've grown closer and I am very reluctant to leave her behind. Marriage is out of the question, her age being one thing, Jimbo's little sister being another.

But it's more than that. I will be gone somewhere for the next four years with only one month's leave per year to come visit, not nearly enough time to keep such a vibrant girl by my side.

By the time I come home for good, she'll be out of school, unless she decides to go to college, at a job and having plenty of opportunities along the way to hook up with someone. This line of thought is very depressing.

Cassi? When Katie asked me if I'd do it with her now, I said, no. The reality is, I probably would. After spending so much time with her, always intrigued and left wanting, I feel like I need some kind of closure, even though this is a girl I'd never marry.

If Katie and I were already together, I wouldn't even consider it. That says a lot about my feelings for her.

Letti? She's special and I'm welcome in her family now. But other than track and our mutual friends, we don't have much in common. She doesn't eat meat, I do. She doesn't smoke dope, I do. And I wonder if she knows that Carlo does.

Would I be like Jimbo if Letti and I were together, needing to sneak out every now and then for a breath of "fresh" air? I don't want to live like that. Do I think she'd make a great wife and mother? No doubt about it. Could I love her for the rest of my life? That's a hard question to answer when I include Katie into the equation. I have to admit, I'm attracted to Jimbo's little sister.

I hadn't seen Letti since that night and called to see if I could pay a visit. We sat beneath an umbrella at a table in front of her parent's store, drinking iced tea. She is radiant, her beautiful olive-colored skin glowing in the light, a contrast to her white, sleeveless top and the bandages wrapped around her left wrist.

"Good to see you, Calvin."

"It's always good to see you. How are you feeling?"

"I feel like I'm getting fat. They told me I'm only allowed limited exercise for now."

"You are not fat. Stunning is a better word."

"You know how to make me blush."

"I don't do it on purpose. It's just that there's so much to like."

"I don't deserve it. How are you doing?"

"I'll be leaving for Lackland soon."

"Is that in Texas?"

"Right."

"Are you nervous?"

"A little."

"How long will you be gone?"

"Basic training is six weeks there. I don't know what happens after that."

"I'll be back in school by the time you come home."

"What's your major?"

"Economics. I think I can grow this business."

"Is that your goal?"

Sipping her tea, Letti studied me for a minute or two before answering. "That's one of them."

"And a family?"

She laughs it off, using the napkin beneath her glass to wipe the condensation off of the side. "Maybe, after I try out for the Olympics."

"I went over to the track at Crawford today and ran the four hundred. I even did a slow practice lap like you suggested. It really helps."

"Yeah? I'm jealous."

"In my mind, you were there with me. Thanks for all of the tips."

"If you don't get into track, you're missing your calling."

"I think the Air Force is going to have something to say

222

about what I do for the next four years."

Letti looked at me with a knowing smile. "And when you get out you'll be twenty-two. What are you going to do, after that?"

"I can't think that far ahead. I don't know what kind of training I'm going to get or where I'm going. I have to get through this first. A lot can change in four years."

Letti held up her glass for a toast. "So true. Whatever's meant to be, will be. Meanwhile, friends forever, Calvin? I don't want you out of my life."

What a wonderful gesture, having freedom in the interim and possibilities in the future. I clinked my glass to hers thinking that there's much more to Letti than what I've seen. "I don't want you out of mine, either."

And here I ask myself, should I marry Letti and later happen across Katie and find that she's ready for a relationship, what would I do? Or, what if it's turned around? These are dumb questions. I'm likely going to lose both of them in the next four years.

"How's Carlo doing at the donut shop?"

Letti reached down and put her hand on mine. "Oh, my God. It's amazing. He loves this work. He's changed from a punk to a business man..., overnight! I think he wants to buy the business. Thank you for that."

"Good. Now you can have all the donuts you want."

"I don't even want them in the house. Already my parents are eating them every day."

"Donuts are a treat for the first few weeks. After that, it gets old."

We didn't talk about going out, dating, anything like that. We both knew that the high school days were over and that we were on new paths into the future.

If opportunity brings us together later on, I'll be ready. Meanwhile, I'll be reading the sports pages and looking for her success. I wish her the best. She's been a pleasure and an inspiration.

Katie and I were out hiking in Cuyamaca Park when we came across a quiet, deserted spot with a view. Stopping in the shade, we laid out a blanket and broke out our lunch. She unwrapped the sandwiches while I opened a Coke and split it between two paper cups. Sitting, she thunked her cup to mine.

"Good luck to you, Calie."

"You want to come with me?"

"Me sleep in the barracks with you and a hundred other guys?"

"You're right, not good."

"Too bad we don't have any liquor to add to the Coke."

"Are you going to be an alcoholic when you grow up?"

"No, but I'm going to enjoy my alcohol."

"What are you going to do when I'm gone?"

"First thing is to wax Jimbo's car."

"That'll take half a day. How about the rest of summer?"

"Go to the beach. I guess I'll have to get a job so I can put gas in the car."

"It's a vicious cycle."

We finished our sandwiches. Each of us ate a Hostess Twinkie and washed it down with Coke. Afterward, I put my arm around her and pulled her in close, both of us watching the clouds and their shadows pass over the rolling hills.

I kissed her. "Katie, I'm the happiest man in the world when I'm with you. You make me crazy."

Now she's kissing me. "You're not dangerous-crazy, are you?"

"Dangerously in love."

"Calie, be honest. I need to know this."

"Katie, I love you and I'm terrified that I'm going to lose you over the next four years. That's as honest as I can get."

She had tears in her eyes. "I was thinking the same thing about you."

224

Katie's kiss is passionate. I love kissing her. I can't keep my mind off of her.

We've spent almost every day together since Jimbo's departure, going to the beach, Scripps Aquarium, wandering around Balboa Park, going to the museums and to the zoo, where I was hoping that we did not run into Letti.

Our time together is coming to an end. As much of a tease as she was those first few times, I'm not sure that sex was ever her goal. She likes to tease but wants to be held, to feel secure, to be included. I want to give her all of those things.

I decide that I'm going to write as often as time permits. I want her to feel like she's welcome in my arms at any moment and I want her to be uncomfortable in anyone else's arms. Don't know how to do that.

We can see if any hikers approach from any direction for several hundred feet. It's a private place, a lazy time after lunch and it's a balmy, quiet day.

I turn to kiss her and find that she has already unbuttoned her blouse. For the first time since we've known each other, we let our guards down, stop the teasing, fall back onto the blanket and explore the limits of our feelings.

Riding the bus to Lackland with fifty other guys, I've got a window seat and what I'm seeing is a lot of downed trees, broken branches, gullies filled with water and signs of severe flooding on both sides of the road.

"Hurricane Beulah," said the guy sitting next to me. "It was only a category three and it didn't hit here, but look at all of the damage. I'm Roy, by the way."

I shook his hand. "Calvin."

Roy had curly, blonde hair, long sideburns and the beginnings of a blonde moustache that followed the curvature of his mouth down to the corners. I still consider it peach fuzz, but it is impressive, me with no facial hair at all. He ran his fingers through his hair and laughed. "They're gonna cut it all off tomorrow. I want to remember what it's like to have hair."

"Where you from, Roy?"

"Redlands, over by San Bernadino. How about you?"

"San Diego."

"Oh, one of the lucky ones."

"How's that?"

"You've got clean air. We get all of the smog from LA. It just hangs over us."

"That's too bad. I never thought about it much."

"Why'd you enlist?"

"I was going to be drafted. You?"

"Same. I graduated early and was starting a business when I got the notice."

"What kind of business?"

"Bicycle shop, Roy's Toys. We had some land out back that was doing nothing, so I turned it into a race track and put up one hundred dollars from my savings as first prize. Ten bucks to enter."

"How'd that work out?"

"I made money the first day and every day since. I charge two bucks to ride the course and you can ride all day long. But I make my real money selling bikes, parts and

226

doing repairs. I used my profits to build a shaded area where they can take a break and hang out. We built a concession stand with electricity and running water. And we sell drinks and snacks. Everybody wants something to drink after an hour or two riding."

"Who's running the business now?"

"My sister, Sally and our little brother, Nick. He's pretty good at sales and repairs, but I only trust Sally to do the books. How about you?"

"Nothing very exciting. I just graduated and have been working nights making donuts."

"That doesn't sound too bad."

"It's good and bad."

There were four busses in the caravan. They stopped in front of a large building about the size of a gymnasium, opened their doors and, standing outside each door were two, mean-looking men in fatigues that guided us toward the entrance. There were no smiles or greetings, just pointing to the door where they want us to go.

"No talking! Anybody talks, you're gonna give me fifty push-ups! Move it!"

Some unfortunate soul mumbled, "Jesus. What a...,"

"Come here, boy!"

They say, "boy." But the word is spit out so that it sounds more like, "Dog shit."

"Did you hear me say no talking, boy?"

"I did, but...,"

"Stand at attention! When you address me, you say, "Sir! Yes, sir!"

"Yes, sir."

"I didn't say, "Yes, sir." "I said, "*Sir!* Yes, sir! You got that, boy?"

"Sir. Yes, sir!"

"Louder!"

"SIR. YES, SIR!"

"Now get down and give me fifty push-ups, boy."

"Sir! Yes, sir!"

"What are the rest of you gawkin' at? You have orders to gawk?"

We didn't quite know how to answer that. Everybody was afraid to say anything. "Sir. No sir," came to my mind, but I wasn't about to be the first one to make a sound. I wondered if Jimbo was going through the same kind of treatment and then decided that I'd better just focus on my own transformation into this new hell.

We were told to file into the rows of folding chairs that had been set out and to be quiet. NO talking, period. It's amazing how just one example can set the tone for everyone. Except for the occasional cough or sneeze, we were stone-faced and quiet for about half an hour while they sorted through our paperwork.

I couldn't help but wonder what Katie was doing. Driving around in Jimbo's car? Smoking a joint? God, Katie. Don't do both at the same time. I've only been in Texas a few hours and already it seems like weeks.

When our names are called, we are told to form a line along one wall and stand at attention until ordered to do otherwise. They divided us into two groups and assigned us a TI, training instructor, who marched us out of the hall, into a formation, everyone is one arm away from everyone else, and off to our new life.

It's dark out. Texas has lots of stars. I never knew. I feel like an ant, marching with, what? Sixty other guys? I have no idea. All of us marching in-step across the concrete, stopping for stop signs, forward marching again.

Except, the guy in front of me isn't keeping in step and, in these close quarters, I have to place my feet where his aren't. I wish the dumb fuck would get it together. It's making it really hard for me.

"Flight! *Halt!*"

Stomp, stomp!

Walking between the rows, TI stopped and glared at the poor kid in front of me. "Boy. You know your right foot from your left?" He has a southern drawl.

"Sir. Yes, sir!"

"Bend down and touch your right foot."

"Sir! Yes, sir!"

I pitied the poor guy. I wanted to watch, but when he

bent down, TI was looking straight at me.

"Boy, point to your left foot. I want to see you touch that toe."

"Sir! Yes, sir!"

I was pretty sure that if I let my eyes drift, even for a second, from looking straight ahead, that I was going to be his next victim. I stared straight ahead, but blanked out his face. I'm starting to figure out how to work this, be small, insignificant, don't draw attention. There is an end to this somewhere.

Dressed in our brand new, olive-green never washed fatigues, we are marched to a building where we are told to line up in single file and remove our shirts so that we can get inoculated. I was expecting needles but was surprised to see that they were using some kind of air gun to inject us, both arms taking hits as you move along.

The guy in front of me flinched as the trigger was pulled. I saw it all very clearly because I was wondering what it did to the skin upon contact. When he flinched, the injection ripped the skin open all the way across his arm. Seconds later, blood was pouring down to his elbow and dripping onto the floor. They pulled him out of the line, used a towel to clean the floor and, done with that, the guy looks at me and says, "Next."

From there, we are marched to a barber shop where we are shaved. We have to pay two dollars for this haircut and he's done in less than a minute. That's pretty good money. Looking in the mirror, I hardly recognize myself.

Accomplishing that, we are marched to our barracks where we are told to put all of our civilian stuff into our duffel bag and hang it at the other end of our bunks, not to be touched again until allowed.

We all have a foot locker at the center aisle end of our bunks that is supposed to contain all of our essential day to day stuff. I thought that was a pretty good idea until I discovered that it had to be in inspection order at all times.

How can you use soap for your shower and still have it look like new for inspection? How to make the toothpaste tube pass inspection? Charles, occupying the bunk next to mine, got some clarification on the subject...,

"Ten-hut!"

When we hear that sound, we have to stand at attention at the center aisle end of our bunks. Don't delay getting there. Our footlockers are opened for inspection. TI stopped at Charles' footlocker, moved things around a bit and appeared to be ready to move onto mine. OK. My heart's pumping. I thought Charles' things were in excellent order and was wishing I'd put more time into mine. But when TI unscrewed the cap on Charles' toothpaste...,

"Boy!"

"Sir! Yes, sir!"

"You see anything wrong with this tube of toothpaste?"

"Sir! No, sir!"

"Look again, boy."

"Sir! It looks fine to me, sir!"

"You need glasses, boy?"

"Sir! No, sir!"

"Then, why do I see toothpaste on the thread of the cap?"

"Sir! I don't know, sir!"

TI took Charles' locker, turned it upside down and kicked the contents across the floor. "When I say inspection, I expect perfection! You got it, boy?"

"Sir. Yes, sir!"

"Give me fifty, boy!"

"Sir! Yes, sir!"

He didn't go to my toothpaste tube, but he did open the lid to my shoe polish and looked for a bit of polish along the rim and on the lid. Fortunately, I hadn't had time to polish my boots yet, so I passed.

There were several other foot lockers that were overturned and their contents scattered while we all stood at attention. Leaving, TI had some kind words for us...,

"You pussies don't know the *meaning* of inspection! I'll be back in one hour. Make it right! Now, move!"

All together now. "Sir! Yes, sir!"

Oh, how my heart aches for Katie. Was it only two days ago that we made love on the side of a mountain? If I knew then what I know now, we'd be in Canada. I'm pretty sure Jimbo feels the same way. Was it only a few weeks ago that we were at the beach with friends, drinking, smoking dope, having fun in that wonderful California sun? It seems like months...,

231

Two hours later, TI returned and ordered us to stand in formation at parade rest outside, facing our barracks. After a minute or two, he wandered off out of our view.

Standing there, we watched the recruits from the barracks next door file out from their building, into formation under the instruction of their TI, who marched into our barracks. For the next fifteen minutes, we listened to them annihilate every inch of our accomplishments.

Exiting our building, they lined up and marched away. Minutes later, our TI returned and went inside to inspect. Coming back out...,

"That's the worst I've ever seen! Get your asses back in there and make it right! You've got four hours! Move it!"

"Sir! Yes, sir!"

Going inside, all bunks were turned over, all beds unmade, all of our stuff thrown together into big piles.

Prior to this inspection, we were all required to put the first initial of our last name and the last four numbers of our Air Force ID on every article in our possession.

We organized a bed crew to get them turned over and put back together, two crews to separate our stuff into upstairs stuff and downstairs stuff and crews at both ends of the stairs to separate even further so each individual didn't have to search through everything for his personal possessions. This is what I'd term, frantic teamwork, kind of like Carlo and me at the donut shop.

The purpose of all of this? I'm guessing that any baggage that we brought with us from home is now secondary to our new set of circumstances. They want us to start fresh from the ground up learning their rules. Got it?

It's all about perspective. If you have an obligation to keep something that you use every day in perfect, inspection order, meaning that it has to look better than new, then you have an almost impossible task.

After the order to spit-shine our boots, our next task is to ensure that our cans of shoe polish look like they've never been used. Right.

Being the clever, industrious person that I am, I decided to buy an extra can of polish, keep an inspection ready can that stays in my locker and another that I carry in my pocket. I showed this to Charles…,

"Man. That's a really good idea. Can I borrow it?"

"Sure."

We're polishing shoes together.

"Where you from?"

"San Diego."

"Me, too. Where in San Diego?"

"Logan Heights."

"Yeah. I know where that is."

"But you probably don't go there, huh?"

"My uncle fixes pin ball machines, jukeboxes. I rode along with him a few times."

"Into Logan Heights?"

"Right. Ten at night on a Saturday night."

Charles laughed. "Probably felt lucky to get out alive, white boy."

"They loved us. Uncle Wally fixed the jukebox and gave them free music."

"Wally's your uncle?"

"Yeah. Why?"

"He bought me a basketball after mine got stolen."

"How do you know Wally?"

"My dad knows him. He told Wally about me and the next time he came around he gave him one to give to me. Tell Wally I said, Hi."

"Who's your dad?"

"Most people call him, Boss."

"Boss? Has he got a friend named, Stitch?"

"No shit. Yeah. You met them?"

"Yeah, in the bar."

"Wait a minute!" Charles burst into laughter. "You must be, Bolt!"

"Wow! I don't believe it! What are the odds?"

The can of shoe polish made its rounds in the area near my bunk. We are starting to become a cohesive group, each telling our stories as we sit around polishing our boots.

Going into the chow hall, we are required to form a single line and remain at parade rest until the line moves forward, at which point we snap to attention and move forward, keeping an arm's length from the person in front of us until the line stops, at which point we return to parade rest.

There are two TI's standing on either side of the entrance into the chow hall. One of them is ours. The other, I don't know. When the line stopped, I happened to be at the front. The TI that is not my TI spotted the shape of the can of shoe polish in my left, front pocket.

"Boy! What you got there in your pocket?"

I snapped to attention. "Sir! Shoe polish, sir!"

"Take it out, boy."

"Sir! Yes, sir!"

He took the can, inspected it and then looked down at my boots, nice and shiny. "You got another one in your locker?"

"Sir! Yes, sir!"

"Anybody order you to buy two cans of polish?"

"Sir! No, sir!"

He showed the can of polish to my TI and then handed it back to me. "Boy. You see that dumpster, over there?"

He was pointing to a dumpster some distance away, about a football field in distance.

"Sir! Yes, sir!"

"I want you to double time it over there and throw it away."

"Sir! Yes, sir!"

I started to go, but my TI shouted. "Stand in line, boy! You answer to *me*."

"Sir! Yes, sir!"

"I *outrank* your TI and I said, throw it away!"

"Sir! Yes, sir!"

"He's not your TI. I am. And I say, stand in line, boy"

"Sir! Yes, sir!"

"Did you hear me, boy? I said dump the can into the dumpster! *Move!*"

"Sir! Yes, sir!"

"Stay in line, boy."

"Sir! Yes, sir!"

OK. They're caught in some kind of loop and don't know how to get out. Without warning, I took off at a run for the dumpster. None of that double time malarkey either. I'm a runner. That's what Letti keeps telling me and she should know.

It was only going to be for a minute or two, but it felt like heaven to be away from all of the bull. Letti? Let's go run! Let's be free of this crap!

Coming back to the front of the line, I assumed a position of attention. They were speechless for a few seconds.

"What did you do with the can, boy?"

"Sir! What can, sir?"

"Boy! I told you to stand in line!"

"Sir! I am, sir!"

I caught a slight smile exchanged between them while keeping my face as straight as possible. This is kind of how I felt when serving donuts to Bill and Kit stoned or during Carlo's and my confrontation by my car. There's a space for getting along. I dared not smile, although I wanted to, but I think I found a chink in their armor.

"Move along, boy. You're holding up the line."

"Sir! Yes, sir!"

Hi Calie,

Harold and I went down to South Mission Beach yesterday and threw the frisbee. Penny and John were supposed to join us, but something came up and they couldn't make it. It's not the same without the whole gang. It makes me sad.

At least I'm back in school. That's a good thing because I'm feeling very lonely right now. I want you here to hold me. We spent so much time together the last two weeks that I don't know anything else. If I knew how good it was going to feel, I'd have done it with you as soon as Jimbo was gone.

I'm taking another art class. Are you still going to pose nude for me? You still want me to pose nude for you? How do you look with your head shaved? Send me a picture and I'll sleep with it. Do you want me to send you my bra?

Anyway, gotta get to my homework.

Love, Katie

XOXOXOXO

Dear Katie,

You are all that I think about these days. Yes, I would love to sleep with your bra, but DO NOT send it. Jesus! You still drive me crazy. Do you do that on purpose? Or, is it just our chemistry?

Yes. I would've done it with you as soon as Jimbo left, right there at the bus station. But I don't want anyone else to see you naked. Maybe, if we drove around the corner? God! I miss you!

I'll pose nude. Do I have to take an art class before you'll pose for me? What else are you taking besides art?

They keep us busy here, mostly inane stuff. You've never lived until you've pulled KP duty. I think it used to mean, knife potatoes. But what I got was dishwasher duty. It's a big conveyer belt that snakes around in a circle. I have to scrape the scraps off of the dishes and put them on the belt at one end while the guy at the other end removes and stacks the clean ones. Every house should have one of these. In any case, it's better than latrine duty.

We're supposed to run the obstacle course tomorrow. I can't wait. I'm tired of sitting around polishing boots, marching everywhere and all of the bull in between.

I ache to hold you. It seems like so long ago already. Have you told Jimbo yet? Are you going to? Do you have his address? If yes, please send it.

Repeat: Do NOT send the bra. I'll get attacked by a hundred horny guys who will want to fondle it. It's a crazy world in here. Can't wait to get out.

Thanks for your letter. You drive me crazy, but you make me happy.

Love, Calvin
XOXOXOXO

Hey, Calvin,

Well, if there's a word lower than sucks, I would use it. The food sucks, morale sucks, everybody's attitude sucks. Shoulda gone to Canada.

Katie gave me your address, says that Blue Beauty is running fine. Thanks for all your help on the car. Doesn't a cold beer and whatever sound really good, right now? I might even let you win a game of chess.

How are things on your end? Be cool,
Jimbo

Hi Jimbo,

Glad to hear you're having such a good time. Yeah, a cold beer and a game of chess sounds great. You might win one, but only in your dreams, sucker.

I'm almost done with basic. It's gonna take a lot of beer and whatever to make it all go away.

Doesn't Cassi seem like she never happened? How are things with you and Annette? I still don't miss working nights. I hope to see you in San Diego soon. Can't wait.

Take care, buddy.

Calvin

I didn't have the heart to tell him about Katie and myself. I feel guilty about this, but after reading his letter, he doesn't need one more thing to worry about.

Hi Calvin,

I'm enrolled at SDSU and have started classes. Accounting, book keeping and income tax are the hard ones. Altogether, fourteen units. I'm hoping to get my degree in three and a half years.

People are always going to have to pay taxes and I think the rules are only going to get more complicated. If I have my license, I'll always have a job. What do you think?

I can apply this to my parent's business and to Carlo's new business, the donut shop. He's a different man. Our parents were so amazed at his change that they decided to help him with a loan to buy the shop. Tony, is that his name(?), was happy to sell after you left. Thank you so much for that. You probably saved Carlo from jail.

I've run the track at SDSU a few times. It feels good to be able to run again. I wish you were here with me. It's fun running with you. You make me try harder because I don't want you to beat me. I'll still give you a kiss for being runner-up, though. Can you see me blushing?

I hear that you have to go through some kind of obstacle course? I'll bet you're good at it. Please write and let me know how you're doing.

Sincerely yours,

Letti

XOXO

Dear Katie,

I don't think Jimbo's doing well. If you haven't told him about us yet, maybe we should wait?

I just learned that I'm being sent to Keesler AFB in Biloxi, Mississippi for the next ten months, even farther away from you. The good news is that I'll be getting some good training that I can use when I get out.

The bad news? I miss you so much already that I can't stand it. Another ten months is beyond hell. Maybe I can find a way to fly home for a week-end once in a while.

Ten months is forever when I think about us. I won't blame you if you want to date, but I'm hoping that school keeps you so busy that you won't have time.

I want to walk on the beach with you, go to concerts with you, make love to you all night long. We've done it a million times in my dreams.

Maybe I shouldn't tell you about that. Any fantasies on your end? Katie, be honest.

Egad! I'm starting to sound like you.

Missing you so much,
Calvin
XOXOXOXO

Hey, Calie,

You've probably already noticed that I sealed our letter with a kiss. Do you like the color of my lipstick? Did you kiss it? I'll bet a hundred dollars that you did. You, and five other postal workers along the way. I'm laughing.

How about the perfume? Is that something you could get close to? I've put it on some secret parts of my body and I want you to tell me where. Is that a game we can play?

Fantasies? Oh, yes. But I'm not going to tell you what they are. Just curious. Would you let me tie you up?

I won't tell Jimbo. Last I heard, he's going to Viet Nam. None of us are very happy about that.

I'm working on a self-portrait. I'm starting to like charcoal.

If I make a mistake, I just smudge it out and make it look like I wanted to do that. Does that sound like me?

I'm just doing head and shoulders like you said. I was going to do a whole-body nude, but then I couldn't send you a picture of it. Maybe I'll do one anyway and you'll just have to come home before you can see it.

Missing you, too. I want to be in your arms.

Love, Katie

XOXOXOXO

Hi Letti,

I would love to go running with you. Just don't embarrass me too much. OK? And if you do, I'll take that kiss. I had a chance to run to a dumpster the other day, about a football field away. I went from zero to full speed and I thought of you and your lessons the entire way.

I guess your wrist is doing OK? Did it leave a big scar? I sure hope it doesn't affect your running. Have you joined the track team? I'm waiting to hear that you made it into the Olympics. I know that you can do it.

How is Carlo doing? Is he sick of donuts yet? He wanted to put in stereo and move all the tables and chairs around. Has he done any of that? Tell him I said, Hi and good luck.

I'm missing San Diego and all of my friends. How are John and Penny doing? Are they both going to State? High school seems like a lifetime ago. What a crazy world.

You're right. Maybe there's a track team I can join after I get out of school. It sure felt good to run, even if my goal was a dumpster. Good luck with your running!

Missing you,

Calvin

XOXO

I was bumped up to an earlier flight and arrived in San Diego hours before anyone was expecting me. I took a cab back to our house, walked through the front door, unlocked as usual and, lingered in the front room.

The repair job on the overstuffed recliner, where Gwen tried to stab Kenny, was starting to show. The duct tape held up pretty well. I'll have to get the black marker out.

I put my bags into what used to be my room. Not sure who's sleeping here now, left a note on the dining room table saying that I was home so nobody needed to come pick me up, walked through the house and out the back door to my car, parked just inside the fence next to the alley. Somebody had just washed it. Thank you!

How odd it feels to get behind the wheel and start the engine. I haven't driven since entering the military and, hearing it idle, I'm remembering all of my trips to the donut shop, down to the beach, Katie sliding across the front seat and kissing me into craziness. Am I really in the military? Has that nightmare passed and am I home for good?

I check my rear-view mirror, see my shaved head and am brought back to reality. No. It's not over. I'm leaving for Japan in a month and I'll be there for two years. As good as it feels to be home, I'm saddened by that thought.

How can I possibly keep Katie under my wing until I come home? She'll turn seventeen a month after I'm gone and by the time I return, she'll be eighteen. Still available? I don't want to think of any other outcome.

I opened the gate and drove out into the alley. I feel like I'm doing something wrong and am waiting for some TI somewhere to jump out from behind some wall and start yelling at me. You get used to things like that, feeling like you're always being watched.

Before leaving Keesler, some old timer Sargent yelled at me for having a couple of hairs touching my ears and brought it to the attention of higher-ups. I was forced to

241

get a haircut before being allowed to leave. I was hoping to have a little hair growing by the time I came home. It was not to be. I wasn't shaved, but it was certainly a military haircut.

I wondered how Harold was doing, him with his long hair and attempts to grow a beard. From what I've seen on the news, Berkley is pretty wild and I can imagine how Harold fits right in.

At least Keesler is behind me. I've got my training, I know what to expect when I go to work and I know that I can do the job. At least I'm not going to Viet Nam. I'm wondering how Jimbo is doing.

Having time to kill, I headed over to the donut shop to see what Carlo had accomplished during this last year. To my surprise, nothing much had changed. I noticed a couple of speakers mounted on the wall over by the cutting table. Carlo had stereo! Everything else was pretty much right where I last saw them.

Cheryl was working behind the counter...,

"Carlo? No. He was drafted. He left a month ago for boot camp."

"Does he still own the business?"

"Yeah. He's paying Dante to make donuts now. But even he just got drafted. He leaves next month."

"Who's taking over after that?"

"No idea."

"Maybe you could get Dante to teach you?"

"No. I've got a life and working nights would kill it."

"Do you know Letti?"

"Yeah. She stops in from time to time. She does the books."

I ordered an old-fashioned donut, a maple bar and a cup of coffee and sat down in one of the booths. The coffee tasted the same. The maple bar was OK. They let it rise too long, so it soaked up more oil than it should have when being fried. They put glaze on the old-fashioned instead of simple syrup, so it came out too sweet.

The counter was the same and I imagined Cassi sitting there on so many nights, keeping me company, short skirt making me crazy about our non-existent love-making. I wondered what happened to her, who she wound up with and wondered if he had to play the same games as Jimbo and I. More power to him if he was getting laid. I knew that he'd worked for it.

I wasn't ever in love with her. She was compelling because she was a mystery and I loved every minute of our time together. But meet a complete stranger, spend time with each other, go to movies, dinners, walk on the beach at night, and leave without saying good-bye? I don't know how to complete that part of my life. It's like losing the skateboard and never finding it. There's a vacuum.

In his very few letters, Jimbo does not mention her at all, nor does he talk about Annette. I imagine that he is too busy to have much time to think about it. I hadn't heard from him in a long time and was getting worried. Katie would be getting out of school soon. Hopefully, she has some news.

On my way over to meet with her, I decided to stop by a flower shop and buy Katie some roses. Going inside, Cassi is behind the counter. When our eyes meet, both of us are transfixed, motionless, just like in the movies. There are other people in the store and the place is quiet.

I didn't know what to say. Looking at her ring finger, Cassi is married. I wondered for how long. Reading her facial expression, I can see that she does not want to revisit the past.

"May I help you?"

"I'd like to buy a dozen yellow roses."

She smiles, a generic smile. "Certainly. Here's a card to fill out while I go get them."

Attaching the card to the roses, she looks at me with a smile. "These must be for a very special person."

A thousand words between our eyes and not one word spoken. "She is. They're for Jimbo's sister."

I knew that I'd hit a nerve. I saw it pass quickly across her face. I thanked her and went out to my car. She followed.

"You forgot your receipt."

243

"Oh, thanks."

"I want to apologize."

"For what?"

"For leading both of you on."

"Were you married then?"

"He was overseas, in Viet Nam. I was so scared..., and lonely."

"You were never unfaithful. I can vouch for that."

"Didn't we have fun, even without sex?"

"Yeah, Cassi. We did."

"You have no idea how many times I wanted to."

"Double that for me."

"How are you doing?"

"I'm going to Japan. Jimbo's in Viet Nam. How are you doing?"

"I'm not out running around at midnight anymore."

"It's about time you settled down."

"This is hard for me to say, especially now since I never even said good-bye, but I want you and Jimbo to know that both of you helped me through some very hard times and I will always love you for that, just not in the way that you wanted."

"I'll pass that on to Jimbo."

She placed her body so that no one from inside the store could see her action, kissed her fingertips and placed them on my lips. "Thank you for all that you did for me. You saved me and my marriage."

"Then, I guess all of our suffering was worth it."

We gave each other a knowing smile and went our separate ways.

It's OK. Everyone does what they need to do to get by. I can't complain about my time with her. She brought a lot of joy to this poor soul working nights.

And I'm pretty sure that I'm going to think about her from time to time as the years go by and smile. I hope that she feels the same way.

Opening the door, Katie pulled me in by my shirt. I handed her the flowers, which she took with a smile, sampling their scent while she placed them on top of the TV and then turned to unbutton my shirt.

"What are you doing?"

"Shut up."

"Where are your parents?"

"Out."

"Wait. When are they...,"

She's laughing now. My shirt is unbuttoned and she's reaching for my belt.

"Wait."

"Calie. You're in my house. You have to go by my rules."

"You know the expression, don't want to get caught with their pants down? That's me."

She's giggling. "Give me your hands."

"What?"

"Your hands. Let me see them."

Like any good soldier, I held them up for inspection. I've been trained!

She took them, placed them on her breasts and held them there. "Tell me, Mr. Boring, are these bigger than the last time you touched them?"

"Jesus, Katie. You drive me crazy."

There is no stopping after that. It felt like the wall of time between us shattered, me breaking out of my military bubble and her from whatever. We were kisses all over, tearing down the days and months between us until we arrived back at this time. Dressing...,

"So..., when are you parents coming back?"

She's laughing. "What do you care? You got what you came for, right?"

"No. I came for you, all of you."

"I think you just got it."

"I want more."

"These roses are beautiful. Thank you."

245

"You need to put them in water."

Katie wandered into the kitchen. "No shit, Sherlock. I've grown a few things in my life."

Smiling, I followed her over to the counter. "Like, what?"

"Grew some cherry tomatoes once, big as oranges."

"That's hard to believe."

"Would I lie?"

"Until it's proven otherwise, I'm with you." I wrapped my arms around her. "I'm with you anyway." We made love again, right there at the kitchen counter.

"So..., when are your parents coming home?"

"Calie? Fuck off with that question. I'm hungry. Let's go eat. Hamburger and fries at Oscar's?"

It does not seem possible that two such different worlds can coexist, Katie, facing me, leaning against the passenger side door eating her hamburger, dipping her fries into a little mound of ketchup without a care, in my life so completely, and compare that to where I was just twenty-fours before.

We drove out to La Jolla, watched the sunset mostly without words, each of us holding the other, alone in our thoughts.

On the way home, she had a desire for some kind of snack and, getting back into the car, handed me a box of Cracker Jacks. At the bottom, I found the toy, a plastic ring.

"Katie? Will you marry me?"

She took the ring, examined it and, teary-eyed, yet giggling, placed it on her finger. "Is this the *best* that you can do?"

"It's all that I've got, for now."

"Then..., it will just have to do."

Knowing that I've got Katie beside me gives me a strength beyond what I have alone. I can handle the time away. After the first year, I'll have a month's leave.

And when she turns eighteen, I'll be back to help her celebrate. We're getting married! I cannot think of anyone who makes me happier.

Hi, Calie,

Is it true that absence makes the heart grow fonder? I'm trying to decide if I miss you more now, or when you left. I think it's the same. The only thing that makes it more is when I look at my ring. Or, when I'm at the kitchen counter where we had sex. Or, when I go to the beach and hear the waves. They remind me of you. Am I being corny, or what?

I'm starting to paint with oils. I love the colors. I think I'm going to have fun with this. My first project will be, guess what? A bowl of oranges and cherry tomatoes! Sounds like us? The canvas isn't big enough for the pumpkins.

If we get married, we can hang it in the kitchen. Where are we going to live? Am I going back to Japan with you? What's it like over there? Do I have to like rice? I'm not eating any raw fish.

I'll be eighteen next month. Are you still coming? This is your chance to get out of marrying me. If you think you made a mistake, now's the time to back out. That's OK. I'll forgive you.

There's a boy in my class, he's a really good artist, that wants me to pose nude. I keep telling him, no. I'll have to teach you how to draw so that I can pose for you. Would you do that for me?

I haven't heard from Jimbo for a while. One of my letters came back. We don't know where he is.

Oh-my-God, I miss you. Please come home. Hurry!
Katie
XOXOXOXO

Dear Katie,

If I thought I could get to San Diego any faster, I'd tape myself to the front of the plane. Once you're in my arms, I'm never letting go. If you want to come back to Japan

247

with me, I'd love it if you did. I'll have to apply for housing. I think there is about a sixty day wait. But I can't apply until after we're married.

I can't imagine us being together without having to look over our shoulders. Ha! Did you parents ever come home?

I haven't heard from Jimbo, either. How is Blue Beauty? Was it you that washed my car when I came home? I never asked who did and thanked nobody because I was so smitten, I like that word, with you.

Katie, you drive me crazy. Of course, I want to get married. Never doubt that. I will always be there for you.

Loving you, dying to hold you.

Calvin

XOXOXOXO

Hey, Calvin,

How's it going? Having a good time, yet? Regretting not going to college? At least you're in Japan instead of the war zone. How is military life?

I made the team. I play for the Aztecs. Penny is not happy about it, but I'm only a sub at this time, so I don't see too much action.

Ran into Letti the other day. She's taking a full load plus some. Penny and I watched her work out at the track. She is amazing! Runs like a cheetah. About the time you think she's going to run out of air, she accelerates! Don't know why she's attracted to you. Ha!

When are you coming home on leave? It sure would be fun to get the gang together down at the beach again. We had some pretty good times, didn't we?

Just wanted to say, Hi.

Take care,

John

Going into my old room, I grab a change of clothes, bathing suit, fins and am about to pack it into my suitcase when Katie tugs at my sleeve.

"Calie? Would you like to make love in your old bed?"

"It's not really my bed anymore."

"OK. Mr. Boring." She starts toward the hallway. "Get your stuff. I'll be waiting in the living room. We still have to stop by my house."

Me, turn down Katie? No way. I grabbed her arm, spun her around and we fell onto the bed laughing. My God, this girl makes me crazy. And she's my wife!

We're off to our honeymoon, two days in a rented room overlooking the ocean in La Jolla. Going into Katie's house, we found the note on the kitchen table...,

Katie Darling,

I'm so sorry to give you this news now, just when you're on your honeymoon, but we've just hung up from the worst call of our lives. Jimbo was killed in action. Your father and I are flying up to San Francisco so that we can be on the plane that brings him home.

My heart aches when I think of all the times that I yelled at him, I just want to kill myself. And my heart aches for you. I should be there with you right now, Katie, holding you. Calvin, we're counting on you to do that for us. You were his best friend. God bless both of you. We'll be home soon.

Loving you more than ever,

Mom and Dad

I pulled Katie into a hug and, feeling the tears roll down my cheeks, was content to hold her as long as she wanted. I could feel her sobbing against my chest, felt her tears on my shoulder.

I don't know when or how we got to the couch in the living room. It was dark when we finally broke apart, her wiping her tears on her sleeve, me staring blankly at the floor.

"I can't believe it, Calie. He's gone."

Somebody said that joy and sorrow are connected. You can't know one without the other. It's true.

"Maybe, it's a mistake. Maybe...,"

"Is he wearing dog tags, like you?"

She was right. I'd heard that when someone dies in the field, they place the tag between the victim's teeth and strike the lower jaw to wedge it in place. I hope that they didn't do this to Jimbo. I did not pass this on to Katie. In any case, if those were his tags...,

"Calie?"

"Yes?"

"I can't stay here tonight."

"That's good, cause we have a place at the beach."

"I want to get drunk."

"Me, too."

"We're too late for the sunset?"

"Right."

"Is there a moon tonight?"

"I think so."

"I want to get drunk and watch the waves. The ocean reminds me of both you and Jimbo. He loved it out there. I want to sit and watch the waves and cry until my tears are all gone."

"Jesus, Katie. You're making me cry."

"Can John buy us some whiskey?"

Sitting out in the balcony of our room overlooking the Coves, John popped open a bottle of champagne and poured it into our glasses. On a table between the four of us, he placed a large Venus Pizza with everything, a large Chef's Salad, garlic bread and paper plates.

John held up his glass. "To Calvin and Katie. We watched you two grow together. We were just wondering when it was going to happen. Congratulations."

We clinked glasses.

"And to Jimbo," said Penny, raising her glass. "I don't want to make everybody cry, but I can't leave without a toast to him."

We clinked glasses and, of course, everybody cried. John

and Penny departed after that, leaving with us a pint of Seagram's and some Seven-Up. We mixed it strong.

"Calie? Let's go down by the water."

"We're drunk. Maybe..., that's not a good idea."

"It's our honeymoon. You have to do what I want."

"Katie...,"

"I want to say goodbye to Jimbo."

"It's already ten. How about tomorrow morning?"

"Tonight. Calie? Please?"

The rocks are always slippery when wet and being drunk didn't help. We sat on what appeared to be a safe distance from the waves and watched them wash across the rocks toward us, splashing and foaming along the way.

"I think the tide's coming in."

"We just got here, Calie. How can you know that?"

"The moon's behind us."

"Oh," She giggles, puts her arm around me. "I guess that's got something to do with it."

"It looks so different at night."

"Like Jimbo. He was dark inside. Something was always bothering him."

"I'm so sorry, Katie. He was my best friend, helped me deliver papers when he found out I didn't have a bike."

She laughs. "Helped me with math, even though he was wrong."

"Nailed Kenny, protecting you."

"He had a temper."

"Turned us both onto dope."

"We found those roaches at the same time, down at that beatnik's house."

"I started to fall in love with you that night, when I saw you dance."

"That was good dope."

"And when we got in that accident. Sitting on the side of Highway Sixty-seven at four in the morning, cooking bacon and eggs, smoking dope and looking up through the telescope."

"I should've been there for that. I'd like to have that

memory."

"Your family still has that scope. We could borrow it and head out to Borrego Springs for a night."

"Skip the accident part?"

"And skip cooking alongside the highway."

She's crying. No..., sobbing. There's nothing more to say. It comes in waves. Times like these, we have to draw from each other.

The wave caught us without warning. I had my eyes closed. Katie's head was buried in my chest. This was one of those waves that comes in low, but has the power of another overtaking swell coming in on top.

We were swamped head to toe in seconds and then hanging onto the rock as the water rolled back out to sea, both of us speechless. Laughing from the shock, we scurried to higher ground.

Another couple, up on the grass and trying not to laugh, shouted. "You guys, OK?"

Slipping and sliding, holding onto each other, I waved.

"Embarrassed, is the word."

"How was the water?"

"Wet."

"Cold," said Katie.

And then we were all laughing.

Making our way back to our room, Calie took my hand.

"Jimbo did that, you know?"

"You think so?"

"He's letting us know he was here. He approves. It's his wedding present."

I put my arm around her as we hiked up the stairs. "I hope so."

We took hot showers, snuggled up in bed, laughing over our drenching, crying over Jimbo, a long and passionate night.

Someone once said that happiness is like holding onto a tiger by the tail. It's fun while it lasts, but it can turn on you at any second. Now I understand.

Rose was bending over him when he opened his eyes, wiping away some smudge or something from his forehead, smelling of fried onions and..., bacon?

"Frankie! Don't close your eyes. George, wake up! Frankie just opened his eyes!"

Looking at her, a stranger, red, curly hair, plump face with happy wrinkles, starry-eyed.

"George, get up! Frankie's awake."

"Workin' on it, honey. I'm no spring chicken, you know?"

"Frankie, they said you might never wake up. Praise the Lord!"

Groaning with the effort, grabbing hold of the bed rail with his leathery, wrinkled hands, George, bald and gray, smiled as he joined them at the head of the bed, opposite Rose.

"It's the arthritis, you know? Can't move like I used to. Hi, son. How are you doing?"

Moving his head side to side, staring blankly at the two of them, he said nothing.

Rose rubbed her hand across his forehead. "He's trying to figure out where he is, aren't you, Frankie?"

"Well, son. You're back in Idaho, right where you belong."

"Our prayers have been answered. The Lord took care of you. I've got your room all ready, Frankie. We want you to come home."

George put his hand on his son's shoulder. "Yep. Work's piling up. It'd be good to get you going again."

"Don't rush him, George. He can't even talk, yet."

"No wonder, after what happened."

"I'm going to tell Faith. Frankie? You remember your sister, Faith? She just graduated from high school, honor student! Can you believe it? Our little Faith, a *smart* cookie." Rose patted him on the head. "Well, she's down in the lobby. I'll send her up. Maybe she'll jog your memory. Thank you, Lord for bringing our son home."

They watched her leave and, after a minute or two, George inched toward the door. "Gotta pee, son. I forgot to take my pills this morning. I'll be back."

The privacy curtain was pulled forward slightly, just enough so that he could not see who was entering the room.

"Frankie? You in there? It's me, Faith."

A tentative smile, a questioning look, raised eyebrows, brown hair pulled back over her Jean jacket, smells of cigarettes.

"Frankie? How are you doing? It's good to have you back. Let me know when you're coming home and I'll bake your favorite pie. Cherry, apple with two scoops of homemade vanilla ice cream, remember that? Did Mama tell you that I graduated with honors? Imagine that, me. I must've had the Good Lord's help cause I didn't think I was doing that good. I've been driving your car, just like you asked. I know you said just to start it up once in a while, but you didn't say I couldn't drive it, did you? Anyway, it's just a small dent. I didn't see that fire hydrant. I did get a DUI, so I'll need the car to go to classes. Other than that, I'm taking good care of it. Remember Billy, the guy you got in a fight with before you left? We've settled our differences and are back together again. Praise the Lord for that, or I'd be back in the house and you'd have to give up your room again. Oh. Your dog died. Fella, remember him? Got hit out on the highway. Don't know why he wandered so far. I just remembered, I'm not supposed to tell you that so, when you hear it from Mama, act surprised. Did you know that Dad had a heart attack while you were gone? Triple bypass. They said that he was lucky to be alive. Insurance didn't pay as much as we thought so we had to put a lien on the place. We won't be getting as much as we hoped when they go, you know what I mean? Bowling alley got hit by lightning and all the lanes got soaked in the last storm so you won't be bowling on Thursday nights for a while. Oh, and old man Perkins died last summer. You remember him? He's got the place next to ours. Don't know who's going to move

254

in next. You can't be too careful these days. Not that we have much say about it. Um, Maggie, remember her? She gained so much weight we all thought she was sneaking extra meals, looks like a butterball. I know I'm not the one to talk, cause I'm kinda heavy myself, but I'm not that bad. Turns out, she's pregnant. Remember Tony, your old baseball friend? She says he's the father, but he's denying it. I can see why. Who wants to be hooked up to her when she looks like that? Wasn't she your old girlfriend back in high school? Anyway, you didn't do it. You were gone. So, how are you feeling? Cat's got your tongue, huh? Oh! Guess who's here? She'll make you feel better, I'll bet."

Lilly, walked around the curtain and stopped at the head of the bed, opposite Faith. She leaned down and kissed him on the forehead. She smells soapy clean, tight skin, very little makeup, frosty, pink lipstick, black hair, styled, cut short.

"Hey, Love. I just heard that you woke up. How are you feeling?"

"He's not talking, yet."

"I'll stay with him for a while."

"Oh, good. Cause I have to get over to the courthouse and pay a fine. See you later, Frankie. Hope you're feeling better! Bye."

Lilly waited until she was sure Faith had gone. "You know where she's going? To fuck Terry, the clerk who works at the courthouse. She'll get him to pull the ticket and that'll be the end of that. Same with her English teacher, Mr. Thomas and her Math teacher, Ben, what's his name? Honor student, my ass. She can hardly add and she gets A's? I wouldn't want her doing my books."

Lilly walked over to the doorway, looked both ways to ensure the coast was clear, returned to his bed and reached under the covers. "Just want to make sure you've still got it, you know? Where we go from here, Love, depends on that."

Confirming that he did, she brought her hand up to his cheek and turned his face toward hers. She kissed him gently on the lips. "It's been a long time, Love. I want you to get well yesterday. I've been good, but I can't hold out much longer. Brad, remember him? Your best friend? He's asked me out several times. Says it's just a friendly date, but I know better. I keep saying, no. Best friends don't do that to each other, do they? I'm counting on you to get well, Love."

He endured the steady string of well-wishers throughout the day, staring blankly at their faces as each told their story, prodding him to remember his past.

And when visiting hours are over, when his room is dark, except for a distant hallway light spilling in through the open door on the other side of the curtain, he hears the whump, whump, whump of the helicopter's blades, the whining of the engine, jumping down into a cloud of dust, rifle in hand, bullets whizzing by, ripping into the helicopter's skin, the whistle of mortars, explosions, the screams of those being hit, the darkness that follows...,

When everyone else is gone, lying alone in bed, heart pounding, his body is covered in sweat.

John turned the key, opened the door and flipped on the switch. Four ceiling lights, located beneath the balcony on the far side of the living room, lit up along with a light mounted into the wall leading up the stairs.

"Kitchen's straight back," said John. "It opens up to a patio on one side and to a spare room on the other. TV's in there. Reception's not very good out here, though."

Katie wandered into the room, stopping at the end of the sectional couch and checking out the fireplace to her left and the bookshelf to her right. "Nice how they built the stereo into the bookshelf."

I followed Katie into the living room and sat on the couch. "Who lives here?"

"Lived. Uncle Lenny died of a heart attack a while back. My parents have been bugging me to come out here once in a while and make sure the place is OK. They come out every couple of months."

"I think I'd live here, if I were you."

"Not while I'm going to State. That'd be a three-hour drive one way."

Penny started up the stairs. "What's up there?"

"Two master bedrooms with baths. Lenny had friends that dropped by from time to time. Sometimes they'd stay for a while. He wanted everyone to have their privacy. Penny, our room is to the left. Calvin, you and Katie have the one on the right."

"This is very cool, John. Thanks."

"Just keep it down to a roar at night." He patted me on the head. "I'm a light sleeper."

"What can I say? It's our honeymoon."

Penny disappeared upstairs. Katie and I followed John into the kitchen where we set the groceries on the counter.

"Looks like we've got enough for a couple of days. Penny and I've got homework. What's your plan?"

"I was telling Katie about our accident out on Highway Sixty-seven. She wants to cook bacon and eggs at four in

257

the morning while we stargaze out on the patio."

"That explains the telescope."

"And the Coleman stove. We're going to cook breakfast out there, bacon and eggs. You're invited."

John laughed. "Four in the morning? Ha! I'll bet you don't make it either."

"He will," said Katie, grabbing my arm and putting it around her shoulder. "We're on our honeymoon. He has to do what I want."

"Ouch! Calvin, you agree to that?"

"Yeah. I'll agree to most anything right now."

John began unpacking the groceries and putting all of the cold stuff into the fridge. "You're leaving, when?"

"Four days."

"Anybody up for one last blast at the beach? Volleyball, hang out, build a fire?"

"Fine with me. Katie?"

"Sure. Except I want to drive down in Blue Beauty."

"Perfect."

Lilly crawls over him, moving away from the wall next to his bed in search of her clothes. She finds her panties at the end of the bed, her pants on the floor in the same area, bra and sweater across the room next to the door.

"Well, Love, you don't talk much, which is good, and you haven't forgotten how to fuck. I think we're on a roll. We've always been good at this, haven't we?"

He is silent, choosing instead to watch her dress, feeling the urge to rip all of her clothes off while she is applying lipstick in front of the mirror above his dresser.

"You hungry, Love?"

He shakes his head, eyes fixed on the pendant, a seagull on the wing, resting at the end of a silver chain in the depression of her sweater.

Watching him, wondering what he must have gone through, she returns to the bed and sits beside him.

"Love? Look at me. We *do* need to talk."

He cannot maintain eye contact for long. Her gaze is too steady, unnerving, reminiscent of the harsh gaze of the drill instructors back in Basic.

"I'm here for you, Love. Do you believe me?"

A quick glance to ensure that she is serious. He nods.

"Then, talk to me. Look at me, not the bird..., me. And say my name."

She has hazel eyes, inquisitive, determined, loving. He knows that this is a test of sorts, that he must make the effort and come out of his shell. Sooner or later, she is going to leave.

He feels tears welling up from somewhere, from some dark place that he dares not go, determined to keep the dam intact, keeping everything at bay.

"Love? I'm begging you. Say my name."

How to feel good about being in the company of such a beautiful woman when there are so many mangled bodies blown to bits, pieces rotting in the dirt, soldiers that are never coming home? How to justify *this?* How to move on as if nothing ever happened while the battle is still raging?

"Love?"

Where did she come from? This room? These people? Is there shrapnel in my brain? Did the doctors miss something? I remember *none* of this. Some part of my life is *missing*. The only part that feels real..., is her.

He reaches up to cup her breasts, but she stops him.

"My name."

He remembers the name, George, the man who is supposed to be his father, but isn't, and Faith, the nut cake that is supposed to be his sister, but isn't, and his own name, Frankie, which is wrong. He does not know the name of the woman with whom he'd just had sex.

"I...,"

After a long silence, she squeezes his hand. "Go on."

"I'm..., I'm not Frankie."

She smiles. "There's a twist. OK, Love. Who are you?"

"I..., don't know."

"You look like Frankie."

"Do I?"

"I wouldn't have had sex with you, if I didn't think you were Frankie."

"You wouldn't?"

"Of course, not. You think I'm a slut?"

"No..., I think you're..., beautiful."

"Do you know my name?"

He shakes his head. "No...,"

"Yet, you had sex with me."

"Yes."

"Does it bother you that you don't know my name?"

"Very much."

"Does it bother you that you had sex with me?"

"No. You're the only thing that's real, so far."

"Love, we're going to have to sort this out. Do you remember anything before waking up in the hospital?"

"No."

"Then..., are these your parents? Is this your house?"

"No."

260

"Well, I'm lost. I don't know what to say."

Somehow it switched from her holding his hand, to his holding hers. "Do I make love like Frankie?"

"Love, after waiting a year, it's all good." She studies his face, moving her hands lightly across his cheekbones, gently down the bridge of his nose. "You look like Frankie. But if I had to compare, this was more passionate, wild. That is, if you're Frankie."

"And..., if I'm not?"

"Then, what can I say? The sex was good."

"You'd do it again?"

"I don't know who you are."

"I'm, Frankie."

She laughs. "You're a fucking liar."

He leans over, kisses her on the cheek. "But we are lovers. You can't deny that. Is it exciting, knowing that I might *not* be Frankie?"

"Love, I can't do this. It's creepy."

"Sexy?"

"Dangerous."

"Thrilling?"

"My name is Lilly. Say my name."

"Lilly, a name I can hold onto. I know you're real...,"

She turns to kiss him. "Love? Shut up."

Falling back onto the bed, pulling her down with him, he slides his hand up under her sweater.

"Lilly, Lilly, Lilly...,"

Lilly flipped on the reading lamp next to the bed and, pointing it away, watched Frankie twitching in his sleep.

She was not going to be the one to shake his shoulder, wake him up and start asking questions. Let sleeping dogs lie. Isn't that what they say? Some people wake up swinging.

Instead, she grabbed hold of the covers and turned away, leaving him bare. Eyes blinking open, he turns and stares blankly at the ceiling.

"Sorry, Love. I'm used to sleeping alone." She gives him back his covers. "Were you dreaming?"

"I was swimming..., in the ocean. I was caught in some kind of current pulling me up into this..., mountain of a wave. And then..., I woke up."

"Do you remember swimming in the ocean?"

"How could I have a dream like that, if I hadn't?"

"Well, Love. Maybe we have our first lead."

"How?"

"You lived near the ocean. Ring any bells?"

"More bells than Idaho."

He reaches over and tries to slide his hand up to her breasts. She stops him.

"It's not all about sex, Love."

"It's working for me."

"What am I going to do if Frankie comes back, huh?"

"I am Frankie."

"And, if you're not?"

"Run away with me."

"To where? For now, this is your home and your name is Frankie."

"I don't fit."

"Where else you going to go? What are you going to do for money?"

"I can't live off of these people forever."

"Yes, you can. Even if you're not Frankie, they think you are. You're doing them a favor."

"I can't live my life for them."

"Yes, you can, Love. You've got a place to stay until you figure out something else."

"What if I remember who I am? What do I tell them, then?"

"Love? George hasn't got two years left. Rose isn't far behind. You could inherit this place."

"Is that why you're sticking with me, for the inheritance?"

"No, Love. For now, it's the intrigue."

"The sex?"

"That's part of it, yes."

"As long as you think of me as Frankie?"

"Both ways, Love."

"Sometimes, I think of you as his wife."

"It turns you on to have sex with another man's wife?"

"Sometimes I'm Frankie. Sometimes I'm me. It turns you on to think that you're having sex with a complete stranger?"

"Love, we both know where we are in this relationship. It's a house of cards."

"Were you and Frankie going to marry?"

"We were working on it, just never got that far."

"So, what are we going to do?"

"I've got a brother that lives in San Diego. I'm invited to visit. Maybe you should tag along?"

"Have I met him before?"

"Frankie never has. Don't know about you."

Travelling south on Interstate 15, Lilly slowed their speed as they worked their way through the stoplights that skirted the business district of Escondido. He had been quiet most of the trip, choosing instead to watch the scenery go by, not really identifying with anything north of this place. But here, he was taking an interest.

"Some of this looks familiar."

"Escondido, Love. You've been here before?"

"Maybe. How close are we to the ocean?"

"Probably thirty miles."

He was quiet again going past Rancho Bernardo, but approaching Interstate 8, he was turning every which way to study the landmarks.

"I remember those oil storage tanks."

"Love, we're going to have to stop and buy a map. Noah's moved since the last time I was here."

"How long ago, was that?"

"About three years."

"Where does he live?"

"On some street called Chamoune Ave. I don't know which way to go on I 8, east or west."

"Chamoune? Go east..., I think."

"East? Well, our chances are fifty-fifty. I have to stop and get gas anyway."

Taking the turn-off to I 8 east...,

"Stay in the right-hand lane."

"You on to something, Love?"

"I can't remember the road's name. But I think I'll know it when I see it."

"OK. Maybe we're on a roll."

"Here it is, Fairmont Ave. Go south."

"Got it."

"What's his address?"

"It's in my purse. Forty-one something. Coming up on El Cajon Blvd. Looks like a major intersection."

"Turn left."

"You're awfully sure of yourself, Love."

"There it is, Chamoune."

Noah motioned for Frankie and Lilly to sit on the overstuffed pillows next to the table in the middle of the room. Hanging from the ceiling and centered over the table, a stained-glass swag lamp with its cord looped across the ceiling, hanging on two ornate, fake brass hooks and down the wall over to the extension cord on top of the stereo.

The ceiling was loosely draped with a black cloth that had hundreds of holes punched into it, letting through the bits of starlight from some unknown rotating source above.

Lying next to the stereo, a large, auburn colored, short haired dog with a jaw that looked like it could break bones.

"This is Krunch," said Noah, going over to scratch his head. "He doesn't say much, but he knows what's going on."

Lilly put the back of her hand out and let him get her scent. "Is he a Boxer?"

"Somewhere between that and Great Dane."

"If I have to get up in the middle of the night, he's not going to attack, or anything like that, is he?"

"He knows I'm OK with you. If I'm OK, he's OK. Frankie, come over here and let him get to know you."

"Krunch does not mind being petted, but he's not about to roll over and show his stomach for strangers."

Frankie put the back of his hand out tentatively. "Is he trained?"

"We have three words between us. If I say "Krunch," I have his attention. If I say his name twice, it means that I want him to do something, so he looks around to assess what needs being done. If I say his name three times, it means, "Help. He talks to me the same way, barking instead. Other than that, we don't say much."

Coming back to the table, Frankie studied the positions of the pieces of a partially finished game of chess.

"Who's your opponent?"

265

"Got a match going with a guy in Germany."

"What color are you?"

"Black."

"Who's turn?"

"Mine."

"What move are you going to make?"

"Haven't decided yet. You play chess?"

"It looks familiar."

"I'm going into the kitchen. Don't move any of the pieces."

Noah returned with a bottle of Ripple, some Seven-Up, three glasses with ice cubes, cut up pieces of hot dogs, plates and a bottle of ketchup, chips and some kind of dip.

"Dig in."

After the initial round of satisfying everyone's immediate needs, Noah studied Frankie.

"So..., Lilly says you're all fucked up. Is that true?"

"I didn't say that."

"He doesn't know who he is. I'd say that's fucked up. OK, Frankie. Who are you, really?"

Lilly topped off everyone's glass with Ripple. "We've already been through all of this."

Noah stabbed a hot dog piece with his fork and dipped it into the ketchup. "How did you know how to get here? Chamoune Avenue is like impossible to find in a city this size, unless you've lived around here."

"True."

Noah stirred his drink with his finger. "So, you're from around here?"

"I guess."

"What street is two blocks east of here?"

"Menlo, I think."

"And after that?"

"Forty-seventh."

Noah looked over at Lilly with a big smile. "I don't know his name, but I think I know where he lived."

"Yeah?"

"How many people will know the names of streets so well

266

unless they have a need? You've grown up, Frankie, or whoever you are. I think you used to deliver newspapers."

Frankie stood, walked outside and looked up and down the street. There was something familiar about this place. Lilly joined him on the sidewalk.

"Hey, Love. Want to go for a stroll?"

"Very much so."

Half hour later, coming back into the house, Frankie finished off his drink. "Noah, you might be right."

"If you are who I think you are, you used to deliver my paper."

"Oh? You said you knew where I lived?"

"I used to have to hunt for my paper every fucking day, never on my doorstep. When you threw the paper into the rose bush and I couldn't get it out, you and I had to have a talk. I followed you home, but watched you save a puppy that had wandered out into the street. I didn't have the heart to talk to you after that. But you were the worst newspaper deliverer I've ever had, if that was you."

"Sorry, if that was me. You followed me to my house? Can you show me where?"

Lilly, driving, slowed down. "Which one?"

Leaning between the two front seats, Noah pointed. "It's one of these two. I left before he went in."

"Shit. I've got to keep going. Somebody's behind me. I'll go around the block."

Frankie leaned back in his seat. "That's OK. I've seen enough. Let's go back to Noah's place."

"Progress, Love?"

"I have to think about it."

Back at the house, sitting around the table with a bucket of Kentucky Fried Chicken, rolls, mashed potatoes, gravy and a bottle of wine...,

"Love, you've been quiet the whole time."

"It comes to me in waves. I don't want to miss anything because I'm talking."

Noah stood, crossed the room, put on the album, *The Doors* and then disappeared into another room. Returning, he placed a water pipe on the table, filled the bowl and lit it. Taking a puff, he passed it on to Lilly.

"I was hoping you had some."

She took a hit and handed it to Frankie. "Well, Love. Let's see if we can jog your memory."

Lilly cleared the table while Noah carefully moved the chessboard in between himself and Frankie.

"I'm going to make this move and I'm open to suggestions. Frankie, you got an opinion?"

"Actually, I do."

"Well, I hope you're better at chess than you were at delivering newspapers."

And for the first time in a very long time, Frankie showed a genuine smile.

Benny had more pallets stored behind his garage and was happy to be rid of them. Katie and I brushed off the Black Widows, cut up the pallets, loaded them into the trunk of Blue Beauty and headed for the beach. John and Penny had gone on ahead to secure a fire ring.

When we arrived, Kenny and Gwen were there, busy cutting up slices of watermelon and hitting up the vodka, adding it to their glasses of grapefruit juice.

Katie and I carried the wood down to the pit, piled it up next to the ring and busied ourselves by pounding down the nails. We split and stacked several pieces into a teepee shape in preparation for the evening's fire and then headed north toward Belmont Park, walking close to the water.

"I don't want you to go back, Calie."

"I have to."

"Let's run away to Canada."

"Katie, it's called desertion. Twenty years is a long time to spend in prison."

"How long before I can come over?"

"Two months."

"I hear they don't have toilets over there. It's just a hole in the ground?"

"They're changing all of that. They do have open sewers, though."

"Is there going to be a toilet in our house?"

"Why? You going to grow some giant, cherry tomatoes?"

She squeezes my hand. "Maybe. What's the dirt like?"

"Good dirt. We won't be there long enough to grow oranges, though."

"That's good. What about the toilets?"

"Every place on base has a toilet, just like here. If you go off-base, that's a different story."

"Can we get hamburgers over there?"

I put my arm around her and pulled her close. We kind of tripped into the next wave as it washed over our feet.

"You're going to love it, Katie. We're going to have our own little place, stove, refrigerator, toilet, shower, all of that."

"Can you take your car?"

"Why? We're going to be back here in a year."

"Can I keep Blue Beauty in the back yard with yours?"

"I'll talk to my parents. We're going to have to figure out what to do with the cars."

"Maybe, I shouldn't go?"

"Seriously?"

"No. I'm coming. I don't want to wait another year. How do you get around over there?"

"Shuttle bus. It takes you all over the base. They have a commissary, so we can get groceries and stuff."

"And off base?"

"Taxi's are cheap, trains go everywhere."

"What's the weather like? Do I have to buy all new clothes?"

"Katie, we're going to do whatever it takes for you to be happy."

"And, you? What about you?"

"I'm happy just being with you."

We walked another half mile and then turned around and headed back. The clouds never really did clear, so neither of us had any great desire to go in the water.

"Being here today makes me sad."

"Jimbo?"

"It's not the same without him. You know what I want right now, Calie?"

"To make love with me right here on the beach?"

"Almost."

"That was my best guess."

"To get stoned and make love with you, not here on the beach."

"If only we had some."

"Jimbo left me a joint. He said when he walked through the front door, to hand him that and a cold beer. I guess it's ours now."

"Smoke Jimbo's joint and make love to his baby sister?"

270

"He did say to watch over me."

I laughed. "I don't think that's what he meant."

"We're married, Calie. You have to do what I want."

"Was that in the contract?"

"Yes."

"Works both ways, right?"

She put her arm around me. "No. You didn't read the fine print. You have to watch over me, Jimbo's request. And you have to do what I want. That's in the contract."

"So unfair."

"Are you complaining, soldier?

"Sir. No sir." And that was such a sad response, a reminder that I was going to be back in Japan soon and that I'd have to leave her behind until we got a house, about two months.

She smiled. "Good. Now give me a kiss."

No more words between us as we headed back to our group, each of us holding the other tighter, knowing the end was coming. They were just starting the fire when we arrived.

"Woof!" Krunch stood, eyes and ears focused on the front door. Noah, not liking the distraction from the chess conversation, frowned as he glanced toward the knock.

"Who could that be?"

Krunch followed him to the door and, after Noah opened it, scrutinized the visitor. "Woof!"

Noah glanced toward Lilly and Frankie, laughing. "One bark means it's OK. Two barks, beware. Come on in, Harold."

Krunch followed them back to the table and, seeing that there were no snacks offered, returned to his mat next to the stereo.

Entering the room, Frankie thought he recognized the man with the thick, Coke-bottle glasses, shoulder length brown hair and scrawny beard, but if so, from where?

Noah made the introductions. "This is Lilly, my sister and that's her boyfriend, Frankie. This is Harold, my math tutor when I was going to State."

Harold shook Lilly's hand and, shaking Frankie's...,

"Frankie? You look like Jimbo."

"And there it is," said Lilly with a big smile. "Jimbo. How easy was that?"

Harold found another cushion and seated himself at the table. "I heard you were dead."

"If, I'm Jimbo."

"If?"

"We have an identity crisis," said Lilly. "He's supposed to be, Frankie."

"Who do you think you are?"

"Not, Frankie."

"I think they're doppelgangers," said Lilly, wanting to clarify everything.

Noah returned from the kitchen with another bottle of wine, Seven-up and a glass for Harold. "Doppelgangers? What is that?"

"Your twin. Supposedly, everyone has one."

272

Harold refused the wine, choosing instead to pour himself some Seven-up. "You're saying Jimbo's identity was switched with his doppelganger?"

"What else can it be?"

"My dog tags say I'm Frankie."

"That doesn't mean shit," said Noah.

Harold was studying Lilly with a big smile. "You're Frankie's girlfriend?"

"Yes."

He laughed. "What happens if this guy turns out to be Jimbo?"

"I know. I know. I'm sleeping with a complete stranger. Shut up."

"It's not a problem. I'll be Jimbo in California and Frankie in Idaho. Both of us have a girlfriend named Lilly."

"And if Frankie shows up...," Harold let it hang there.

"I don't want to think about it."

"That is an interesting question," said Jimbo. "What would you do?"

"I'm going to ignore that question."

Noah, with a devious smile, refilled the water pipe, lit it and passed it on to Harold. "This is getting interesting."

It went around the table once. Harold declined a second hit. "Do I look like someone you know?"

"It's hard to tell with all that hair," said Jimbo. "But I remember your thick glasses and you have a kind of sarcastic smile. Yeah. Maybe."

"Anybody else?"

"Throw something at me."

"Calvin? You two always hung out together. Both of you used to work at the donut shop."

"Donuts? My, God."

"You bought Calvin's old Dodge, got in a wreck and bought a Buick. You called it, Blue Beauty. Any of this ring a bell?"

"Keep going."

"We have some of the same friends. John, plays football. Went to Crawford. Penny is his girlfriend. You went to

273

Hoover. How about Gwen and Kenny? You gave Kenny a black eye."

"Why would I do that?"

"You thought Kenny was putting the make on Katie, your little sister. Do you remember her?"

"Oh, my God." Jimbo put his head in his hands, staring blankly at the table. "Oh, my God! Jesus!"

Lilly put her arm around him, pulled him close and gave him a hug and a shoulder, rubbing his back. "It's OK, Love. Let it out."

In the silence, Noah got up and put on The Rolling Stones, *Aftermath*, keeping the volume low.

Minutes later, Jimbo, pulling away and wiping his eyes, recomposed himself. "It's like there's a cloud between here and there."

Lilly started laughing. "What did you think when you woke up and everyone called you Frankie?"

"Speechless. Give me some of that wine, will you?"

Harold poured a round. "Do you remember where you live?"

"Yeah. But I'm not going there tonight."

Harold laughed. "That would be interesting, if you did. What are you going to do?"

"Tonight? Lilly? Care to take a walk on the beach?"

"I wouldn't mind. It's stuffy in here. You know any good places, Harold?"

"We used to go to South Mission Beach."

"Can you tell me how to get there?"

"No. But I can show you, if I can hitch a ride."

"I'm not going," said Noah. "Lilly, I'll get you a spare key. When you come through the door, Krunch will greet you. He knows who you are. But just to be safe, say his name when you come in. Your bedroom's on the right when you get to the hallway."

"Thanks, Noah. No idea when we'll be back. But we'll be quiet, I hope."

Kenny and Gwen left soon after the marshmallows. John and Penny lingered for another half hour and then bid their good-byes. We had a few pieces of wood left and Katie wanted to watch the fire burn down to the coals. Smoke was drifting toward the parking lot, so we sat north of it, looking south.

"When do you leave, Calie?"

"Day after tomorrow, early morning."

"We won't even get breakfast together, will we?"

"We'll get up early. Is Aunt Emma's still up on Fifty-fourth and El Cajon? They used to be open twenty-fours."

"And miss last minute sex? No. Let's just buy some donuts on the way home. We'll eat them on the way to the airport."

"Grocery store donuts?"

"Still can't eat them, huh?"

There wasn't much more to say. We'd crammed all of our thoughts and concerns into the last thirty days. All that was left now was the knowledge that our time together was coming to an end.

We'd had a bit to drink, thank you, John, and our walk had worn us out. The sounds of the surf mingled with the magic of a dying fire. All too soon this moment would be over, signalling the next stage of my departure, so we were in no hurry to leave.

Not far away...,

"Park anywhere along here," said Harold from the back seat. "If you want to walk the beach...,"

"I do," said Jimbo. "I can smell the ocean, I love it."

Lilly found a spot and parked. Getting out, Harold looked north.

"If we go that way, we'll run into Belmont Park."

"I don't want to see a lot of people," said Jimbo.

Lilly grabbed his hand. "South, it is."

Hearing the waves crash onto shore, Jimbo breathed in a long, deep breath. "Oh, my God. I *love* the ocean!"

They headed south carrying their shoes, pants rolled up, walking in and out of the water as the waves washed up and over their feet.

"I'd go for a swim if I had a suit," said Jimbo.

Lilly grabbed his arm and poked him in the ribs. "No, you won't, Love. Not at night. I've already lost one of you. It's bad for my reputation, if I lose two."

"So, I'm like a spare tire?"

"Exactly."

"What if Frankie shows up? You never answered that question."

"And I'm not going to."

"Do you still love Frankie?"

"Love, how can I possibly answer that?"

"You're right. Dumb question."

"We're on a roll, Love. Sex, drugs and now we're walking the beach in your old stomping grounds. What more could you want?"

Harold, walking in front, talked over his shoulder. "We used to get together way down at the end. Do you want to walk that far?"

Jimbo nodded. "Anything that helps fill in the gaps."

Harold, noticing that Lilly and Jimbo were slow to keep up, was feeling like he shouldn't have tagged along. This was their discovery now. He had done his part and it was time for him to bow out, something he would do if he had not hitched a ride with them.

Deciding to walk on ahead, approaching their old party spot, he noticed a young couple sitting together next to the fire, their backs to him. He couldn't be sure, but is that Katie?

It had been almost two years since he was last in San Diego and appearances change, men grow beards, their voices deepen, young girls fill out and..., is that Katie? My God, she's grown up, if that's her. And if it is, who is she with, some soldier home on leave? Military haircut.

Staying near the water, he walked past them, turned and, walking further up on the beach, headed for the fire pit.

Approaching...,

"Katie? Is that you?"

The voice was familiar, but looking up at the long-haired, bearded face flickering with the light of the fire, his glasses reflecting the flames, she did not recognize him. "Who are you?"

"It's me, Harold. Calvin. Is that you?"

Calvin stood, pulling Katie up with him. "Jesus! Harold, I didn't recognize you."

"Yeah. It's the hair. Man, you look like a government official."

"Don't judge a book by its cover."

After handshakes and hugs, Harold sat so that he could see Jimbo's and Lilly's arrival. Looking past Katie, they were strolling his way, not hurried, still down by the water. They wouldn't leave without him. He was pretty sure of that. "Are you two together now?"

Katie smiled. "We're married."

"Wow! When did that happen?"

277

"The day after I turned eighteen."

Harold laughed. "We could all see it coming. John and Penny know?"

"They were just here. Gwen and Kenny, too. We've still got a couple of hot dogs left, if you're hungry."

Jimbo and Lilly were leaving the water's edge, coming up toward the fire.

"No, thanks."

"How is Berkley?"

"A riot." Harold laughed. "Literally. I'm going back in another week. We've got a big protest march coming up."

Calvin pulled a couple of marshmallows from the bag, offered it to Harold, along with a coat hanger, and then stabbed the two he was holding and held them over the fire. "Protest what?"

"Everything," said Harold, stabbing his marshmallow. "The Establishment's thinking is backwards. It's time to move on. We want peace, not war."

"I'm with you on that. What's the biggest concern for you, right now?"

Harold smiled. "The biggest thing? What's going to happen in the next minute."

Katie took control of the clothes hanger. "You're holding it too close, Calie. I don't like mine burned."

I was confused. "Oh, like, live in the now? I've heard about that. You can't change the past and the future hasn't happened, so why worry? That kind of thing?"

Harold looked like he was about to reveal the biggest secret in the world. He pulled his marshmallow away from the fire, turned it so that it was charred all the way around and then blew out the flame with a devious smile.

"Sort of. You can change the past, sometimes."

"How?"

"If what you believed about the past was wrong, and then you found out the truth, wouldn't you view the present differently? That's how my Philosophy instructor puts it, our reality is based on what we believe."

"Jesus, Harold. Berkley's really having an effect on you."

278

"Let's put it to the test."

"How?"

"Look toward the water."

Turning, I saw this couple approaching, not identifiable yet, the girl anyway. They were not in the light of the fire, so I couldn't tell much about him and was wondering why Harold would say such a thing with two strangers approaching.

It's amazing what you can't see if you don't believe your eyes. Looking at the guy, I thought I recognized his posture and profile, but..., *what?*

Seeing my reaction, Katie twisted around to see for herself. She, too, was in doubt. And then she screamed, dropped the marshmallows into the fire, scrambled to the other side of me, looking over my shoulder and staring at what we thought was a dead man walking.

"Katie?" His voice is soft, inquisitive. "Is that you?"

She's screaming. *"Jesus! Holy Jesus!"*

"Calvin? Who...?"

"Oh, my God!"

Is there a time when you refuse to believe your eyes? How can he be standing there when we have the official piece of paper saying that he is dead? I trust my eyes more than anything..., yet. Standing..., "Jimbo?"

"Calvin? Holy *fuck!*"

It went from a hand shake to a hug, both of us teary-eyed. I don't like to think of myself as soft and I know that Jimbo isn't that way at all, but sometimes you just can't help yourself. We opened our embrace to include Katie and the three of us stood there crying for I don't know how long.

Harold is right. The present is definitely defined by the past. Get off on the wrong foot and everything else is messed up after that.

John and Penny, as a final gift, left Katie and I with the rest of the bottle of vodka and we still had a couple of soft drinks left in our cooler. We rinsed out the cups and poured drinks for a toast.

I raised my glass. "To Jimbo, for coming back from the dead."

He raised his. "To Calvin, for taking care of my baby sister."

Everybody drank to that.

Harold, cleared his throat. "Did you know that they're married?"

"*What?* You two are *married?* When did that happen?"

"The day after I turned eighteen."

"Do Mom and Dad know?"

"Of course. Do they know you're alive?"

"I'll talk to them tomorrow."

"My, God, Jimbo. They're your parents."

"Which is why I'll talk to them tomorrow. It's been a long day, Katie. What are you doing with this loser?"

I put my arm around her. "Loser? Now that you're back, I'll have someone I can easily beat in chess."

"In your dreams, sucker."

Lilly laughed. "Jimbo's come home."

Harold raised his glass. "To, Lilly. Without her, none of this would be happening."

We raised our glasses. "Here, here. To Lilly!"

Of course, now that Jimbo is alive, I'm wondering about Lilly and Jimbo's old girlfriend, Annette, who probably doesn't know that he's alive, yet. I'm wanting to ask, but probably not a good question in front of Lilly, which brings me to her.

"How do you two know each other?"

"Um, that's kind of a long story. She visited me in the hospital up in Idaho."

"Why would you visit him?"

"I thought he was Frankie."

280

"Oh. Does he look like Frankie?'

"Very much."

"Jimbo, how did you get to be Frankie?"

"Fuck if I know. Everybody was calling me Frankie when I woke up."

"Wait..., you're Frankie's girlfriend?"

"We've been through this, many times, yes."

"So..., are you now Jimbo's or Frankie's girlfriend?"

"Yes."

"Yes, what? Both?"

"Yes."

"One of us is dead," said Jimbo.

"So, is that Frankie in your grave?"

"There's a grave with my name on it?"

"Mom and Dad flew up to San Francisco to bring your body, *somebody's* body, back to San Diego."

"That was nice. I'll have to thank them for that."

Lilly laughed. "Jesus, Jimbo. They're gonna have other things to talk about."

"I'm going to have to go in first," said Katie. "You can't just walk in the front door."

"Yeah. Dad would shoot me."

"They'd both have heart attacks."

"Looks like we're not going anywhere for a while," said Lilly. "I've got some snacks and stuff in the trunk of my car, stuff we didn't eat on the way down, if somebody will give me a ride. Then, I can bring my car back here."

Harold stabbed another marshmallow with a clothes hanger. "I'll stay with the fire."

On the way up to the car, Katie pulled the keys out of her pocket and handed them to Jimbo. "You OK to drive?"

"Why would I drive?"

Katie didn't answer, choosing instead to wait until Blue Beauty came into view. Approaching the car, Jimbo became very quiet. "Oh - my - God! Jesus, Katie. You've got her all shined up. She's beautiful!"

More tears. He drew Katie into a bear hug. "Thank you, baby sister! Thank you!" Setting her back down, he handed her the keys. "But..., I'm not ready to drive, yet."

Getting in, Katie taking the wheel, Jimbo and Lilly riding in the back, me shotgun. When she turned the key and the engine roared to life...,

"I remember that sound! Calvin, you and I put this baby together!"

I laughed. "And it's still running in spite of us."

We gathered up all of the munchies, went back to the fire ring and, as it popped and crackled down into an orange, fiery glow, and to much laughter, heard everybody's side of the tale.

Sometime in the middle of all that, Harold quietly lit up a joint and passed it over to Jimbo, who had no problems about taking a hit, nor did Lilly or Katie.

When it got to me, I had to think about it. Could I help it if some second-hand smoke got in my lungs while my friends were celebrating Katie's and my marriage and Jimbo coming back to life? No!

Somebody once said, "It's the journey, not the destination." Tonight, being with friends, holding the love of my life, hearing the surf and watching the fire burn down to coals, there is no place that I'd rather be.

Tomorrow, we'll all be off doing other things, Harold going to march in a protest, Jimbo and Lilly doing whatever it takes to make a new life, Katie and I going through the throes of a temporary separation. Most of the time, life is moving so fast it's all we can do just to get by.

Every once in a while, a pearl comes along, a moment in time that is impossible to forget, a night like this. It's the little things.

* * * *

Credits

I cannot imagine the 1960's without all of the wonderful, creative music that we enjoyed. These songs helped define the mood of our generation. How hollow our lives would be if we couldn't hum these tunes when we think of the past.

Listed below in the order in which they appear in East Side, the titles of the songs. Thank you for all of your fabulous work.

Louie, Louie – The Kingsmen
Mama Said – The Shirelles
Do you love me – The Dave Clark Five
Love Potion Number Nine – The Searchers
He's a Rebel – The Crystals
Loco Motion – Little Eva
I Like It Like That – The Miracles
Girl from Ipanema – Stan Getz and Astrud Gilberto
Under the Boardwalk – The Drifters
A Hard Day's Night – The Beatles
Glad All Over – The Dave Clark Five
Suspicion – Terry Stafford
We'll Sing in the Sunshine – Gale Garnett
Hello Dolly – Louis Armstrong
The Way You Do the Things You Do – The Temptations
Come a Little Bit Closer – Jay and the Americans
Baby, I Need Your Loving – Four Tops
Dancing in the Street – Martha and the Vandellas
Wishin' and Hopin' – Dusty Springfield
You Don't Know Me – Ray Charles
Money. (That's What I Want) – The Kingsmen
Dawn (Go away) – The Four Seasons
I Get Around – The Beach Boys
It Hurts to be in Love – Gene Pitney
Everybody Loves Somebody – Dean Martin

I

Dancing in the Street – Martha and the Vandellas
Baby Love - The Supremes
Do Wah Diddy Diddy – Manfred Mann
A World Without Love – Peter and Gordon
Game of Love – Wayne Fontana
Hang on Sloopy – The Vibrations
When a Man Loves a Woman – Percy Sledge
Come On, Let's Go – Richie Valens
La Bamba - Richie Valens
That's My Little Suzie - Richie Valens
Donna - Richie Valens
The Doors – The Doors
Aftermath – The Rolling Stones

About the Author

Dave Riessen earned his Associate's Degree in Electronics at San Diego City College and then attended San Diego State University where he changed his major to English and focused on creative writing.

Other novels by D. D. Riessen:

You Gotta Have Wings - young adult fiction

On Standby - adult fiction

Sometime Tomorrow - science fiction

The Other World - fantasy and science fiction

Borrowing Time - sequel to *The Other World* - fiction

* * * *

Dave's work revels with the fanciful, ponders the inscrutable and enigmatic and examines the human character.

To learn about the history behind the stories, please visit his web site at:

www.ddriessen.com

I appreciate your comments. I always strive to make each story the best that it can be and I love that you take the time to read them.

This is my passion.

Thank you